★

They were all huddled around something wet that lay on the ground. At first it looked like just a bundle of clothes. Then as I got closer, the men seemed to part and I recognized a leg—white, sickly looking, like wax with dark hair on it. Black shorts. A turquoise shirt. A Sage Country Club shirt.

Tim Michelik was dead.

There was a question I had to ask. "Did he drown?"

There was a moment of silence before Mac said, "No, Jolie, it looks like he was shot and then put in the water."

★

"This is a refreshing mystery...the storyline is good and the characters both realistic and enjoyable."

—*Mystery News*

"Smith's characterization of her detective, in fact, is so intimate that we're made to wonder how fictional Jolie Wyatt, mystery writer, really is."

—*American-Statesman*, Austin, TX

"Smith's tale offers a rewarding connection with modern life."

—*Arizona Daily Star*

Dust Devils OF THE Purple Sage

BARBARA BURNETT SMITH

WORLDWIDE.®

TORONTO • NEW YORK • LONDON
AMSTERDAM • PARIS • SYDNEY • HAMBURG
STOCKHOLM • ATHENS • TOKYO • MILAN
MADRID • WARSAW • BUDAPEST • AUCKLAND

In *Dust Devils of the Purple Sage,* there is a great deal
about mothers and sons, and the special bond they share.
With much love I would like to dedicate this book to my
own son, W.D., who is simply the best.

DUST DEVILS OF THE PURPLE SAGE

A Worldwide Mystery/April 1997

First published by St. Martin's Press, Incorporated.

ISBN 0-373-26234-5

Printed in U.S.A.

ACKNOWLEDGMENTS

Special thanks to Sheriff Dwain Hensley of McCulloch County, who offered his technical expertise for this book. If there are mistakes it's because I didn't ask the right questions, or didn't take the advice given. I would also like to thank Joan and Ed Keeling, who gave me my first job in radio and taught me how a real KSGE might operate.

Wilmot County is fictional, as is Purple Sage. None of the characters in this book is real, yet their spirit can be found in any one of a dozen counties in Texas. That spirit shines through whenever I travel around doing research, and while I can't name all the names, I'd like to thank the many people who have answered the millions of questions I've asked.

Also, my dear friends, the Black Shoes, offered invaluable help and support in the writing of *Dust Devils of the Purple Sage;* much gratitude to Susan Rogers Cooper, Jeff Abbott and Jan Grape.

And I have to thank Carol Ruff, Bruce Burnett, Stacey Bridwell, Caroline Young Petrequin and my love, Gary Petry. No matter how hard I try, I just can't seem to do everything myself, and, luckily for me, they've always been there to help.

DUST DEVIL

A dust devil, or *remolino* as they are known in Spanish, is a spinning column of wind that can crop up almost anywhere. Caused by a bubble of heat between two layers of air, some have been said to whisk up and whirl away animals, billboards and even vehicles. Dust devils are much like people—they can appear when least expected out of a clear and cloudless blue sky, and they can be playful or dangerous. There is simply no predicting a dust devil.

ONE

As I SAT in the news booth there were two buttons and one toggle switch in front of me on the console. During my first week at KSGE I had been sure that if I hit the wrong one it would send an atomic missile shooting toward the Middle East or eject my chair into outer space. Or turn my microphone on when I was having a personal conversation. Luckily, in my three-week tenure, my mis-hits had not caused any global repercussions. Nor had the good citizens of Purple Sage called for my impeachment, or whatever is comparable for a newsperson, so now I wasn't quite so terrified.

When Dan, the engineer on the other side of the glass, pointed at me, I took a breath, flicked the toggle switch to open the microphone, and started in:

"This news bulletin is brought to you by Jackson's Funeral Home and Ambulance Service—home owned and operated for over fifty years.

"Twenty-year-old James Elliott Jorgenson, a former resident of Purple Sage, escaped from a minimum-security unit of Huntsville Prison sometime during the early morning hours. According to law enforcement sources, Jorgenson escaped from the farm unit, which is located south of Victoria, in a light green pickup and was last seen traveling at a high rate of speed on Highway Eighty-one.

"He was with a female companion, believed to be his sister, eighteen-year-old Sharon Alice Jorgenson. Speculation is that the pair are headed back toward Purple Sage. They are considered armed and dangerous.

"James Jorgenson was serving a ten-year sentence on two counts of burglary and had been a model prisoner until the escape.

"This has been a K-Sage news bulletin and I'm Jolie Wyatt."

I pushed the button on the far right and miraculously the commercial for Jackson's Funeral Home started. Dan was giving me a thumbs-up sign and a grin. I shook my head in wonder.

As part-time newsperson I had covered the garden club's meeting on the care and feeding of bromeliads, the YMCA's pancake supper, and I'd even written the copy on a three-car fender-bender on the square, a rarity in Purple Sage. But this was actual, hard-core, honest-to-goodness news. Not just the kind that went into a newscast, but news that rated a bulletin, a first in my short experience. I kept looking over my shoulder, expecting to see our news director, F. Rory Stone, appear at my elbow to tell me how I should have done it better, right, and his way. All three are the same with him.

But Rory, the boy wonder, was out, unable to be located, so I had followed the explicit directions from his latest memo. It had clearly stated that if a felony or violent crime was committed within the K-Sage listening area a bulletin was to be aired immediately. And that was what I had done.

As I took off my headphones I realized that, strictly speaking, the felony hadn't been committed within the area. It was merely *heading* toward our area and, in Rory's book, that could be a whole different thing. Or not, depending on his mood. It would mean a lecture, not that a lecture would be anything new. With Rory they were like vitamins: one a day. And for me they were going down harder and harder, which was exactly what I intended to talk to Rory about as soon as I found the right moment.

Since he wasn't at the station, this wasn't the moment. I told myself there was no need to think about it and that I was wasting time and focus on the wrong male. I pushed aside the nagging worries about Rory and turned my attention to the self-freed James Elliott Jorgenson. All I had were the barest facts on the escape that I'd gotten off the police scanner; what I wanted included background and those interesting tidbits that kept listeners listening.

KSGE doesn't run to a morgue, although they do have three tall filing cabinets filled **with** old news stories. Unfortunately there was no order as to how they were filed. Past news on Jorgenson, if there was any, could be under *J* for Jorgenson, *C* for Criminal, or *M* for Misfiled. Not to mention a thousand other places.

Obviously the file cabinets weren't worth attempting, and I didn't have any idea whose jurisdiction a prison escape fell under, so I went into the crowded office that held both my desk and F. Rory Stone's. I pulled out a notepad and pen before I dialed the number of Mac Donelly, the sheriff of Wilmot County.

"Jolie Wyatt, to what do I owe this pleasure?" he asked as soon as I got him on the telephone. The welcoming tone was genuine and used universally.

"Oh, just business as usual," I said as I flipped open the notebook. "I need some help if you don't mind; I heard that a man by the name of James Elliott Jorgenson—" I was interrupted by a bark of laughter coming over the phone line.

In the past I once expected more of Mac than I should have; I suppose citizens do that with their public officials. When I had gone into news, I worried that Mac would allow that past incident to stop us from developing a working relationship. "Am I missing something?" I asked.

"You been doing some eavesdropping on the police monitor? I expect you'd call it *official* eavesdropping." I could hear his smile, so apparently the concern was only on my part, not his.

"Exactly," I said, allowing a smile of my own, "and it goes with my new territory. They actually make me listen in. I could become a helluva spy."

"I reckon you could. So, you need to know something about James Jorgenson?"

"Everything," I said. "What about his background? I understand he grew up around Purple Sage."

"You could just about say he grew up in my office." Mac almost sounded nostalgic.

"Then we're talking about juvenile crimes, is that right?"

"You may be, but I'm not."

Juvenile crimes can't be discussed. Sealed records and all that. "Then how come James Jorgenson spent so much time in your office?" I asked. "Selling Boy Scout cookies?"

"Not hardly; he was the original Huck Finn and then some. James was in and out of every kind of mischief you can think of. Cherry bombs were his speciality."

"Like in mailboxes?"

"Mailboxes, toilets, soda-pop bottles, whatever. You could say he was a creative genius of a very unique sort. I remember one time he lit one, stuck it on top of a cream pie, and carried it in to his sixth-grade teacher singing 'Happy Birthday.' 'Course he ran; took the teacher with him before it blew up. They had to cancel class for a week to get the whip cream off everything."

"Real charmer," I said.

"Actually, he is, kind of. He made sure the teacher got out so she didn't get hurt; far as I know, he's never hurt anyone."

"The warrant says he's armed and dangerous."

"I know what it says, but I don't know why. Truthfully, Jolie, I can't figure out why they added that, unless someone saw him with a gun, and that just don't seem likely. Maybe it was just a precaution."

"Interesting," I said, scribbling notes. "I still don't understand how he went from cherry bombs to Huntsville. A fugitive from Huntsville. On the police scanner they said he was only twenty, but he'd already been in prison for three years on burglary charges—is that possible?'' I asked.

"It is. They tried him as an adult at seventeen because he was what they termed a habitual criminal.''

"Then he must have done something.''

"Another troublesome birthday. That kid had more than his share of those. Anyhow, he hit seventeen and celebrated a bit too heartily, if you know what I mean. He ended up breaking into the school and doin' a whole lot of damage. By the time we found out about it, he'd gone underground, just sorta disappeared. Guess he figured that kind of life suited him because next he broke into a package store, then a grocery. He was convicted on two counts of burglary and got a ten-year sentence. He'd of been out in less than five.''

"Mac, I don't ever remember hearing his name before.''

"Well, except for the school break-in all his other burglarizing took place in San Saba County. The public defender figured James couldn't get a fair trial out there so they got a change of venue to Victoria.''

I'm a city person at heart—I grew up in Dallas and spent most of my adult life in Austin; in those places a criminal like James Jorgenson would be considered a minor problem, certainly not anyone worthy of public attention and a change of venue. However, here in the sparsely populated area of central Texas where crime rates are low, I could see how he would be something more. He must have seemed like a reincarnation of Clyde Barrow, and there were probably dozens of Close-Encounter-with-Jorgenson stories that people told. The fact that he had broken out of prison would only increase the legend. Which reminded me of something else I didn't have. "Mac,'' I said, "have you heard how he escaped from Huntsville? From what you've said, I assume it wasn't at gunpoint.''

"I already talked to the officials down there,'' Mac said, and I could hear the smile coming back to his voice. "This is off the record. You see, James was in a minimum-security farm unit. It's not quite so prisonlike as a lot of places, so he put pillows under his blanket, picked the lock on his cell, and disappeared 'over the wall,' as they say."

"I don't get it; what's so secret about that?"

"It's how he learned to pick them locks."

"Okay, I'll bite—how did he learn to pick them?"

"They taught him," Mac said with a bark of laughter. "It was his trade for rehabilitation."

I caught myself grinning. Maybe James Elliott Jorgenson *was* a charmer. "Anything else you can tell me?" I asked.

"This time James may have gone a mite too far," Mac said, suddenly somber. "His sister, Sharon, just turned eighteen and hasn't even graduated from high school. She hadn't had so much as a tardy slip until today. Her being involved is not going to set well with anyone."

"You think James forced her into helping him escape?"

"Nah, coerced her, maybe."

It made me wonder why kids in general, and James Jorgenson in particular, didn't look beyond their actions to the consequences of them. A true parent speaking. "One more question, Mac. They said that he was moving in this direction. Do you really think he's coming back to Purple Sage?"

"Knowing James I expect he is."

"But why?"

"Because that's the way James is." There was silence, which Mac finally broke. "Damn," he said softly. "I just hope this doesn't turn out as bad as it could."

"Me too," I said. I waited for Mac to add something, but when the silence remained, I said, "Thanks, Mac, I really appreciate your time."

"You could return the favor."

I was game. "Okay…"

"Go easy on the kid in your story."

I nodded. "I promise."

THE RADIO-STATION BUILDING is shaped like a horseshoe. The right-hand side has a big open area where the two salespeople and our traffic person work. Beyond that are a closet, coffee room, bathroom, and then Lewis Hilger's office; he's the owner of KSGE. The left side of the horseshoe, our side, has a production room, news booth, control room, and finally two offices that serve as the record library and news room, respectively. Lewis had supposedly been in the middle of renovating the building when he ran out of funds, so his side is gorgeous with wainscoting, Ralph Lauren-looking wallpaper, wooden desks, and a plushy hunter green carpet. The walls on our side are mostly glass and soundboard that I suppose was white once upon a time. We also have a tritone shag carpet in shades of orange left over from the fifties.

We do have our own door with a push-button security lock. There was a regular key-style lock but the elderly gentleman who used to do news habitually lost his key. He is now eighty-seven and only comes in on Sunday mornings when he reads, on the air, the comics from the *Dallas Morning News*. Honest.

Visitors to KSGE come in the central concrete walkway to the front door. Behind that door is the receptionist's desk, only we don't have a receptionist, so our bookkeeper, Michelle Kleinsmith, sits there. Michelle is in her early twenties with the richest brown eyes and hair I've ever seen in my life. She also has delicate ivory skin, as well as an almost unbelievable figure.

On my first morning at KSGE, Rory took me around and introduced me to the rest of the staff. When we walked into Michelle's office she was in the midst of a big stretch and yawn—Rory took one look at her and had a testosterone reaction that was practically nuclear. It was not a pretty sight.

I had decided to dislike Michelle on general principles, and then discovered that under her drop-dead gorgeous exterior, with its bigger-than-life-size bosom, beat the heart of a real feminist. She doesn't make coffee, and she doesn't take guff off anyone. She's also very good at her job, and that includes bookkeeping, typing, answering the phone, and keeping track of the rest of the staff. Which is why, as soon as I had finished writing the full story on Jorgenson and the prison break, I picked up my purse and headed to her office.

"If anyone calls, I'm out for a few minutes. I'm going over to the *Tribune*," I told her.

"Got it," she said. "Oh, and hey, Jolie, I heard your bulletin. Good stuff; you're catching on pretty quick."

"Thanks."

"Of course, that may not be a good thing," Michelle added, with a wicked grin. "You know how Rory is and he's gonna be pissed as hell. You have whipped that over-weight chauvinist hog in his own pen! So to speak."

"Damn. You think I shouldn't have done the bulletin?"

"Basically, you shouldn't do anything, because Rory wants to do everything himself. He loves the sound of his own voice." She must have seen my lack of enthusiasm because she added, "Maybe you could sneak out early."

"I don't see how," I said, checking my watch. It was 11:30. I left at noon, Rory did the local news at 12:15. He was always back in time to edit my stories and give me a lesson on "how we write real news."

Rory is not the hard-bitten news veteran he'd like to be—in actuality he's straight out of broadcast school and barely out of his teens. He couldn't be more than twenty-two at the most, and he's not mature enough yet to realize that he doesn't know everything. It was especially difficult for me to take since he's only a few years older than my own son, Jeremy.

"You don't have to put up with him, you know. Why don't you just quit?" Michelle asked. "It can't be the money." She was referring to the fact that my adorable husband, Matt, has a rather large ranch and an even larger portfolio of business interests. "Lewis isn't paying you enough to put up with the aggravation," she added. "I'm not trying to be nosy, but I can't help but know what Lewis is paying you." Michelle made out the paychecks.

"It's okay. Lewis says that since the station isn't involved in any interstate commerce he doesn't have to pay minimum wage. Is that true?"

She shrugged. "Beats me."

It was one of those things I intended to look up at some point, but my three weeks had been busy and, so far, I hadn't had time. Besides, it wasn't the money. I happen to love radio.

Back in the days when my son was little I had gotten a job with a small station in Dallas. I did news. A little news. Mostly I typed things for people, but I had big visions. I kept seeing myself on television sitting next to Dan Rather. Like I said, a big vision—the jumbo economy size.

Then the ratings came out and half the staff got fired. Three months later the station was sold and eight more people were terminated without warning. I had made it through both purges but, being quick on the uptake, I realized that radio was not a place to look for job security. Since I was the sole support of my young son and myself, I took my writing skills to the first place that would have me—an advertising agency that put me to work writing commercial copy and news releases. It wasn't exactly the fortune and glamour I'd planned on, but they didn't fire people for no apparent reason. I like that in a company I work for.

I have to admit, though, that the six months I'd spent in radio had been wonderful. I'd responded to the constant deadlines like a racehorse at the gate. I liked writing news, too, and if I were willing to tell the whole deep, depraved truth, I loved being on the air.

Michelle didn't need to know all that. "I want this job,"

I said. "I love this job. It's F. Rory Stone who's the problem. But don't worry, I'll learn to get along with him."

"If I had to put up with him the way you do, I'd kill the guy."

"That's Plan B and it is under consideration," I said. "See you in a little bit."

With a wave I headed out the front door, ignoring my car, which was in the parking lot, and, instead, walking toward the Purple Sage *Tribune*.

Some time back tourists discovered other central Texas towns, like Fredericksburg and Kerrville, and those places had grown because of it. Purple Sage, with its five thousand mostly charming residents, had remained a relative secret— except to the hunters who came through every fall wearing their camouflage clothes and paying enormous sums for the right to shoot dove, turkey, and deer, all in the appropriate season, of course. Then, slowly, other less purposeful tourists began to wander through, and now Purple Sage has its first bed-and-breakfast. The economy is beginning to pick up. The square, which was just a few blocks away on my right looked better than it had when I first moved to the town three years before. Some of the buildings had even been restored to their premodernized glory. From my vantage point I could see Henshaw's Hardware, with its white limestone walls glowing softly in the morning sun. Joan Henshaw had a display of wheelbarrows, hay bales, and blue crockery out front to attract business. Beyond that was Miz Priddy's, an arts and crafts store, and then the little drugstore. The far end of the block had been one large building, a dry-goods store, that had been divided in the fifties. Today the reddish marble façade was again visible, lending a touch of authentic beauty, but it was still no competition for the elegant, three-story, limestone courthouse that reigned in the center of the square.

I looked both ways before I crossed East. That's not usually a necessity, but somewhere in the back of my mind

I was visualizing a light green pickup screaming down the street. Of course there wasn't one, and I wasn't really surprised; it was actually hard to imagine James Elliott Jorgenson on the loose in Purple Sage.

As I stepped up on the sidewalk I could feel the heat coming through the soles of my flats. It wasn't officially summer yet, at least not by my definition since school still had another week to run, but the warm weather had already settled in. Only the sporadic thundershowers seemed to cool things off. I shaded my eyes with my hand and glanced up at the sky. There was nothing but an expanse of blue. Not even a wisp of a cloud.

"Am I missing something up there?"

Rhonda Hargis had come out of the old three-story *Trib* building and was looking at the sky, just as I had been. She was dressed as usual in something made of lycra, her blond hair pulled back into a ponytail. She had a camera on a neon green strap slung across her chest.

"I was looking for rain," I said. "Or maybe just some cool."

"Didn't you read the paper? The story's on page two. We've got a cool coming—just stick around until October. Can't miss it."

Rhonda is a good reporter, an excellent aerobics teacher (maybe a little overzealous for those of us who aren't physical fanatics), and a member of my writers' group. Most of us write mysteries while she goes in for dark fantasy and horror. Her stories don't particularly appeal to me, although I do like Rhonda. Usually I don't get her humor at all.

I put a quarter in the old-style newspaper rack and took out the latest edition of the *Trib*. "Hey, did you hear about the prison break? Isn't that something?" I asked, tucking the paper under my arm. "I talked to Mac and he was telling me—"

"Jolie, we're not supposed to exchange information. As

long as you're working for the radio station we're competitors.''

I looked at her for a few seconds to see if she was serious. She certainly appeared to be. "That's like saying apples and oranges are competitors.''

"That's right,'' she said, "they are. After all, they're both going after the same fruit dollar.'' She turned around and began to undo the lock on her bike while I just stood there, staring.

Rhonda's logic was beyond me. First of all, the *Tribune* came out twice a week, Mondays and Thursdays. It could be cut up and put in scrapbooks, taken to school for Current Events, and used to line the bottom of the birdcage. You can't do that with radio waves, but K-SAGE had other attributes, like immediacy. We were on the air every day, sixteen hours a day. A story was still fresh news when we aired it. Although sometimes I swore the grapevine was faster.

And as for the fruit analogy...

Rhonda was already positioning herself on her bike. "Well, see you later,'' she said. "Tuesday.'' Writers' group.

"Right.''

She started to pedal off, then flipped her head back around and added with a cocky little grin, "Oh, and give my love to Rory.''

She was around the corner before I could think of a response.

I shook my head anyway, flipped open the paper, and started back to the station, reading as I went. There was nothing new in the *Trib;* it was composed mostly of pictures of the graduating class, a story on the senior trip, a report on the city council—all things that we had either covered earlier or weren't going to.

I may not have gained any news, but getting out and walking had helped me relax and clear my head. I needed that; when I got back I wanted to talk with F. Rory Stone and I wasn't looking forward to it.

I folded the paper back up. As I turned at the KSGE parking lot, I heard the unmistakable sound of a Volkswagen bug engine. My body reacted automatically, my stomach tightening, my breathing a little quicker. The fight-or-flight syndrome.

The little car whipped past me, with Rory at the wheel. He was driving fast, so intent on where he was going that he didn't even notice me. He pulled into his preferred parking space next to our side entrance and the little Volkswagen shuddered to a halt. When Rory got out, he slammed the door so hard the car rocked. Then he barreled toward the back door.

If his body language reflected his mood, F. Rory Stone was at less than his charming best.

TWO

RORY WASN'T ANYWHERE to be seen, not in the news booth, nor in our office, not the control room, record library, or production room. Dan was still on the air, and I popped in to ask him where Rory might be.

He had a rueful look on his boyish face before he said, "He was hunting for you, Jolie, and he wasn't happy."

"He's never happy. Did he say anything?"

"He was kind of mumbling...."

"So are you. Come on, Dan, I can take it. What did he say?"

Dan kept his eyes on the VU meter rather than on me as he said, "I'm sure he was just rambling.... It was something about how he'd had it and this was the final straw, and it was a disappointment, too, because he'd prayed over this and prayed over this." He shifted his eyes up to mine, then looked away again quickly.

"He'd prayed over this?" Over me?

"He's a jerk. He's probably hiding out in the bathroom; just ignore him," Dan said.

The latest Tanya Tucker song was ending so I backed out of the control room heading toward my office.

I needed to talk with Rory—I'd been grinding my teeth for a week now and that is not what my mother would call a lady-like habit. Although I certainly wasn't going to go charging into the men's room to have the conversation. So I waited. And while I waited I tweaked and edited the prison-break story on our old, slow but reliable Apple IIE. Then I rewrote the blurb about the YMCA pancake supper. As soon as I'd printed a copy of each I made sure I saved them on disk and labeled it just the way Rory liked. Whenever Rory couldn't find a story on disk he became down-right computer surly.

After another few minutes of pretending to proofread what I had just written, I picked up the phone and buzzed Michelle at the front desk.

"Rory didn't slip out that way, did he?" I asked.

"Nope; he's still back in the bowels of the building somewhere."

"I'm in the bowels of the building," I said, "and I don't see him."

"Then face east and say a prayer of thanksgiving. Gotta go." And with that she hung up.

I felt like some kind of sly predator, lurking around the hallway. I was about to give up my vigil and leave when the bathroom door opened and Rory emerged. He was white, that awful color skin turns when the stomach inside it has rebelled all the way down to the bile.

"Are you okay?" I asked.

Rory sat at his desk across from me and nodded. Rory is about five-ten, a little overweight, with pudgy arms that he had crossed in front of his body. I'm sure he was at-tempting to appear stoic, but it made him seem young and pitiful.

"You don't look very good," I said, jumping up, my moth-erly habits coming out despite my better instincts. "I could call the drugstore and get you some—"

"No, that's okay; I'm fine. We need to talk. Sit down."

"It can wait until tomorrow," I said, refusing to obey the command. Besides, I wanted him at full strength so I wouldn't hold anything back out of pity.

"Now is better. Please, sit." Since he'd added the "please" I did so. He went on, "It's about the bulletin you did. Conjecture is not news, as I'm sure you would have realized if you'd used a little common sense—"

"Wait a minute, your memo said—"

He snapped his fingers at me to stop; the police monitor was blaring again and he cocked his head to listen. I whipped around toward it, my eyes focused across the room so the fury radiating from them wouldn't sear a hole through Rory. I had to take a few deep breaths before I could tune into what was being said.

"Base here, go ahead."

"Loretta, didn't they say that Jorgenson's pickup was a light green?"

"Ten-four."

"So what year is it? Over."

"Eighty-one or Eighty-two. You got something, Andy?"

"Not anymore. Unit Two clear."

"Base clear."

Rory looked noncommittal as he turned back to me. "Now, what was it that you were saying?"

"It's not important."

"Well, as I was saying, you needed more information. You didn't have enough facts to—"

"According to your most recent memo, I was to go with what I had. I did; I used everything that came over the police monitor. Facts." I snapped out the last word.

"Apparently you misinterpreted my memo, because the bulletin wasn't enough. I didn't like the way it was worded, either; news is different from advertising writing and you don't seem to be getting the feel of—"

"I have written several thousand press releases in my career."

He didn't acknowledge that I had spoken. "I know you're not happy here and I want you to know that I understand. Not everyone is cut out for—" Rory stopped as Lewis Hilger, the owner of KSGE, came walking in the back door. Lewis has a huge presence that fills and alters any space he occupies.

"'Morning," Lewis said brightly.

"Uh, Mr. Hilger—Lewis—" Rory was on his feet, although none too steadily. He bent over slightly and my first thought was that he intended to kiss Lewis's ring and genuflect. Then I realized it was far more likely he was going to pass out.

Lewis raised one hand in a kind of benediction, but his face puckered as he took in Rory's complexion. "Rory, you don't look good."

"It's nothing." He did sit down again, though. "I'm just having a bad day."

"You must have eaten something that didn't agree with you," Lewis said, perching himself on the edge of the desk. "I did that last year in Amsterdam. Ever heard of *pommes frites?* They're a kind of local french fry that's sold on the street from kiosks and why I ate them I will never know. I was sick for three days. The rest of the tour group said I had Rembrandt's Revenge." He chortled. "I still can't believe I was eating greasy french fries, and did I mention that they serve them with mayonnaise? It turns a yellow color from the heat. Really disgusting."

The visual image turned Rory a yellow color, too.

Lewis looked at me. "By the way, I heard your news bulletin, Jolie, and I thought it sounded great. I love the way you write. And this time you really stirred up some excitement—now that's the way to get people used to tuning in to KSGE. Don't you agree, Rory?"

And that settled that. He could only nod at Lewis. "Uh, sure."

"Titillating, that's the word," Lewis went on. "Jolie teased our audience into tuning in to the noon news. I can just feel those advertising dollars starting to pour in." I half expected him to clap his hands and bark like a sea lion— which is what he reminds me of, large and sleek. "Maybe we should have Jolie do the noon news since you're feeling so puny, Rory."

"No," Rory said, rising slightly like a mortally wounded soldier making his last stand. "I can do it."

Lewis waved him down. "No, no, Jolie will. You can stay a little late, can't you, Jolie?"

At quarter of one I was meeting Matt at the lawyer's office. Since we don't have title companies in Purple Sage that was where we would sign the papers to close on some land we were buying. The whole procedure would require about four signatures and ten minutes. Matt says God intended all business transactions to be that easy, which is a little simplistic for a man with a Harvard MBA, but I have to agree.

After the closing we were having lunch with Diane and Trey Atwood. Diane is a member of my writers' group, and my best friend. Trey is the mayor pro tem of Purple Sage, almost. But that's another story.

"I can stay," I said to Lewis. "I don't have to leave until after the newscast."

Rory started to say something, mumbled "excuse me" instead, and hurried off to the bathroom.

"Must be something he ate," Lewis said. "Anyway, Jolie, this afternoon, if you have the time, you might want to go out and talk to their grandmother."

Any conversation with Lewis is a challenge, but he seemed particularly obscure at that moment. "What? I'm not sure what we're talking about here. Whose grandmother?" I asked.

"Fergusons'."

"Who? Oh, wait, do you mean Jorgensons'? She's here in Purple Sage?" I don't know why I was so surprised by it, but I was.

Lewis had tipped back his head and made himself more comfortable on the desk. "As far as I know Mrs. Toffler still lives right where she used to. About a half mile down the road from my cousin, Elmira. I don't recall much about it, but I'm pretty sure that she raised James and his sister from the time their parents were killed in a car crash. That was some time back. They were just little. I'll bet James wasn't more than four or five."

"You knew him then?" I asked.

"Oh, no. I've seen Mrs. Toffler maybe once or twice, of course, but I doubt that I was ever formally introduced to her. She kept pretty much to herself. I never knew James, either, but I do remember seeing him a couple of times. One time specifically comes to mind; it couldn't have been but a couple of months after Corinne Toffler, or I guess I should say Corinne Jorgenson, and her husband were killed. I was driving out to my cousin's and the three of them, Mrs. Toffler, James, and the little girl, were out picking wildflowers alongside the road. I can still see that little girl, so serious and wide-eyed, in her little pink dress. She was holding out a bunch of bright blue dayflowers to her grandmother. I slowed the car way down so I wouldn't kick up caliche dust on them."

He'd created another strong image and I couldn't help but see it myself. Mrs. Toffler must have been devastated by the death of her daughter and son-in-law. Any mother would be, to lose her daughter like that just when she thought the child was grown and safe. My own child, Jeremy, who is fifteen, has been known to create havoc in my life, but to lose him would be more painful than anything else I could imagine. At least Mrs. Toffler had had her two grandchildren for comfort in her grief, two warm, cuddly little bodies who needed her love and hugs more than at any time in their young lives.

But who was going to comfort Mrs. Toffler now?

"I'll talk to her in a few days," I said.

"No." Lewis shook his head. "Jolie, I think it's something you'd best do now. Strike while the iron is hot. TV reporters are always on the scene immediately."

I was almost physically repulsed by the idea. There was no way Lewis Hilger or anyone else was going to get me to bother Mrs. Toffler on that particular day. Maybe not any day. "Lewis, I have a problem with that," I said, carefully. "I just don't think there's much you can ask someone right after a tragedy. And what can you expect them to say?

You know what I mean." I picked up a pen and held it in front of my mouth like a microphone. "Well, Mrs. So-and-so, now that your entire family has been wiped out and your house is lying in splinters all around you, can you tell us how you feel?" I shook my head as I put down the pen. "I can't do that. It just isn't kind, and the people of Purple Sage would be incensed if I did it."

Lewis nodded his head thoughtfully. "Maybe you're right," he eventually conceded.

Rory returned from the bathroom, and he seemed better now.

"Rory," Lewis said, "I tried to call you on your cellular—got some weird message—"

"Uh, yeah. That's been a problem." Rory ran a pudgy hand over his still pale face.

"Do we need to have it fixed?"

"I already sent it off," Rory said. "I meant to tell you."

"Good. So how are you feeling?"

"I'm okay," Rory said. He reached over to pick up the news stories from my desk. "You can go ahead and go home, Jolie."

I could only stare at him for a moment. He was such a series of contradictions, and I was beginning to think most of them were either selfish or just plain evil. If I stayed, rather than doing the newscast, Rory would have me retyping stories with him dictating. I preferred to make my exit.

"Well, since you're better," I said, "I guess I will go. Have a good afternoon." I had said it generally, but Rory chose to respond.

"Don't worry," he said. "We'll talk tomorrow."

I had thought Lewis said everything that needed saying. Apparently Rory thought otherwise.

THREE

"HELLO, MY LOVE," I whispered discreetly in my husband's ear. Technically I should say my *ex*-husband's ear. After three years of marriage he and I had separated and then divorced in what must have been temporary insanity on my part. I did eventually come to my senses a little over a month ago, and now Matt and I are back together and happier than ever. We haven't remarried yet, which means, I suppose, that we're living in sin. Frankly, I like it.

I was being discreet because we were in the lawyer's office and it's so old-money-stuffy with huge leather chairs and oriental rugs that I'm always intimidated by it. I think I should behave properly and I have no idea how that is.

Matt started grinning as I slipped behind his chair and into my own. "Hi," he said. Then he leaned over and gave me a quick kiss that perked me up.

Did I mention that Matt's eyes are dark, warm, and sexy? And that in contrast, his hair turns blond at the mere mention of the word *sun?* The rest of him is gorgeous, too, but I'll admit I'm prejudiced.

"How did your morning go?" he asked. He's also a genuinely nice person—to everyone.

I curled one lip.

"Didn't your mother ever tell you that your face would freeze like that?"

"Yes, and I ignored her."

He smiled, then shook his head. "I assume the look means that Rory is at it again."

"Matt, he never stops." It was getting so that just hearing Rory's name was enough to push my frustration level up near the ozone layer. I purposely kept my voice light.

"I've considered poison, a curare-tipped dart, and shoving him out a fifteenth-story window. Unfortunately, poison's been done, curare is not available at Henshaw's Hardware, and we don't have any fifteen-story buildings. I think it would be obvious to drag him to Austin to find one. What do you think?"

"I think it's going to make a helluva book," he said, taking my hand in his.

"Yes, well, if he keeps it up, I'll be writing it in prison."

Ellis Kramer, who is both a district judge and Matt's attorney, came bounding into the room. Ellis is barely forty, and yet he's managed to make himself seem one of the old guard in Purple Sage. He also looks like one of the old guard, with a round, domelike head that frankly could use a lot more hair. He also wears plastic-framed glasses like something out of the fifties. You'd expect him to prefer brown suits and striped ties, but Ellis does have his quirks. His suits are exquisitely tailored and his ties are always unusual to the point of bizarre. This particular day his tie was wide and red with an embroidered Mickey Mouse on it.

"Did I hear you mention prison, Jolie?" Ellis asked. "You don't even have to think things like that; my role is to keep you on the streets, regardless of what you've done." Since most of his clients were elderly, and staunchly religious to boot, he'd probably never handled a criminal case in his life.

"If I get caught I'll call you, Ellis." I let go of Matt's hand and tried to get in a "bidness" mode. That's *serious business* in the South.

"Doubt it will come up." He sat behind his massive dark wood desk piled high with folders and patted Mickey's tummy to center his tie properly. Suddenly his eyebrows came together in a frown. "Wait a minute, you did get mixed up in something a few months ago. When the Judge died you were—"

"Almost," I said, cutting him off. That's the problem with people in small towns, they have long memories.

"And aren't you part of the writers' group here? You're supposed to be a pretty good mystery writer. Is that true?"

"Well, I do write mysteries." I forgave him for remembering my brief brush with the law.

"Sold any books yet?"

"Not yet," I said.

"Jolie's agent says she could sell something any day now," Matt offered. Is it any wonder I love that man?

"Well, if you need me to look over the contracts, just give me a call," Ellis said. He picked up some long documents. "I guess we'd better get down to business here. I told you, didn't I, Matt, that the Hammonds have already been in? All I need is the check and a couple of signatures, and we'll have you out of here in a jiffy."

I tuned out the conversation as he and Matt began to discuss the intricacies of the purchase. Legal contracts give me a headache. As a former copywriter for radio, TV, and print advertising, I have this philosophy: If it can't be said in two paragraphs, you've got too much crap in one document. Think about it—the Gettysburg address was only a little over two hundred words. The Sermon on the Mount was shorter than that. So why do lawyers have to take twelve pages to say that these people are selling property, and these people are buying it? Maybe we should stop paying them by the hour.

Besides, I was busy thinking about James Elliott Jorgenson and his younger sister. And their grandmother. I was considering the afternoon ahead. We were meeting Diane and Trey for lunch at the country club, but after that I had nothing planned. Maybe I would take a short drive, just a quick trip past Mrs. Toffler's house. I wouldn't stop, but I wanted to put her and her grandchildren into perspective. There was always the off chance that I'd spot an older-model green pickup tucked away somewhere nearby. And if I did, what would I do about it?

Of course, the idea was crazy. The sheriff and his men had probably gone to Mrs. Toffler's first thing. Might even still be there.

"Jolie?"

I looked up at Ellis. "I'm sorry, did you say something to me?"

"All we need is your signature right here on this second line and here and we'll be finished."

I took the pen he was holding out and signed where he'd indicated without even complaining that he'd put me on the second line. "That's it?" I asked.

"That's it," he said. "You and Matt are now the proud owners of three hundred and fifty acres of ranch land, and the Rom Cursed Cave."

"The what?"

Matt laughed. "I'd almost forgotten that story." He leaned back in his chair and the leather creaked softly. "We have a cave with a Rom curse."

"We do? Really?" I asked. "Does this mean that the fleas of a thousand camels are going to infect my hard disk?"

Matt said, "Not that kind of Rom. Romanian as in Gypsy. It was a Gypsy curse."

I didn't get it. "The Hammonds weren't Gypsies," I said. In fact, they were very nice Baptists, who were in their seventies, if that counts for anything. He was a deacon in their church and she had once brought me a homemade dewberry pie. It may not be solid legal evidence, but it made me believe they were unlikely candidates to put a curse on a cave. "Why did the Hammonds curse their cave?"

"It wasn't the Hammonds. It was way before their time," Matt said. "Ellis, do you know the whole story?"

"I grew up over in Pontotoc, so the only things we heard

about Purple Sage were gossip. Well, okay, I do know a bit about it.'' Then he grinned again, leaned back in his chair, and his eyes took on a dreamy, unfocused look. ''When I was in high school, we used to sneak out and drive over there to spend the night. You know, like sleeping in a haunted house, only it was a haunted cave. One night there was an owl back in that cave and it nearly scared the bejesus out of us!'' He sat up and shook his head, still grinning. ''That was our last trip to the Rom Cursed Cave.''

''But how did it get cursed?'' I asked. ''This is Texas, for God's sake!''

After several ''no, you go ahead''s from both of the men, it was Ellis who finally began the story. ''The way I heard it, a wagon load of Gypsies had come through Purple Sage somewhere in the mid-1800s. Maybe a little later. Back then the town was very small and a fundamentally religious one, even more so than now, and the sight of a wagon full of 'heathens' got things pretty stirred up. Being sensitive people, the Gypsies stopped in town, just long enough to buy a few supplies and then they traveled on. Problem was that back then, you couldn't get far what with the bad roads and all.''

''When they got to the pass in the hills,'' Matt added, ''which is now the Hammond place, they discovered the cave. That's where they stayed for several days.''

Ellis was nodding like mad. ''I heard that it was the spring and that the weather was hellacious. They'd already had enough rain to cause mud slides up there. That's why the Gypsies decided to make camp. The thing is, they were just minding their own business, but it was the townspeople who started coming out to visit them. First in trickles— having their palms read, buying up special lotions and potions, you know. Then a group of citizens, actually more like vigilantes, decided to put a stop to it.'' He leaned forward and his voice dropped as he went on. ''A whole band of men rode up—it was midday but it was ready to storm and they say the skies were black. Like midnight at noon. The vigilantes were carrying torches, and waving their guns. The Gypsies were peaceable people and it scared them no end. They scooped up everything they could and ran into the back part of the cave.

"Remember, these were women and children as well as men. They were unarmed and terrified. When the townspeople came chasing into the cave after them it must have been chaos what with kids screaming and everyone pushing and shoving." Ellis shook his head sadly. "There is some kind of drop-off in the back of the cave, and in the crush, a little Gypsy girl, about three, went over the edge. She died instantly from the fall. As the story goes, the Gypsies left that night, but not before the little girl's grandmother put a curse on the people of Purple Sage and anyone who entered the cave after them." He finished simply, "Which is why you now have the cave with the Rom curse."

Little girls seemed to be the theme of the day. First Sharon Jorgenson, who was left without parents, and now a little Gypsy girl. I let out a long breath. "Sad."

Matt touched my cheek. "The story may not be true. Maybe there were no Gypsies and no little girl at all."

I nodded. "Right. But what was the curse?"

"That every person who entered the cave would be visited by evil spirits and then they would die," Ellis said. Suddenly he grinned, showing delicate white teeth. "And if you look at it historically, eventually, all those people *have* died. But the real point is that the cave became a challenge to every kid who lived within fifty miles of here. They all had to come out and spend the night in there, like some kind of rite of manhood."

"Which means you'll be busy putting up 'No Trespassing' signs this afternoon," I said to Matt.

"The Hammonds had a few and I think I'll let it go at that. I haven't heard anybody talk about the Rom Cursed

Cave in twenty years—I really don't think anyone even knows about it anymore.''

Ellis agreed. "I think you're right. Seems like the stories have died out."

Jeremy had never mentioned the cave, or the stories, and, since the Hammond place adjoined ours, I was pretty sure that he would have if he'd known about it.

"You ready for lunch?" Matt asked me.

"Past ready; I'm starved." I also needed a little R and R, and lunch with Diane and Trey would provide it, I hoped.

FOUR

WE SAT on the patio at the country club, listening to the squeak of tennis shoes on the hard court surfaces only thirty feet away. There is another patio, which overlooks the golf course, and I usually prefer it, but the decking was being treated with something that smelled obnoxious, so instead we were here with the persistent *whompf* of racquets hitting tennis balls.

The Sage Country Club is hardly the kind of place you find in those glitz-and-glamour books. Millionaires don't pull up in Rolls-Royces and gloriously wealthy widows don't waltz through wearing diamonds as big as the Ritz. You do see a lot of cowboy boots, jeans, and Stetson hats. Baseball caps sporting local business names are also popular.

The club does have linen napkins at dinnertime, but not at lunch. There are massive windows in the pink, native stone walls. The floors are tile and the decor is southwestern with lots of glass, stone, and light wood furniture.

We belong to the club because Matt is a tennis fanatic. He plays at least three times a week when he's in town. The club also offers the only real socializing we have in Purple Sage. For example, they have dances twice a month with country bands. Everyone from age two to two hundred shows up and has a wonderful time. I wasn't much of a two-stepper when I moved to town, but I can hold my own with the best of them now. The club also has golf tournaments, poker nights, and the largest swimming pool around.

The main reason the club is private is that in our county liquor by the drink is illegal. You can go to a liquor store, or a package store as they call them out here, and buy a bottle of any alcoholic beverage you want, but we don't have bars, clubs, or any other places that would normally serve liquor. Except the country club. Since this is a private establishment the rules are different.

"Just a Caesar salad and some iced tea," I said to Tim, our waiter.

Diane looked up from her menu, a frown on her patrician face. "If you're eating salad I suppose it would look bad if I ordered a chicken-fried steak with fries. Maybe I'll just have a sandwich. Without mayo."

"Have what you want," Matt said. "Jolie is just doing that to impress us."

"You didn't let me finish," I said. "Tim, for dessert I'd like strawberry pie with extra whipped cream." I handed over my menu while Matt and Diane both ordered club sandwiches.

Tim wrote as fast as he could then flexed and stretched his arm, his shoulder muscles rippling impressively under his aqua Sage Country Club T-shirt. I had first met Tim when we had moved to Purple Sage a little over three years before. That was right after Matt and I married. Tim had been about seventeen at the time, and he'd been the batting coach for Jeremy's Little League team. He'd also been my first encounter with a small-town kid. In Austin, the kids had always called me Jolie. Tim always called me Mrs. Wyatt or ma'am. The ma'am I could have done without, although Tim himself was a godsend. As soon as he noticed that Jeremy was the new kid without friends, he had taken him under his wing. He would drive all the way out to the ranch to pick Jeremy up and take him into Purple Sage for a Coke at the drive-in where the kids hung out. And he always brought Jeremy back when he said he would. After a few afternoon Cokes he had started gathering up more of the team members so Jeremy could make some friends his own age. Tim really made that first summer a memorable one for Jeremy, so I had a special spot in my heart for him.

"So what are you planning for the summer?" I asked Tim as he finished writing Matt's order.

He slipped his pen into the back pocket of his black knee-length shorts before he said, "Well, I was going to take some classes at the junior college in Brownwood, but time just got away from me." He looked a little sheepish as he shrugged his shoulders, causing another impressive ripple. "You know how life sometimes just gets out of hand?"

I laughed. "That's normal at our house. You just have to keep going in spite of it. Or maybe because of it."

"Well, Miz Wyatt, I'm giving it my best shot." He grinned at me, then held up his order pad. "I'd better get this turned in if you want to eat anytime soon." With that he zipped off toward the kitchen.

"He's really matured, hasn't he?" Diane said, watching Tim leave.

"Those are just muscles, Diane," Matt said, "not maturity."

She swatted at him with her napkin and said, "Let's change the subject, shall we?" Matt laughed as Diane turned her slender body toward me. "So, how is Rory? Oh, and by the way, I heard the bulletin you did and it sounded great."

"Thanks. Lewis thought so, too."

Matt looked at me. "But not Rory?"

"Well, he was sick so it doesn't count."

Diane cocked her head to the side. "With any luck, he'll die."

"I doubt it, but since he spent so much time in the bathroom he didn't get to criticize every story I wrote. Or have time to make me rewrite them."

"That is ridiculous," Diane said, her dark brown eyes filled with annoyance. "Jolie, why don't you simply remind him that you were hired because you are a professional writer? Not only that, but an award-winning writer? Has he forgotten that you have four Addies?''

Diane remembers more than most of us have ever really heard. She can tell you the exact date and day when John Kennedy was elected and how far it is from Düsseldorf to Bonn. Not to mention the fact that she remembers the awards I have garnered in my past. This is not a woman you want to play Trivial Pursuit with.

"I got the award over four years ago," I said. "Rory considers them something from my youth. From the dark ages back before they had real copywriters. He also dismisses them because they weren't for news."

Just then Diane's husband, Trey, came hurrying up to the table. He was running late, as usual. Trey is a nice man and I enjoy his company, but if he were my husband I'd put a cow bell on him so I could find him once in a while.

He's a little over six feet tall, with thinning brown hair and an elegance that nicely matches Diane's. Although once you get to know Diane you discover that she grew up on a ranch, and is still a tomboy at heart.

"Here you go," Matt said, pulling out a chair for Trey with one hand. "So, how's the Mayor today?"

Trey rolled his eyes as he sat down and unfolded his napkin. "Not yet; can't call me mayor yet."

"Could we call you Mayor Pro Tem?" I asked.

Diane laughed. "I call him Mayor Possible. Or Mayor Impossible."

"Electorally challenged?" Matt offered with a grin.

Trey had won the Democratic primary for the mayoral position, and since the Republican Party in Purple Sage consisted of about ten people, he basically had the job.

I leaned forward and said, "You don't seriously think there will be a Republican candidate, do you, Trey? You do think you're going to be mayor, don't you?"

"It ain't over 'til it's over," he said.

"I don't want to have to start campaigning again," I

said. "I'm not in the mood, at least not in this heat." I had served as Trey's campaign manager and, while I suppose I would do it again, it wouldn't be anytime soon.

Apparently Diane felt the same. "I gave up campaigning for Lent."

"That's over," Trey said.

"And for Advent, Saint Patrick's Day, and every other day."

Tim reappeared and gave Trey a menu, before starting to pass around tall glasses of iced tea to the rest of us.

I picked up my tea glass; it was already sweating and the ice was melting fast.

"Oh, Jolie," Trey said as he glanced at the menu, then at me, "I heard the news bulletin you did this morning. That's something about that prison escape."

"Isn't it?"

"I remember hearing about James Jorgenson when he was arrested several years ago. As I recall he wasn't all that bad a kid—at least he doesn't kill people." He shook his head. "What I can't get over is his sister helping him escape. Sharon Jorgenson was—"

There was an explosion of sound as a glass slipped from Tim's hand and slammed onto the tile. Tim's eyes grazed downward, then back up to look at Trey. He appeared stunned. "I'm sorry," Tim began. His voice simply stopped there.

I jumped up and took the tray from him. He was shaking. "Tim," I said, "are you okay?"

He nodded his head but his mouth remained open as if he might not be able to breathe if he closed it. He still didn't talk.

"Maybe you'd better sit down." I tried to push him into my chair but he was rigid. "Tim, what is it?"

He mumbled something, took the tray from my hand and, with a terrified look, hurried out. He didn't even notice the puddle of tea and ice or the shattered glass. He stepped right into it and kept on going into the club building.

I watched him all the way in. "Do you think he's okay?"

Diane puckered her features into a frown and said, "I think he knows Sharon Jorgenson." She looked at me, then at Trey. "Did they date, maybe?"

"Oh, hell," I said, sinking into my chair. Obviously this was the first he'd heard about the escape and if they had dated, then of course, he was shocked. "Poor Tim."

"It's not your fault," Matt said. "He would have found out eventually."

I took a large swallow of my tea. "It must have been horrible to hear about it like that. And he's such a nice person."

"I'm the one who brought it up," Trey said.

"Exactly," Diane agreed. "He's the motormouth. Besides, we don't know for sure what caused Tim to react that way."

I could only nod and say, "You're right."

A blast of air-conditioned air hit me as the door behind us swung open and Lurline Batson, the manager of the club, came whipping out onto the patio. She was carrying a fresh drink. "Tim said there'd been a slight accident." She deftly placed the glass in front of Matt, then signaled to someone inside the club. It turned out to be another waiter, this one older and not someone I knew personally.

Lurline pointed to the tile. "We need to get this cleaned up right away," she said as he hustled off, presumably for the proper tools to do the job. Then she turned to us. "So, what can I get for anyone?"

Her tanned hands wrote quickly as Trey gave her his order. From a distance, Lurline always reminded me of a surfer kid with her straight, bottle-blond hair and wide-set baby blue eyes. Up close and in the bright sunlight, I could see that she was probably nearing forty. The short skirts and low-cut sweaters she wore showed off her tan and her figure, but they also revealed skin that was getting leathery. Maybe from all the sun, maybe from a life that was tougher than most of us would want. That was speculation on my part, but as a writer I'm allowed.

"Sorry about the problem," Lurline said when she finished taking Trey's order. "Tim isn't feeling too well, but he'll be fine in just a few minutes."

"It's my fault," I said. "I mentioned that James Jorgenson had escaped from prison—"

"James Jorgenson?"

"Yes. But it wasn't just the escape. Jorgenson had some help; they think it was his sister, Sharon."

Lurline stared at me for a moment, then cocked her head and flashed a smile. "Don't worry about Tim. He's young, he'll get over it. Well, the drinks are on the house, and your food will be out in just a minute, so y'all enjoy." And then she too hurried off.

Half an hour later the tile floor was spotless and not even damp. The ice in our tea glasses was melted and the plates in front of us were empty. Lunch had been a little quieter than usual.

Diane reached for her tea. "I almost forgot why I called this meeting."

"You didn't," I said. "I did."

"Don't bother me with details! We're supposed to be celebrating and we haven't been." She raised her glass. "To you two and your new acquisition. May you enjoy it in good health."

"And prosperity," Trey added, as we all clinked glasses. "I assume we're talking about the Hammond place. You did close on it?"

"About an hour ago," I said. "We now own a Rom Cursed Cave. Did you know about that?"

Diane almost choked on her tea. She set the glass down and coughed a few times into her paper napkin. When she'd regained her breath, she said, "You own the Rom Cursed

Cave? I used to hear about that when I was a kid, but I never knew where it was. I can't believe you actually own it! It's on the Hammond place?''

''That's right,'' Matt said. ''About three miles from our house, as the crow flies. About ten miles by road, I suppose.''

A gleam was starting in Diane's dark brown eyes and I knew we were in for something. ''I think,'' she began in a voice that was almost a whisper, ''that we should pay the check as fast as we can, go home and change, and spend the afternoon exploring the cave! What do you think?''

I looked over at Matt. I could see his childhood fantasies coming to life even as he tried to sound nonchalant. ''Well, I guess I'm game,'' he said. I made a snorting sound, although a delicate one, and Matt looked at me with a grin. ''Okay, I'll admit it, I'm dying to go out there.''

''That's what I thought,'' I said. ''What about you, Trey?''

He looked up from his plate. ''Count me in. Although I've been there once or twice already,'' he added with a smug look. Macho male stuff.

''Actually, I don't know about this,'' I said. ''If we go into the cave the Evil Spirits will visit us.''

Diane snorted, not nearly so delicately as I had, and said, ''Big deal! We have teenagers—how much worse could evil spirits be?''

I reached for my purse while Matt reached for the check. Before he and Trey could do their usual argument over whose turn it was to pay (more macho stuff), Trey snapped his fingers and said, ''Bramble B Ranch.''

Matt looked up and let out a groan that made him sound like a kid who just remembered a big test. ''We have an appointment to see those Charolais heifers.''

''Now?'' I said.

''Can't you postpone it?'' Diane asked.

Trey shook his head. ''This guy is harder to catch than

the Fugitive. We've been trying to get with him for months.''

"When do you have to go?" Diane asked.

Matt looked at his watch, then at us. "If we don't leave in the next ten minutes, we won't make it. It's over an hour's drive." He turned to Trey. "What time do you think we'll be back?"

"Seven-thirty. Eight. Maybe later."

"Sorry, honey," Matt said, looking at me. "I guess the cave is out." Like I was the one who was disappointed. And maybe in a way I was.

"If we can't go now, then what about tomorrow?" I asked.

When they say that men are just grown-up little boys, they aren't kidding. Matt's face lit up like it does when I wear my French bustier. "That's a great idea!" He turned to Trey and Diane. "One o'clock, okay? Meet us at our place and we'll drive over together."

With that he signed the check, kissed me quickly, and headed for the door with Trey.

"What are you going to do this afternoon?" Diane asked me as I gathered up my purse and took a last swallow of my iced tea.

"I suppose I'll write."

She nodded. "Yeah. Me, too." Then she looked at me squarely. "Does it feel like we're waiting for something? Just marking time?"

"Just because Matt and Trey left? That's crazy."

"Oh, I know, and I didn't mean because of that." She stood up and I joined her as we started out toward the parking lot. "Never mind. Maybe it's just the weather." She looked up at the sky. "Like we're waiting for a storm."

"We always are this time of year." I tossed my purse in the car and waved a good-bye. "See you." As I drove toward the highway I have to admit that I did have a twitchy feeling as if I were waiting for something. Or maybe it was something coming toward us, looming on the horizon. Jorgenson? My impending talk with Rory?

I turned the air conditioner up a notch. Maybe it was just a storm.

FIVE

THE FEELING hadn't gone away and the temperature hadn't come down. Jeremy was clicking his pen against his teeth and it was adding to my tension; what with checkups, cleaning, fluoride treatments, and the pulling of two molars, I have a lot invested in those teeth.

"Jeremy, please stop that before I have to kill you."

"Sorry," he said.

We were on the back deck, enjoying the evening shade that cut the heat some. Above us wisteria covered the trellis, and behind us soft jazz played. Antonio Carlos Jobim. I closed my eyes and tried to imagine that I was on a beach somewhere in South America.

A cow mooed loudly in the distance. Not quite a South American beach, but almost.

Jeremy was sitting at the white wrought-iron table, books scattered in front of him. I was stretched out on the swing, a tall glass of iced tea in my hand and the new Milt Kovak upside down on my stomach. Even my hero Milt couldn't hold my attention at that moment. My mind kept slipping back to James Elliott Jorgenson. And his younger sister, who wasn't even out of high school. Might never graduate now.

I had spent the afternoon working on my book. I love writing—it's as natural to me as breathing; besides, if I show up at my weekly writers' group empty-handed I get these fish-eyed stares. It's the equivalent of showing up at school without your homework, and no matter what excuse you have it always sounds as lame as if you'd said, "My dog ate it."

That afternoon it had been a fight keeping my mind on

my characters. Especially because Diane had called twice. Apparently the Purple Sage grapevine had gone into red alert with everyone trying to top everyone else's brush, however minor, with James Jorgenson. I'm not well fixed "on the vine," as it were, because I never seem to have the time or the patience for that sort of thing. Besides, Diane is much nicer than I am, and she'll stay on the phone mumbling "oh"s and "uh-huh"s for hours. Then she passes the best stuff on to me. It's a very efficient system, I think.

That afternoon she called with two stories that I have to admit were pretty good. Both had taken place about four years before, and one had been about real estate signs that disappeared from homes on the market, and reappeared elsewhere. Inappropriately. The other was about a brand-new motorcycle in a dealer's showroom that one morning suddenly had over a hundred miles on it, as well as a coating of mud on the tires. James Jorgenson had been a rounder all right, but Diane made it sound like everyone talked about him with affection.

"Mom, what do you think was the cause of the Civil War?" Jeremy asked, interrupting my thoughts. "Was it because of economic differences or humanitarian reasons?"

"Neither. I think it was caused by macho posturing and an overabundance of male hormones."

"Mo-om!"

"Sorry, but they got bored and didn't have anything else to do; cable hadn't been invented yet. So, the men decided to create hardships and ruin people's lives with a war. Happens all the time. You're taking history, you should know that."

He turned around to face me. He was wearing an old T-shirt of Matt's from Harvard that should have been thrown away years ago, and jeans that were at least three inches too long so they buckled several times over his tennis shoes. That's how he likes them and I decided to quit arguing about it. One thing I've learned is that you can buy a kid any kind of clothes you want but you can't make him wear them. Besides, I keep thinking that maybe Jeremy will grow into the jeans and by that time it will be stylish to have them fit. Could save me scads of money.

At that moment his light brown hair looked almost gold because he'd spent so much time in the sun. My hair, which is the same murky brown, never turns that rich a color. He also has hazel eyes like mine. The similarities end there. He's growing almost daily, so that now he's a good five inches taller than my five-four. He was also scowling, something I avoid doing because it makes me look unattractive, not to mention older.

"I don't know why I bother to ask you questions," he said. "You never give me straight answers."

"Ah, but maybe what I said is right and what they said in the books is bullshit."

"You'd slap me if I said that."

I had to grin. "Right again."

"What's with all the man-bashing, anyway?" His voice took on a morally superior tone. "This sexist attitude doesn't become you, Mother."

That's the problem with raising a socially conscious child—they end up using it against you.

"Okay, okay," I said. "I'm sorry."

"So, why are you being that way? Did you and Matt have a fight?"

"No." I stopped to consider. "Maybe it's because I'd like to murder Rory and I'm sublimating my feelings."

"Then put him in your book and kill him off."

The phone rang, saving me from trying to respond. I didn't bother moving; Jeremy had the cordless phone sitting in front of him on the table. I knew he would answer it first and the odds were that it would also be for him.

"Hello? Yeah. Yeah. Sure," Jeremy said, and when he paused I expected him to take the phone into the house to finish the conversation. Instead he held it out to me. "It's Wiley Pierce, Mom."

My heart did a few heavy beats before I remembered that I was in the news business now, and a phone call from a sheriff's deputy didn't necessarily mean there had been a death in my family. I sat up, carefully closing my book, and placing it on the swing beside me. I put my tea on the table.

"Thanks," I said to Jeremy as I took the phone and spoke into the receiver. "Wiley, hi. What's up? Have you caught Jorgenson?"

"Not yet, but we'll get him, you wait."

"I don't doubt it a bit. So, what can I do for you?"

"Well, I was hoping you might be able to give me a little information," he said, then cleared his throat. "I heard you talked to Tim Michelik down to the country club today. Is that right?"

"That's right. We had lunch there. Matt and I, and Diane and Trey Atwood. We only talked with him for a few minutes. Why? What's going on?" Jeremy had moved back to the table, but I suspected that his attention was on my conversation.

"You haven't by any chance talked to Tim since then, have you? He isn't out there at your ranch, is he?"

"Tim? No, sorry."

As soon as I said the name Tim, Jeremy turned to watch me, listening openly.

"I heard he got kinda upset by something someone said," Wiley went on. "Could you tell me what that was about?"

I was tempted to ask more questions, but that hadn't gotten me anywhere the first time I'd tried it.

"He was our waiter," I began. Then I told him how Tim had dropped the tea when he heard Sharon Jorgenson's name and how he'd behaved afterward. Jeremy's face grew grave as he took in what I was telling Wiley.

"Did he ask you anything about Sharon or her brother?" Wiley wanted to know.

"No. I don't think he said anything at all after he dropped the tea. I'm sorry, but I'm not sure. You might call Diane Atwood and see if she remembers anything else."

"He didn't say where he was going when he ran off?"

I caught myself shaking my head. "No. He didn't say anything; he just ran inside the club. Why? Where is Tim? Has something happened?"

Wiley is fairly young and, according to Mac Donelly, very bright. Mac says he knows the law and also has an excellent feel for dealing with people. Up to that point you couldn't have proved it by me, but Wiley changed his tactics.

"Miz Wyatt, as far as we know nothing has happened to Tim. He just isn't around and some people wanted us to check up on him."

"What do you mean, 'he isn't around'?" I asked.

"Well, he left the country club right after he dropped the tea and no one's seen him since."

Since Tim is very levelheaded that didn't seem too ominous. "Maybe he's just off thinking somewhere. He was pretty upset."

"Yes, ma'am, that could be, but you see, he volunteers out to the Boys' Ranch every Thursday startin' at five o'clock. Has for years and he's never missed a time, not even in that big snowstorm we had two years back." The Boys' Ranch was a home for orphaned boys about thirty miles south of Purple Sage. Wiley went on, "He didn't show up this evenin' and they got kind of concerned. We can't do much just yet—he's only been out of pocket for half a day—plus we've got every man possible huntin' up Jorgenson, but I said I'd make a few phone calls."

"Have you tried Lurline?" I asked.

"She was the first person I called, and she said he'd been

gone since nearly two. She's the one told me I should give you a call.''

I sat there for a moment, taking it all in. Jorgenson was on the loose with his sister, Sharon. And now Tim Michelik was missing.

''Wiley, do you know if Tim ever dated Sharon Jorgenson?''

''Yes, ma'am, I believe I heard somethin' like that.''

''You don't suppose that somehow he found...'' I began, but I stopped when I saw Jeremy furiously shaking his head and mouthing the word *no!*

Wiley had already figured out what I'd been about to say. ''You thinking Tim might have hooked up with the Jorgensons?'' he asked.

''It was just speculation.''

''I don't rightly know how that'd be possible, but I suppose he coulda done it. Well, thank you for your time. If you should hear from Tim, you'll let us know, won't you?''

''Of course. And I'll call you in the morning when I'm at the station. Just to see if anything has happened.''

''Mac'll be here then. He'll tell you what he can.'' And with that he hung up.

ALTHOUGH I SLEPT WELL, curled up around Matt, I awoke in the same antsy mood I'd gone to bed with. It hovered around me, clinging like some poisonous fog all the way to the station. When I drove into the lot only a luminescent, practically glow-in-the-dark pink pickup was there and since I knew the pickup belonged to one of our part-timers, I surmised that F. Rory Stone wasn't there yet. Since it was only quarter of six I wasn't surprised.

I should explain that KSGE has the authority to broadcast twenty-four hours a day, but doing so would require that someone be there twenty-four hours a day, and since everyone else in Wilmot County is asleep, Lewis thinks it's a waste of money. Instead, we sign on at five a.m. for the early-rising farmers and ranchers, and sign off at midnight. That's for the three or four people who stay up *really* late.

Usually when I get to the station, the jock has already pulled any pertinent stories that have come across the news wire, which is mostly none, and has put the news folder on my desk. That gives me about fifteen minutes to update the crucial stories before I do the first cast at six o'clock. The whole system doesn't work all that well, but Lewis won't officially consider me on duty until six, making the fifteen minutes before six my daily gift to him and KSGE. It's like donating diamonds to Elizabeth Taylor, so I try to do as little of it as possible.

That morning when I came in the back door I was greeted by the soft sounds of the new Garth Brooks song. There is a hushed quality to the station at that time of day, as if the jock doesn't want to wake up yet. I waved to him, he mumbled something that I couldn't hear through the double glass windows, and then I went to my desk to start the early-morning round of phone calls. I was looking for some news of Tim Michelik, and certainly something on Jorgenson. Something.

"Trina?" I said after I got through to the dispatcher at the sheriff's office. "Is there any news this morning?"

Normally I don't bother trying to make conversation with Trina. She is not helpful or even responsive in most situations. Her under-five-foot body is built along the lines of a miniature sumo wrestler and if the milk of human kindness had ever run through her veins, it had curdled long ago. It was a mistake to think that just because we had escapees on the loose she would be willing to spare a little of her time and energy to save that of the actual law-enforcement officers. When Loretta came on at ten, information would be easier to obtain. I wasn't sure I could wait that long.

"Who's this?" she demanded.

"This is Jolie Wyatt from KSGE," I said. "Is Mac available?"

"No one's here."

"No one?"

She didn't even bother to answer that, just let out a sound that resembled a grunt.

I tried again. "So, is there any news on Jorgenson?"

"No."

"Have they been hunting him all night?"

"Yeah."

"And they haven't seen any sign of him?"

"No."

I felt like I was having a one-sided conversation with the only living Neanderthal left on the planet.

"Okay, so what about Tim Michelik?" I asked. "Wiley Pierce called me last night and said he was missing. Has he turned up yet?"

"No."

"So…is there anything else happening at all?"

"No."

Her one-syllable answers were sounding testier, as were my questions, so I tried for a little levity. "I'll take anything at this point, Trina. What about a complaint call on Miss Alice Rooter's cat? Has it howled at the moon lately?"

She hung up on me.

That meant that my newscast was mostly national news. Afterward I made the rounds, walking to the police station, the sheriff's office, the courthouse, and even the Sage Cafe, all on the off chance that I could pick up some gossip that might lead to real news. Maybe bump into Tim, or James Elliott Jorgenson. Possibly see an accident. Or cause one.

Unfortunately, it was a morning of emptiness. Even F. Rory Stone didn't show up. When I called his apartment I got nothing but his self-important voice on his answering machine, so I didn't leave a message. By that time it was ten o'clock and I was beginning to think I had wandered into an episode of *The Twilight Zone*. Then the phone rang, two lines at once, and suddenly life had resumed as normal.

"KSGE News," I said, picking up the first line.

"Mom, it's me," Jeremy said by way of hello. "Have you heard anything about Tim?"

"Nothing yet; can you hold on?" The other line was still blinking and buzzing.

"Okay."

I grabbed the other line and heard Lewis's voice before I even had a chance to say hello.

"Jolie, I just ran into the sheriff a few minutes ago at the bakery. He was going home after hunting Jorgenson all night, but then his radio went off. It seems that someone just found a body out at the lake. Suspected drowning, I think, but Mac didn't say much before he took off."

"Where exactly at the lake, Lewis?"

He gave me some reference points and I was ready to hang up and grab my car keys when he added, "Jolie, it's a young man, white Caucasian and they think he was in his late teens or early twenties."

I was very grateful that Jeremy was holding on the other line. "Any more description than that?" I asked.

"None that I've heard. Guess it could be Jorgenson."

"Could be," I said. There were other options, too, like Tim Michelik, or F. Rory Stone. "I'll head straight out."

"I'll meet you there," he said as he hung up.

I picked up the other phone line. "Jeremy?"

"Yeah, I'm here."

"Uh, honey, I, uh, need to run. Lewis just called and there's a story out at the lake that I have to cover. If I hear anything about Tim, I'll give you a call."

"Yeah, okay."

"And, Jeremy. I love you."

There was a long silence before he said in a slightly puzzled tone, "I love you, too, Mom."

SAGE LAKE WAS about fifteen miles out of town. It was man-made some thirty years before and has the lovely and expensive Sage Lake Estates on the north shore, with the public cabins and boat docks on the east. I was moving toward the south end, where there were older homes and a few weekend places. None were fancy, nor were they expensive, since most were fairly small, but they were set far apart and surrounded by huge old trees. If you knew where to look there were some really beautiful spots on the south shore where you could fish or picnic.

I drove slowly, trying not to think about what the sheriff's office had found. In the past, my experience with news had been writing press releases for an advertising agency. Those were stories about exciting upcoming events. Death is not an exciting upcoming event. Nor is it a common occurrence, at least not in my life. I'd never seen a dead body before, except those that had been cleansed and made civilized by a mortician. I wasn't sure I wanted to see the other kind. And I was afraid of who it might be.

I had thought about stopping at the *Tribune* to see if Rhonda needed a ride, but decided against it. With her attitude toward competition, she wouldn't be interested. Besides, I had a bad feeling about this, and I wasn't sure I could handle that and the driving and keeping up a casual front for her benefit.

About a half mile past the dam I turned in at Fisher Road and followed it as it wound down and around toward the lake. Lewis had said there was a second road that I would come to, and I spotted it after a few miles. One more turn and I saw all the official vehicles, as well as the DPS mobile lab.

Here the trees and underbrush were so thick the road almost disappeared. The foliage overhead blocked out the sun, making the temperature several degrees cooler with a dampness that verged on clammy. I parked immediately, nodded at an officer I knew, and then walked past the ambulance, downhill toward the water.

Several men were there: Mac Donelly, Lewis, and Wiley Pierce, as well as the justice of the peace, Sandy Winterly, Skip Jackson from the funeral home, and two others I didn't know. They were all huddled around something wet that lay on the ground. At first it looked just like a bundle of clothes. Then as I got closer the men seemed to part and I recognized a leg—white, sickly looking, like wax with dark hair on it. Black shorts. A turquoise shirt. A Sage Country Club shirt.

I stopped five feet from the men and the ground seemed to tilt up toward me. I reached out to stop it, whirled, and fell hard against a tree. It felt good, both the pain and the solidness. I closed my eyes to stop the world from spinning, took a few deep breaths, and bent my knees, sliding down the tree. My head went forward automatically, my arms wrapping around my body.

Tim Michelik was dead.

He was lying over there on the ground, just a few feet away. The nicest kid in Wilmot County, the person who'd befriended Jeremy, had died alone in a desolate part of Sage Lake.

Now I was shaking so badly that my teeth were chattering. Even though the temperature was in the high seventies, I felt as cold as Tim. I wanted to cry for him but I couldn't. Couldn't feel anything but a terrible chill that penetrated all the way to the bone.

My eyes were still tightly closed, so I sensed rather than saw the men moving off up the hill. There were other sounds. Plastic crinkling, a sporadic rumble of voices, a zipper, a squeak of what I presumed was a stretcher, so they must have moved Tim, too. Then I felt a hand gently press against my back.

"It's just me, Jolie." It was Mac.

He put his arm around me and held on tightly, almost

cradling me, until I could feel the heat of his body beginning to penetrate my own. I didn't look up, didn't open my eyes. He began to speak in a quiet, gentle, matter-of-fact tone.

"It's real hard to have to face some things in life, and I still have trouble sometimes, even after all these years. I've learned, though, that however it takes you is okay. Some folks cry, and some yell, and some throw up. Don't much matter, 'cause we're all human and we all got to handle the pain.

"I remember first time I ever had to face a tragedy. I was just twenty-four, just graduated as a DPS trooper and I was real proud of that, and real proud of the uniform. Then my second night out I came up on a wreck. Two cars, two families. A head-on collision.

"I burnt that uniform the next day, cuz I knew I'd never get the smell or the blood out of it. Didn't think I'd ever get rid of the terrible vision of that wreck, either, but God was real smart, and he really did give us time to heal up our wounds. And it took some time for me to forget, but I did eventually."

I nodded, but I stayed where I was. I wanted to take in as much of his warmth and strength as I could before I had to stand up and face the reality of what I'd seen. Mac didn't move, just gave me the time. Eventually, my legs started to cramp and I rose carefully. Mac rose with me, kept his arm around me, until he was sure I could stand on my own. He didn't say anything. I was the one who finally spoke.

"He was good to Jeremy."

Mac nodded.

I was still cold, but I'd stopped shaking and Mac moved his arm, then took a step away from me. "He was a real special young man."

It took a few minutes for me to get my breathing under

control; when I did there was a question I had to ask. "Did he drown?"

There was a moment of silence before Mac said, "No, Jolie, it looks like he was shot and then put in the water."

SIX

ALL THE MEN who'd been at the site had gone on, so Mac drove my car back into town. I sat in the passenger's seat, letting Mac's words and the isolation of the car form a barrier around me. It wasn't going to drive the emotions away, just hold them at bay for a while and that was the most I could ask for.

"It was a Mrs. Anderson who lives out at the lake that found him. She was walkin' her dog—it was actually the dog came up on the body." We followed the curve on the road then turned inside the city limits. Mac's voice continued, slow and soothing. "She went straight back to the phone and we got the call about nine-forty or so."

He stopped talking so I nodded, not knowing what else to do.

The radio was on in the background, a Billy Ray Cyrus song, just a thin substitute for conversation. Earlier Mac had asked me questions about Tim, but I hadn't been able to answer any of them. Jeremy had kept up with Tim; I hadn't. I knew him from a distance, like you do so many people in a small town.

We arrived at the courthouse, and Mac carefully set the emergency brake before he slid out of the Mazda. "Why don't you call me before you do the noon news?" he suggested. "I may have a little more for you."

I nodded as I walked around to the other side of the car. After I got in the driver's seat, I paused before closing the door, saying, "And, Mac—thanks."

He accepted that with an easy nod of his head, then turned toward the front of the courthouse. He didn't ask me if I was okay to drive, and he didn't refer to how I'd reacted to Tim's death. I was grateful for that.

I headed toward the radio station, thinking about Jeremy. I was going to have to tell him about Tim and I wanted to do it in person. Mostly I wanted to be there to comfort him, if he'd let me. He was getting to the age where he wouldn't be needing a mother much longer, and I wanted to do whatever I could to keep the bond between us for as long as I could.

Jeremy was at home today, some kind of teachers' in-service workday.

From the radio came a tinny siren signaling a KSGE news bulletin. I turned up the volume automatically, probably like half the people in the county.

"This K-SAGE news bulletin is brought to you by Jackson's Funeral Home and Ambulance Service—home owned and operated for over fifty years." It was Rory's voice.

"There's been a death in Wilmot County; the body was found on the edges of Sage Lake early this morning. A Sage Lake resident was walking her dog around nine-thirty when she discovered the body of a young male. According to County Justice of the Peace Sandy Winterly, the man was probably between the ages of eighteen and twenty-two and had been dead for at least eight hours, possibly more. The identity of the man has not been released by officials, pending notification of survivors. We'll have more information for you as it becomes available, so stay tuned.

"This has been a K-SAGE news bulletin, and I'm F. Rory Stone."

I was already pulling into the station parking lot. Half the county would have heard the news bulletin, and the other half would know about it within the hour. Many would assume the dead man was James Jorgenson; others would guess it was Tim. I could only hope that Jeremy was out in a pasture somewhere, riding Diablo, so that he missed it.

I went in the back door and straight into the news office.

"Well, it's about time you showed up." F. Rory Stone was at his desk, his fingers hovering over the keyboard of the computer, the phone wedged between his ear and shoulder. Apparently he was on hold. "This town has blown up with news and I've been trying to handle it all with just the telephone. I could use a little help."

"I've been out at the lake," I said. The second phone line rang and I picked it up without conscious thought. "KSGE News, this is Jolie."

"Jolie Wyatt?" asked a woman's voice.

"Yes."

"This is Grace Gordon. Used to be Grace Michelik," she said, her words coming fast. "Jolie, I just heard the bulletin, the one about the body at the lake? Well, you know Tim's missing...that wasn't him was it? That they found out there?"

My hand began to shake. I was seeing Grace, Tim's mother, as I'd last seen her, sitting in the bleachers at the Little League field. She was an attractive woman, tall, dark haired, with the same smile as Tim's.

I had to swallow twice before I could speak. "Grace, I'm afraid I can't help you. We don't have that information." I hadn't contemplated the lie; it had just come out.

"Jesus, Jolie, isn't there someone at the station who knows? Maybe that Stone guy? I'm going crazy."

My voice came back as flat as the lake had been that morning. "They haven't released that information, yet, Grace. I'm sorry, but you'll have to call the sheriff's department."

"Fine." She put down the phone quickly. Her reaction had been anger, but I knew it wasn't directed at me. She was afraid, and she had a horribly good reason to be.

"Another nutcase wanting to know who the body was?" Rory asked. "Jeez, don't they listen? I said we couldn't tell them—they think they're special just because they can dial a phone?"

I looked at Rory and paused before I said, "That was Tim's mom."

He ran his pudgy hand through hair that looked oily. "Oh." He shook his head.

I only hoped that someone from the sheriff's office made it to Grace's home before she got them on the phone. That wasn't the kind of news to get thirdhand. Then I remembered Jeremy again.

It was time to ask for a favor, my first from Rory, and probably a mistake. It couldn't be helped. "Can you handle the noon news alone?" I said. "I have to break the news to Jeremy."

"Couldn't you just call him?"

"He's a friend of Tim's," I said. "Was."

"WHAT DO YOU MEAN he's dead?" Jeremy was standing stone still, the currycomb in his unmoving hand.

I took a step forward. "They found his body at the lake this morning. A woman found him when she was out walking her dog." I touched his arm tentatively, but Jeremy didn't move. "I'm so sorry."

"It could be a mistake."

"Jeremy, there's no mistake. I, uh, I saw him."

He whirled around and furiously threw the comb across the small stock pen. It hit the metal fence with a reverberating clang and Diablo jumped. Jeremy wasn't watching the horse; he was staring fiercely up at the sky.

I stepped toward him, but he didn't want comfort, at least not now, and not from me, the source of his pain.

He whirled around to face me. "Did he drown? Is that it? He drowned?" Jeremy demanded. "Because that couldn't have happened; he was a Red Cross instructor. Did you know that?"

"Yes," I said, quietly. "I knew that. He didn't drown."

"I didn't think so. He was just too good a swimmer. I mean the very best." He said it frantically, as if by convincing me he could change things.

"You're right," I said.

"So how did he die?"

I took a breath. "He was shot."

"And then they put his body in the lake?" he asked. I nodded, but I'm not sure Jeremy noticed. "Somebody killed Tim? But why? Why would they do that? Did they rob him? Was it for money?"

"I don't know, honey. At this point, I don't think anyone does."

He shook his head, again denying that such a thing could happen. I slipped an arm around him and held on as his whole body began to quiver. He never shed a tear, instead he just murmured no, over and over, while the pain washed through him in physical tremors.

I DON'T UNDERSTAND life and death. I know that it's all part of the nature of things, that everything that lives has to die, but it has never really come clear for me. Life is a never-ending mystery that I avoid peering at too closely, I guess because I'm afraid I'll see too much. I do know that there are momentous times in every person's life. For me, Jeremy's birth was one of those. I think that's when I learned to love unselfishly and, while it may sound terrible, I never felt such a deep, all-consuming love for my parents or my sister or brother. I also know that the death of my father was one of those things. I kept looking at the casket after the funeral, thinking, Okay, Dad, get up, it's over now. We can go home. But, of course, he didn't get up, and his death wasn't over. It's gone on ever since. And even though I've adjusted to the fact that he isn't alive anymore, his death is not something that I can go past, because in my vision of him there is nothing beyond that moment.

When Jeremy went inside the house I saw that Tim's

death was one of those times in his life. Teenagers always think they are invincible. Every generation has thought that way, believing they can mimic movie stunts and defy natural laws without consequences. This was the moment when Jeremy realized that he and his friends lived by the same laws of nature that bound the rest of us. Even though we didn't know why Tim died, Jeremy knew for sure that he was no longer invincible.

He walked toward the house, his body rigid, his face blotchy from tears held inside too long. I followed more slowly.

It was a little after twelve-thirty and Rory must have been given the okay to release Tim's name, because Jeremy's phone began to ring. The calls seemed to come one after another. I didn't pick them up, and I couldn't hear his conversations from downstairs, but his line rings in the den, too, so I knew about them all. He and his friends were dealing with their grief by talking it out. Or so I thought at the time.

When Matt arrived for lunch, he'd already heard the news on Bart's radio as they drove in.

"I'm sorry, honey." He put his arms around me, and we held each other tightly. I still couldn't cry, didn't even want to, but there was a loneliness forming inside me that I wanted to stave off as long as possible. Tim's death had made me realize again how precious Jeremy and Matt were to me.

"How's Jeremy taking it?"

"I don't know. He seemed pretty upset," I said, leading Matt toward the kitchen. "I think he's on the phone right now; his line has been ringing like crazy."

Matt kissed me lightly on the cheek. "I think I'll go up and just let him know that I'm here. I doubt there's anything I can do for him."

"I'll fix you something to eat."

"Thanks."

He hadn't been gone more than a minute when I heard a car pull up out front. I didn't go outside since I was slicing fresh fruit, and my hands were sticky. The kitchen is at the back of the house and whoever was arriving, presumably one of Jeremy's friends, would come around to that door in a minute anyway. I was rinsing my hands in the sink when I heard the knock.

"Come in."

Diane and Trey breezed in, both in jeans. Randy, their teenage son, was right behind them. He said hello with a wave then zipped past me toward Jeremy's room.

"Thank goodness he's gone. We didn't tell him a thing about the cave, honest," Diane began. She looked at me and stopped. "You forgot. We were supposed to explore the cave today. What's wrong? You look terrible."

"You haven't been listening to the radio?" I asked.

Trey shook his head. "We've been in San Angelo."

"We were listening to an Angelo station," Diane added. "What's happened?"

I REMEMBER the rest of that day in fits and starts, like little bits of old film pieced together with large chunks missing. I do remember having to break the news of Tim's death to Trey and Diane. It was easier that second time since they hadn't known Tim quite as well as we had.

Next I have a memory of all of us sitting around the oak table in the breakfast nook, the sunshine disappearing as heavy clouds rolled overhead. Spring thunderstorms arrive and disappear quickly, only this time their shadows felt heavy and frightening. The four of us talked about going to the cave, concluded the weather wouldn't hold, and Diane and Trey decided to leave so they could stay ahead of the storm. They called up the stairs for Randy, but both boys were gone; there is a back staircase on the outside of the house and apparently the two had used it. I expected to find them sitting in a pasture, throwing rocks, or maybe saddling Diablo and one of the other horses for a ride. They weren't, though.

I don't recall our harried search; my next clear vision of that day was when we finally found Randy and Jeremy behind the big barn. They were loading Matt's old four-wheel-drive pickup. The truck has been in several wrecks and the color used to be green, although now there is more orange rust than paint. We only use it when we're going into the roughest country and don't want to scratch up anything more valuable. Jeremy is allowed to drive it on our property if he asks permission first. He hadn't asked this time.

Gusts of wind had started, and the sky was a pale gray with darker clouds boiling up on the horizon. Neither Jeremy nor Randy had heard us approach and they both looked guilty when they saw us. Matt walked over to Jeremy at the side of the pickup bed. Randy was still holding a sleeping bag in his hands; the other was loaded in the bed of the truck and under it was a box of some kind.

It was Matt who began talking. "Looks like you're going out for a while."

Jeremy ducked his head. "We've got some things to do." I could hear the bravado.

Trey stepped up beside Matt and pointed to the bedroll. "You were planning on being out all night?"

"Yeah, maybe," Randy said.

"Were you going to tell us you were leaving?" Trey pushed.

The two boys exchanged a glance. It was Randy who finally muttered, "I guess."

"So where are you going?" Matt asked without any reproach in his tone.

Randy tossed his sleeping bag in the back of the pickup and it hit the other one, knocking them both off the top of the box. In the wind the flaps of cardboard box flew open and I could see two handguns and enough ammunition to refight the Alamo.

"What in the—" I blurted out, but Jeremy was already talking.

"We're going to find him, Mom! We've got to do it."

"Find who?" Matt asked in his quiet, reasonable way.

"Jorgenson. He killed Tim, I know he did. We're going to find him." He looked at me, his expression defiant. "Don't say we're too young, either. People fight wars at our age."

There was a crack of lightning followed by a pounding roll of thunder. The raw elements added a fierceness to the scene. A scene that frightened me, because a hundred years before it could have happened just that way. Boys, young men, going out to right wrongs. To fight wars and no one would have stopped them.

"You don't understand, Mom, but this is important."

SEVEN

MATT FINALLY GOT everyone moving toward the house. He simply reached into the pickup bed and got the box of guns and ammunition, plus the bedrolls.

"If it rains in the next few minutes, we don't want these ruined."

He said it as if taking everything inside were merely the next step as dictated by common sense, but I could tell Jeremy viewed the maneuver as the gates of freedom closing. He didn't yell or put up a fight—he never does with Matt—but he walked ahead of us, his neck and jawline taut, never looking to the right or left. His fists were clenched into tight balls, the very picture of rigidly leashed fury.

Most telling, he didn't offer to help Matt carry anything. Randy, on the other hand, was complaining loudly to his father. "Don't you get it, Dad? We have to do this." Like it was a mission, another of those rites of manhood. Or maybe he was just doing it for Jeremy.

"And if you find Jorgenson, just what do you think you're going to do with him?" Trey demanded.

Randy's eyes narrowed. "An eye for an eye and a tooth for a tooth."

"The way I learned it, only God shall wreak the vengeance. It's not your place."

The argument sounded like a battle of wits that they carried on because it was expected, not because it mattered to either one.

Diane wasn't saying anything, but she looked relieved, as if the worst of the confrontation was over. For her it probably was; Randy hadn't idolized Tim the way Jeremy had. He hadn't needed that older-brother-friend and confidant like Jeremy had, either. Randy could probably begin to let go of the emotions coming from Tim's death, but Jeremy wasn't that far along yet.

We reached the screen door to the kitchen and Jeremy flung it open violently, then remembered that I was right behind him. He caught it just before it slammed into me. His jaw was still tight and he didn't speak.

"Let's go into the den to talk," Matt suggested.

Everyone went in that direction except Jeremy. "I'm going to my room," he said. He cut right and I grabbed him by the arm. He shook my hand off so quickly I caught my breath. "Don't," he snapped.

"All right," I said. "But I want you to know something, Jeremy; you are not going after Jorgenson, you understand? Not today, not ever. It's just not happening."

He stared at me.

"I mean it," I added, but I didn't like the look on his face; there was a determination that didn't leave room for compromise. It didn't leave room for understanding or love, either. I could almost feel the rift slashing through our relationship.

"Please, Jeremy," I said, "you can't go after him. You don't know that he killed Tim. And if he did, that's even worse—he might kill you, too."

"Why don't we go and sit down and talk about it?" Matt suggested again.

"There's nothing to talk about," Jeremy said as he slammed up the stairs.

Matt turned around to look at me. I think it was the first time Jeremy had openly challenged him and it had to be disconcerting. Matt was Jeremy's adopted father—Steve, my first husband and Jeremy's biological father, had left when Jeremy was just a baby. Growing up, Jeremy had wanted a dad desperately, and when I had married Matt a little over three years before, Jeremy had latched on to him joyously. The feeling had been reciprocated by Matt. In

some ways Matt was almost a hero figure to Jeremy. It
made their relationship special and not one to be taken for
granted. I, on the other hand, am just "Mom." There's a
big difference: Jeremy doesn't have to be careful with me,
because he knows I'll always be there. Sometimes even
when he doesn't want me. With Matt there's a touch of
fear that he might go away.

Both anger and hurt showed on Matt's face as he stood
looking up the stairs. "Is this when you go in for tough
love?" he asked. "Or is this when I'm supposed to come
up with something brilliant?"

"Can you think of anything brilliant?"

"Not a goddamn thing." Matt rarely swears in my presence, so I took that as a bad sign.

Even though we had split most of the parenting duties
fifty-fifty, I still held fifty-one percent of the stock in Jeremy, which meant that I was ultimately the responsible
party. Or maybe in this case, Jeremy was.

Someone touched my arm and I turned around to find
Diane standing behind me. "Jolie," she said. "We're going
to head home. If there's anything I can do…"

I reached out and gave her a hug. "Thanks."

She smiled at me ruefully, then looked at Matt. "Welcome to parenthood."

"It's not like the movie," he said.

"Yeah, well, what part of real life is?" Then she hugged
me again and said, "I'm serious—if you think of anything
that we can do to help, let me know."

"I will," I promised as she left.

I'D LIKE TO GIVE Matt some credit for my idea, but he left
shortly after Trey and Diane. Bart, our foreman, was moving stock from one pasture to another and, while he could
have done it alone, it would be much easier with some help.
Matt kissed me good-bye distractedly and left with a frus-

trated look on his face. Obviously the ball had been left in my court, as they say.

Initially I sat on the back patio to think. And, if I were totally honest, to watch the back stairs to make sure that Jeremy didn't sneak out again. Around four I went in to start a roast—and that's when I had the idea.

I picked up the phone and called the number of the sheriff's office. I knew it by heart now.

It was Mac himself who picked up the phone. "Donelly here."

"Mac," I began, "I didn't really expect to find you there. I won't take up much of your time."

"Not to worry. I can spare at least thirty seconds. Anything more and it will have to keep 'til we get things sorted out." He sounded tired, the kind of weary that invades your mind as much as your body. "So, what can I do for you?"

"I have a strange request." In as few words as possible I explained about Jeremy's relationship with Tim and the unfocused anger he was dealing with now that Tim had been murdered.

"How old is Jeremy now?" Mac asked.

"Fifteen. He'll be sixteen in another couple of months."

"Hard age." Mac knew a lot about boys that age. He'd been an umpire at the ballpark for years until his knees gave out on him. These days he did some announcing when he had the time.

"So what I was wondering," I said, "is if you could use some help hunting Jorgenson. I thought maybe Jeremy could go with you to help search." I was trying not to sell my idea to Mac, but that was hard. This was important, both for Jeremy and for my relationship with him. "Jeremy is very responsible," I found myself adding. "And he'd be another pair of eyes for you. If he got in the way or didn't follow your instructions exactly you could send him home. It would just help a lot for him to be doing something constructive."

"Is he thinking that Jorgenson had something to do with Tim's death?"

I let out a long sigh. "Mac, I don't know that he's thinking at all. At least not very logically. He's hurt and he's angry, and there's no place for that anger to go."

"That's tough for a boy."

"Very tough," I agreed. Then I waited for Mac to say yes or no. Finally he spoke.

"Okay, Jolie, he can go with me tonight. It'll be about midnight; think that'll suit him?"

"It'll suit him."

Mac told me to have Jeremy at the sheriff's office a little before midnight and he would bring Jeremy home. Then we hung up. I hoped this would let Jeremy see that I was on his side.

I went up the stairs quickly and faced his door with more than a little trepidation. I was afraid that he would lash out at me again before I could say anything, and it would be another big obstacle for us to get over.

There was no sound coming from his room, no computer-game noises, no music, no conversation. My heart began to sink. What if he'd gone out again?

I tapped on the door. "Jeremy? I have some news for you." There was no response. "Jeremy? Did you hear me? I've got some news that I think you need to hear."

Finally his voice came back, thick and heavy. "What is it?" Jeremy had been crying.

I didn't ask him to open the door, nor did I suggest that I come in. Instead I said, "I called Mac and asked him if you could help with the search for Jorgenson. He said you could. I'm supposed to take you to the sheriff's office tonight; we'll have to leave about eleven-thirty. Is that okay?"

"Yeah, okay."

I waited a moment then said, "You might want to get some sleep now, honey. You'll be up all night."

There was a long pause, then his voice came back even rougher than before. "Thanks, Mom."

I WAS SURPRISED when the alarm woke me a little before five. Surprised because I hadn't thought I'd sleep at all that night.

Dropping off Jeremy at Mac's office had felt much the same as the day I had dropped him off at kindergarten for the first time. Jeremy had insisted that I stay in the car so he could go off alone to his classroom. My most vivid memory is of him standing on the walkway, his blond hair gleaming in the sunlight, his five-year-old face radiant with excitement. He'd been wearing new jeans and a T-shirt, with a cardigan sweater around his shoulders. Why I'd insisted on the sweater I'll never know. The temperature probably got up to ninety-five that day, but Jeremy had worn the sweater like it was one of the things you did to get to go to school. At the last moment he'd flashed me a grin that shot straight through to my heart. Then, grin still in place, he'd flipped me a little wave before he turned and set off for his classroom. I, on the other hand, had to keep wiping my eyes as I drove out of the parking lot so I wouldn't run into anything.

At the sheriff's office the night before Jeremy had not been grinning; instead his face had been tense with anticipation. But he had flipped me that same little wave before he started solemnly up the sidewalk to the door.

I had somehow stopped myself from saying all those motherly things like "Be careful" and "Do exactly as Mac tells you" and "If you want to come home early, just give me a call." I don't know why I think I have to keep repeating those things, but I do. Like Jeremy didn't hear them the first hundred times I said them. But, for once, I didn't utter a word—just a silent prayer as I backed away from the curb and started for home.

The drive home had been dark and lonely, but at least when I got to the ranch Matt was waiting for me.

When it had been just Jeremy and me living in Austin, we'd worked out most of our problems, and the world's, in the kitchen. The room was too small for a table, so we'd sat on the counters to discuss everything from Jeremy's grades to hunger in Africa. The one who was not having the problem, or who was the most conciliatory, would fix hot tea. Sometimes mint, sometimes chamomile. And then we'd sit and talk until all was right with the world.

When Matt and I had started dating he had drifted right into our informal ritual. At first he'd just leaned against a counter and visited. Then one night he'd volunteered to brew the tea. Finally he was sitting up there with the two of us, just like he belonged.

Last night he must have known what my mood would be because he'd fixed some chamomile tea. Rather than stay in the kitchen, though, he'd led me to the living room and we'd sat on the couch, my body curled up close to his. I used to complain that Matt didn't communicate sufficiently, but I've finally come to realize that when there are problems Matt *thinks* things through, rather than talks them through. Later, if I'll listen, he talks. This time I didn't mind the silence; I was grateful for his physical presence.

Eventually he'd said, "Are you about ready for some sleep?"

I had let out one of those long breaths. "I don't think I can sleep tonight."

"Don't you have to work tomorrow?"

The next day was Saturday. I only had to work three hours, but those hours started at six. "I still can't sleep," I said. I shook my head. "You know, yesterday at this time I thought I finally had it all."

He touched my hair lightly. "Which all is that?"

"Oh, you know. I had you and Jeremy, and I didn't have to worry about money or whatever." It's Matt's money, so

I thought I'd better explain. "It's not that money is all that important to me but…well…"

"It is important, since it means you have a place to live and food to eat. I knew what you meant."

I curled up a little closer to him. "Anyway, I felt like I had everything. My writing, even a job that I liked."

"And a news director that you hated," he said. I could hear the undertone of amusement in his voice.

"Maybe an enemy is important, too." Then I sighed again. "I guess I was taking it all for granted. And then suddenly, everything changed."

"Because Tim was killed?"

I nodded. I was looking across the room and out the window to the darkness of the hot summer night. Jeremy was somewhere out there, looking for a man who might be a killer.

"Tim's death," I said, to stop my own thoughts, "seems to change things. I know I didn't see him all that much but he was part of our world. An important part of Jeremy's, and now he's gone. His death leaves a hole. Especially because he was murdered."

"No man is an island," Matt said softly.

"I guess it does sound pretty trite."

"No, it's profound. We realize the truth of it over and over again in our lives; that's what makes it profound."

His arm was wrapped around me and I gave it a squeeze. Then we lapsed into silence again, just enjoying the togetherness, the safety of each other's presence.

After about fifteen minutes I felt Matt's body twitch slightly. I moved as carefully as I could, turning around so I could see him. His eyes were closed, his breathing soft and regular; he was sound asleep. He couldn't comfortably stay there all night, so I rubbed his arm gently. "Matt. Matt, you need to wake up."

His eyes opened but without much enthusiasm. "What time is it?"

When someone wakes me up I always ask that question, too. Like it matters. "It's a little after one. You need to go up and get some sleep. You've got to get up in a few hours."

"What about you?" he asked.

I shook my head. "I may never sleep again."

"Could you write?"

What a concept. I don't know why I hadn't thought of it myself—it is the perfect thing to do when your life is not going the way you want it to. After all, it's a whole new world where the circumstances and the characters are in your control, at least in theory.

"Good idea," I said, getting up from the couch and stretching. "We'll see if my characters are cooperative."

Matt stood up and slid both arms around me, kissing me lightly. "If they aren't, you can always come to bed. I promise I will be. Cooperative, that is."

We left a couple of lights burning and went up the stairs; at the top, after one more kiss, Matt turned right and I turned left toward my office. The soft hum of the computer and the draw of the mystery I was creating eventually pulled me in and I spent the next two and a half hours turning out six pages. Then when my body finally gave out, I went to bed and apparently didn't hear a thing until the alarm. Now it was morning and Jeremy was safely back home.

I hoped.

EIGHT

I SLIPPED OUT of bed and tiptoed toward Jeremy's door only to find it closed. I couldn't remember whether it had been shut the night before or not, so I cracked it open, flinching at the noise it made. Jeremy was there, an arm flung over the covers, his head only partially visible. It was wonderful to have him home and I had to resist the temptation to walk over and stroke his hair or cover up his arm; instead I pulled the door closed and hurried back to my room to get ready for the day.

A faint trickle of light came in the bathroom window and somehow it made me feel better, as if the day before were just a bad memory, and one that was fading. I knew it wasn't over, knew there was still much to be faced about Tim's death, but for the moment I was willing to take my small pleasures where I could, and enjoy them.

Matt didn't even stir as I kissed him gently, so I quietly slipped down the stairs. While I was microwaving a cup of water for tea I heard a sound behind me. It was Jeremy; he looked tired, but more settled than he had the night before. As if he had come to grips with his emotions, or at least set them aside for the moment. Maybe like his mom had.

"Hi," I said, still speaking quietly. "I didn't expect you to be up so early. What time did you get in?"

"Around four-thirty." He sat down at the table and yawned.

"Did you find Jorgenson?"

"No." The microwave dinged and he got up and began to fix my tea. I just sat and watched, afraid to say anything for fear of breaking the early-morning spell of camaraderie. "Mom, have you ever ridden around in a cop car?"

"Only once, after an accident. And Mac drove my car yesterday—is that the same thing?"

"I don't think so."

"Why do you ask?"

"It's weird; it's like the whole world looks different." He stopped dunking the tea bag and set it on the edge of the sink, then added cold water to the cup before handing it to me. "It's still kind of hot," he said. He sat down at the table beside me. "In a cop car you see more. Or it's like everything is in real sharp focus. I can't explain it."

I sipped some tea. "What kind of things did you see?" I asked.

"Oh, you know. Mostly people on the highway. Only you start to wonder what they're doing out there at that time of night. And Mac calls in the license number of almost every car after about one o'clock, unless he knows them. He says that in a big city you have people working three shifts, you know, in hospitals and clubs and at big manufacturing companies, but out here, it's different. Most regular people are home asleep."

"Some people must have a reason to be out."

"Oh, yeah." He almost smiled. "Like Mrs. Tichenor," he said. "She's not going to get to finish the school year like she wanted to."

"She went into labor!"

"Yeah, we saw them about three o'clock in the morning. They flagged us down, so we gave them an escort to the hospital. Her pains were already two minutes apart when we helped her inside." He sounded very knowledgeable.

"You helped her?"

He nodded slowly, almost as if he didn't believe it himself. "Mom, I was right outside the door when she had the baby. I could hear Mr. Tichenor telling her to breathe and everything Dr. Baxter was saying. It was just..." He stopped and looked at me as if the words were too much for him. Finally, he said, "She had a little boy. Tyler Morgan Tichenor."

The continuance of life, even as he mourned a death.

I didn't say anything, just watched as Jeremy took a deep breath. "I got to hold him. Tyler."

Perhaps it was the birth of little Tyler Morgan that had given Jeremy his new serenity. I could almost hear Mac's soft voice saying it just might be God's way of hurrying the healing process.

We were silent for a while, me sipping my tea, Jeremy staring out the window, still with a look of wonder on his face.

Finally, I asked, "Did anything else happen last night?"

"Huh? Oh, no, nothing as exciting as that." He got up and poured himself some juice. "We did see the guy from the radio station. Around two o'clock in the morning."

"What guy from the radio station?"

"Your boss—Rory Stone."

"What was he doing out? Did you talk to him?"

"Mac waved him over and we talked to him for a little bit. He said he couldn't sleep and was just out driving around, but Mac thinks he was looking for Jorgenson, just like we were."

"And you didn't see any trace of Jorgenson?"

"Nope. But I'm going out with Mac again tonight." He put down his glass and said, "If that's okay with you."

It was like an apology and an acknowledgment of who I was all at the same time. I nodded slowly. "Sure. It's okay." I watched him drink his juice and then said, "So, how are you doing this morning?"

He shrugged. "I'm fine."

"I know you're fine—I wondered how you were feeling—"

"I said, I'm okay." He must have regretted the snap to his voice because he added, "Mac says it'll just take time."

Apparently Mac was the new hero around our house. I

wasn't sure how I felt about that, but I suppose Jeremy could do worse.

"Hey, Mom…"

"Uh-huh?"

He paused. "Oh, nothing."

"It's okay, you can tell me."

"Never mind." He looked at the clock. "You're going to be late."

"Oh, shit," I said, as I grabbed for my purse and keys.

"Wiley Pierce is going to be out south, so if you want to go a little over the speed limit it should be okay."

I rolled my eyes, then gave him a quick kiss on the cheek as I raced out the door. He hardly flinched.

I GOT TO THE STATION at ten 'til six and went straight to the computer, waiting impatiently for its little voice to say, "Hello, Commander, computer reporting." Since I already knew that no one had spotted Jorgenson or his sister during the night, I did what I could to fill out the stories I had. I can pad or stretch almost anything, a talent that had made me very popular in high school when term papers were due.

Then it was time for the six o'clock news. I had Dan, the morning guy, play a couple of extra public service announcements to fill up any extra time. When it was over I had a cup of hot tea, scanned the national and international news from the wire, then left on foot to make my rounds.

It wasn't quite seven yet, but the temperature was already climbing as I walked the two blocks to the square. The courthouse stood in the center, in all its regal glory, just as it had for over a century. Surrounding the building was a thick carpet of grass and sixteen stately pecan trees, like sentinels. I knew their exact number because I had counted them on more than one morning walk. The Beautify Purple Sage committee must have been busy recently because the flower beds next to the courthouse, which had held faded pansies, were now filled with brilliant pink petunias.

Even this early there was activity around the square. Cars were beginning to appear as the owners of the small shops arrived for the day. Two blocks away I could see Webers Grocery, the parking lot already filling up. Wilmot County depends primarily on farming and ranching for its income and things start early in Purple Sage. For example, most grocery shopping is done in the morning on Wednesdays and Saturdays. According to Matt, that's when the stores used to give double trading stamps. As he tells the story, every Saturday morning when he was little his family would get up at five, do their chores, then pile into the car and head for town to do "errands." That meant his mom would shop for groceries at Piggly Wiggly while his dad drank coffee and visited at the Sage Cafe. The Piggly Wiggly, as well as the trading stamps, have been gone for years, but the tradition of early Saturday shopping remains.

Having been raised in Dallas, I don't always recognize Purple Sage traditions until I'm practically knocked over by them, and then I don't always like them. For example, if I had my way, the major newscast would be at noon. I doubt that it will ever happen, at least not in my lifetime. Things change slowly out here in "ruralmania," as Jeremy sometimes calls it.

The front door of the courthouse isn't unlocked until eight, so I went in the side door and up a flight of wide stairs to the sheriff's office on the second floor. As I suspected, Mac wasn't in. Instead I found Linc Draper behind the wooden counter. He was sitting at the scarred, dark oak desk, thumbing through a file. Linc was older than the other deputies, probably early fifties, with thick graying hair and a heavy, muscular body. When a new dentist, doctor, or CPA moves to town there is a write-up in the paper, and often a reception to welcome them and their family. The common people don't get that same treatment, so Linc had slipped in practically unnoticed several months before. All

I knew about him was that he'd been with the Albuquerque Police Department before coming to Purple Sage.

"Good morning," I said.

Linc lifted his head and eyed me a moment before saying, "'Morning."

"I don't know if we've officially met; I'm Jolie Wyatt from KSGE. The radio station. I do news."

"Linc Draper. Deputy." He didn't hold out his hand and he didn't smile, but he got up and moved to the counter. "What can I do for you?"

"I was wondering if you had any information on the search for Jorgenson." I already had pen and paper at the ready for notes.

"Nobody's found him yet," Linc said.

"I'd heard that; my son rode with Mac last night." I didn't know if that would win me points or take them away. "I was hoping that you could give me some other information," I went on. "Like, how many men are out. Where. How long they're going to be looking for Jorgenson. Whatever you can tell me." The taxpayers like to know that sort of thing, since their money buys the gas and the tires.

Linc rubbed his chin slowly before saying, "It's not really much of a search at this point. We haven't pulled in anyone from the other counties to help. Not even from the police department. No reason to. Jorgenson could be a thousand miles from here—nobody knows."

Which made perfect sense when you thought about it. "But wasn't Mac looking for him last night? And aren't there some others searching?" I asked.

"We've only got five officers total and I'm working on the homicide."

"Oh." I hadn't forgotten about Tim's death, but I had pushed it back to some dark corner of my mind. I took a breath and tried to switch to business mode, to sever the connection between heart and mind so that I could deal with anything he said as if we were talking about a stranger.

I looked straight at Linc. "Is there anything new on the murder?"

"Not much, yet."

"What *do* you know?"

With a bit more prodding, he told me that Tim had died from a twenty-five-caliber bullet. There were three wounds in his chest; the bullet that had killed him had pierced his heart. There had been no water in Tim's lungs or stomach, so Linc believed Tim had already been dead when he went in the lake.

"We don't know for sure where that was," Linc added, "but I suspect it was pretty close to where we found him."

"Have any witnesses come forward?"

"Not a one." He didn't sound happy about it. "Must be sound sleepers out there."

"Must be. Do you know what time he died?"

Linc gave me a hard look. "Let's just leave that part out for now."

"Okay." I finished writing my notes. "Well, thanks for your time."

"Don't mention it," he said.

I gave him one final, halfhearted wave and headed out the door. Next on my list was the police station, but that turned out to be a total wash. The door was locked and a sign said that the dispatcher was out for fifteen minutes. If you had arrived because of an emergency, it suggested, you try the sheriff's office.

The chief of police, Bill Tieman, isn't someone I've depended on for a lot of information, anyway. Only a month or so before he had run on the Democratic ticket for mayor, against Trey Atwood. I had been Trey's campaign manager. Worse, a murder case was being investigated by the PD at the time and I had made it clear that I felt the investigation was biased. I never said anything against Bill personally, but I'm sure he took it that way. I would have.

Now, since Trey won the primary, Bill is stuck as the

chief of police. That makes two strikes against me, so I don't find it surprising that no one at the police department has ever gone out of their way to help me with a story or offer me a cup of coffee.

At least by then I had shaken off, or at least set aside, the horrible sense of loss I'd been overwhelmed with; I was walking a little faster, feeling a little better. I stopped at the drugstore for a quick cup of tea, and then headed back to the station. When I got to the news office F. Rory Stone was already there, sitting at his desk, the police monitor squawking away.

"Good morning," I said loudly to be heard over the monitor.

He hardly noticed, just sort of waved me away like a fly.

"I just left the sheriff's office," I said. "Do you want to hear what I got?"

"Is it important?"

"Well—"

"Shit!" He jumped up and reached for his keys, his pudgy body moving like Michael Jackson's.

I was about to demand that he explain what was going on when I heard the voice of Linc Draper coming over the monitor using the words *roadblock* and *Jorgenson* in the same sentence. Half an hour ago nothing had been happening, now there was action. I grabbed my purse and I was right behind Rory by the time he got to the door.

"Stay here," he said.

"No!"

I was in his little VW turning on the police radio before he even had the driver door closed. He started the car and I said, "Have they mentioned a location?"

"Highway Eighty-one." We were already out of the parking lot and speeding down the street.

"Where on Eighty-one?" I asked.

"Where it meets Five-thirty-seven. North of town."

"Then turn left up here. We'll cut around the back and

take the old Farm to Market Road,'' I said. ''Where's Jorgenson now?''

Rory was pressing the car forward. Our tires spun and threw gravel as we whipped around the corner and onto a narrow caliche road.

''They spotted him near the airport.''

''We can beat him if we hurry.'' I noticed my voice was shaky. I rolled up the window to keep out the dust and fumbled with the seat belt. Rory was driving like a demon—same as I would have been.

The police monitor started up again. *This is Unit Twenty-three, we're about five miles from the intersection on Jones Road.*

That meant we weren't far behind them. The cop finished by asking, *''Is there another unit responding?''*

There were two. *''This is Unit Four. We're coming in from Delton.''*

Delton is a small community about eight miles out of town.

''Unit Seven. We're in position.''

I suddenly realized that with luck they would apprehend Jorgenson. ''Have you got a recorder?''

''In back,'' Rory said. I undid my seat belt and leaned over the seat as he swerved left onto the Farm to Market Road and we hit a chuck hole that almost bounced us off the pavement. ''Hang on,'' he said.

I sat back down and buckled myself back in.

Ahead of us I could barely make out the lights of the police car as it braked at the highway.

''There,'' I said. ''That's it!''

Rory slowed the little car then whipped it off into a shallow barrow ditch that ran beside the road. There were fallow fields on two sides of us and a maize crop stretched out as far as I could see on the other side of the highway. Two cars were lined up across the asphalt of the intersection: one was from the Department of Public Safety, one was a sheriff's car. A uniformed patrolman was putting down flares to warn other drivers of the obstruction. Rory just sat there watching.

"I'm getting out," I said, reaching for the door handle.

"You don't get it, do you?" he snapped. "Someone is very likely going to die out there. If you get in the way it could be you."

His words skidded across me like ice across a sunburn.

He had to be wrong. Jorgenson would see the roadblock and stop. The kid wasn't stupid.

Some primal instinct was drawing me and I couldn't resist it. I opened the door and got out. "I'll be behind the car."

Off in the distance I could hear a siren; it had to be coming from the police unit that was chasing Jorgenson. A buzzard circled lazily above. A pickup came screaming down over a rise, then disappeared as the highway veered behind a clump of trees. The troopers took their positions.

Wiley Pierce, one of the sheriff's deputies, got down in the brush across the narrow road from me and leveled his pistol, as if waiting for a target. A police officer crouched beside him, and a DPS trooper picked a spot behind some bushes not five feet in front of me. I moved farther back.

The pickup was in sight again, tearing toward the roadblock. Jorgenson must have seen what was waiting for him—the flares, the cars, the guns—but he didn't seem to care. I saw the front end of his pickup bounce as he hit the accelerator. The cop in front of me swore.

When Jorgenson was less than thirty feet from the police cars he slammed on the brakes, skidded slightly, then swung wide, aiming for a spot between the far sheriff's car and the fence. The pickup hit the tail end of the sheriff's car and dust flew everywhere. The pickup began to swing wide, but Jorgenson didn't flinch. He fought the steering wheel for just a moment, and then must have slammed the accelerator all the way to the floor because the pickup bucked up onto the pavement. Then he was speeding down the highway again.

There was suddenly a lot of movement and swearing.

"Goddamn son of a bitch—I should have just shot his ass!" It was Wiley, flailing his arms in frustrated rage.

Another of the DPS troopers was already running toward his car. "Let's go!"

The cop car that had been chasing Jorgenson was stopped in the intersection. He couldn't get through without doing more damage to the other official vehicles. The first state car was already backing up, ready to take up the pursuit. As soon as it hit the highway the sheriff's car tried the same maneuver, but with less luck. It snagged the wire fence and hung. When the fence finally snapped, the car jerked forward only to have the rear tire explode. Apparently when Jorgenson hit the back end of it, he'd pushed the fender into the wheel.

I swung around and headed for the VW. "Come on," I said as I jumped in the car, but Rory wasn't there. I piled out of the car again. "Rory? Rory!" A sound came from behind a huge tumbleweed. I didn't have to get any closer to know what it was; our hard-bitten news director was throwing up his breakfast.

"I'm ready." Rory was pale, and sweaty.

"Are you okay?"

"I'm fine. We'd better go." The hand dangling his keys was shaking.

I reached for them. "I'll drive this time," I said.

"It's a stick shift—"

"We're losing them."

"They're still chasing him?" He turned around to look toward the highway.

"Yes," I said, my hand still out for the keys, "and if we hurry we might be able to catch up."

He tossed me the keys, while he raced around to the passenger's side. I started the engine, tested the clutch, brakes, and so on. As soon as Rory's door closed I took off. It was not with a mighty roar, or a great deal of speed.

"Hit it," he said as we swung onto the highway. "You won't hurt her—just push it!"

NINE

I WENT THROUGH the gears as fast as I could and only ground them for a millisecond. "Do you see them?" I asked. My foot was flat on the accelerator and we were going seventy-two miles per hour. In that car it seemed fast.

"I see the DPS car," Rory said. "I'll navigate."

I followed his directions, right on a two-lane Farm to Market, left on a caliche road, curve left and up on another Farm to Market. The DPS car was always well ahead of us and I never could see Jorgenson. Listening to the police monitor was no help—no one was talking. We covered the countryside, winding in and out until I was thoroughly lost.

After half an hour or so of that, the DPS car pulled over and eventually I caught up and slid in behind him. The trooper was already walking back toward me. I rolled down my window.

"Did you see where he went?" he asked, scanning the horizon. He adjusted his hat and sweat glistened on his forehead.

I shook my head. "Sorry, after he left the roadblock, I never saw him again. We were trying to stay up with you."

"Damn. I lost him about ten minutes ago, back at the four-way." He was scowling. "It's like he went down a damn rabbit hole."

"He's young and he's got lots of guts," I said. "They'll probably get him killed."

The trooper looked at me for the first time. "You're with the radio station, aren't you?"

Rory was up and out of the car in a flash. "I'm Rory Stone. The news director."

I stayed where I was. "And I'm Jolie Wyatt."

"Matt's wife?" the trooper asked.

"Right."

He thought for a moment before he said, "Follow me back to town, okay? I'm out of gas." He started toward his car, then turned to add, "It's going to take me a minute. I've got to call in."

Rory got back in the car and we sat silently, listening to the trooper radio directions and additional information to headquarters. A sheriff's car was coming out to join him in a few minutes. Seems with all the doubling back, we had ended up only about four miles out of Purple Sage.

We heard the dispatcher call to the trooper and ask him to wait where he was. Now they were going to start a full-scale search and the trooper could show them where to start.

"We might as well go," I said, starting the car and moving forward slowly. I pulled up even with the DPS car and the trooper waved us on.

"Think I'll make this trip a little slower than the last one," I said, glancing at Rory. His head was leaned back against the seat and his eyes were closed. "Are you still sick?"

"Huh?" He opened one eye and looked at me. "Just tired. Didn't sleep much last night. If you don't mind I'll nap on the way in." With that he closed his eyes and began a soft whistling snore, which I wasn't buying for a minute.

As soon as the Volkswagen came to a halt, Rory's eyes popped open and he headed straight into the station. And into the bathroom. I took my keys out of my purse and tried to muster the energy to go home. The last twenty-four hours were beginning to take their toll on me.

"Well, hey there, Jolie," Lewis Hilger said as he came into the news office. "Heard I just missed a real bang-up meeting with Mr. Jorgenson."

"How did you know about the roadblock?"

"Heard about it on the police monitor," he said, pointing to the one mounted near my desk. "I got one for my car, and it's a real education! Then I went over to the cafe for coffee and that's all anyone was talking about."

I looked down at the wire basket that held our news stories and wondered why we bothered. Maybe for the shut-ins who couldn't get to the Sage Cafe or the country club.

"So, what was everyone saying?" I asked, putting my keys and purse back on top of the desk.

"Oh, just that the kid's a rounder," he said with a laugh. "Always has been and always will be."

I was hearing the kind of admiration that folk heroes get. "Like how? What are you hearing about Jorgenson?"

Lewis sat on Rory's desk. "Well, you know, Jolie, some people just aren't born to settle down, or live in houses and lead everyday lives. I can identify with that some, because I'm a little that way myself. When Mrs. Hilger was alive we pretty much stayed in Purple Sage and lived our lives, but I always wondered what we were missing out there in the world. About eight years ago, she died; the kids were grown and gone, and I'll tell you something, as much as I love Purple Sage, I can't stay here too long at a time, anymore. Home is where I settle in, rest up, and then repack between trips, because, frankly, I want some adventure in my life. I think when Jorgenson was a kid he wanted some too, but he was stuck here, if you know what I mean. So he created his own excitement."

"With cherry bombs?"

"Not just cherry bombs, although that is how he started. Have you ever heard the story of how he escaped from the Wilmot County jail the first time?"

First time? "When?"

"When he was just sixteen years old."

Which explained why Mac hadn't told me—it was a juvenile offense. "No, I guess I haven't," I said.

"This is a great one!" Like a kid he squirmed around,

his grin almost as broad as his round face. "I love this story! You see, Jorgenson was in jail, the old jail, off Main, the one that's a museum now."

I knew it well. It was a three-story red-brick building with a crenellated tower. It was built in the 1800s, and had served as jail, gallows, and apartment for the sheriff for many years. It had been antiquated in the forties, but hadn't been replaced until about three years ago.

"Our writers' group meets there every Tuesday night," I said. The lower floor has been restored to a polished and pristine state that is probably nothing like it had been in its heyday. The cells upstairs still have graffiti scratched on the brick walls. My personal favorite says *Help, I'm being helt prisoner.*

Lewis said, "You can imagine poor Jorgenson trapped up in that place. It just wasn't for him, and so one night he begged the deputy to just let him stick his head out the window and breathe some outside air. Now the deputy was young and not too bright, although he swears he told Jorgenson no at first. Then he decided that if he handcuffed Jorgenson, nothing could go wrong, so that's what he did.

"Once he had Jorgenson out of the cell, and nothing bad happened, he decided that maybe they could play some dominoes. The deputy was bored, Jorgenson was bored, so why not?"

"This story is getting weirder and weirder."

"And I haven't gotten to the best part yet." Lewis was loving every second of it. "After a few games the deputy decided to take the handcuffs off Jorgenson. That worked out okay, so he let a little more time pass, and then he decided it was hot and he needed a cold drink. They were in the refrigerator in the kitchen." The kitchen is just off the main room downstairs, close to the front door. "No one knows why, but it turns out that there was a six-pack in the fridge."

"And the deputy got drunk?" I guessed.

"He swears he didn't, but Jorgenson did keep bringing the beer—''

"And the deputy had to go to the bathroom!"

"Exactly. Several times. The third time, Jorgenson unplugged the police dispatch unit, grabbed the keys, and took off in the deputy's car. By the time the deputy came out of the bathroom, Jorgenson was long gone and the deputy knew he was in deep trouble. He tried to call another unit for some help and he couldn't figure out why the radio wouldn't work. He thought it just broke at the worst possible time."

"So Jorgenson got away."

"Actually, it wasn't a clean getaway. Jorgenson zig-zagged around so much to avoid being followed that he didn't get far before the sheriff—it was Rayburn Elsby back then—spotted him. Rayburn was just coming from the movies with his wife, and when he saw Jorgenson he went straight into pursuit. There was one hell of a chase and Jorgenson ended up driving through a fence and into a ditch before he finally gave up. As the story goes, Mrs. Elsby, the sheriff's wife, gave Jorgenson a piece of her mind for putting her and the sheriff in danger and then slapped him good with her purse. Several times. Jorgenson told someone later that the law-enforcement officers in Wilmot County weren't worth worrying about, but he hoped he never ran into Mrs. Elsby again." Lewis started to laugh, then suddenly sobered. "Damn, I hope that kid doesn't get himself killed this time."

James Jorgenson was barely out of his teens and he was baiting law-enforcement officers like a puppy might bait a bull. It was the kind of action that could prove fatal if a lawman lost his temper or made a mistake. It might not even take a mistake—Jorgenson might get himself killed pulling the kind of stunts he had earlier that morning.

"Was his sister with him?" Lewis asked.

I stopped to recall the memory of that blazing pickup

roaring down the country road. The driver's side of the pickup had been toward me, and I didn't remember seeing anyone else through the open window. That didn't mean that Sharon Jorgenson hadn't been crouched down on the floorboard. That's where I would have been had I been riding with James Jorgenson.

"I'm not sure," I said, then explained what I'd seen to Lewis.

He nodded, his eyes focused on some far-away spot. When he spoke his words came out slowly, his voice quiet. "This just has all the earmarks of something that could end in tragedy."

"And we've already had one of those," I said.

He seemed startled, then finally nodded. "Tim Michelik, you mean. Everybody says he was a hell of a nice kid." I was about to agree when Lewis went on, "Then again, I guess not everybody says that."

"What?" The words didn't even want to register. "Tim didn't have any enemies—everyone loved him." In my surprise I couldn't form sentences.

"It's not good to speak ill of the dead," Lewis said, rising. "And I'm holding you up. You need to get on home. Did Jeremy catch up to you?"

"Jeremy?"

"I thought I saw him coming down the sidewalk here about eight this morning. While you were out making rounds. Maybe I was mistaken," he said, as he started off down the hall. "Have a nice weekend."

"Right." I was still too stunned to do much more than stare after him. What could he possibly have heard about Tim that I didn't know? I picked up my purse again. Tim had been wonderful to Jeremy, and great out at the Boys' Ranch, in fact, he had been just generally a terrific person. How could people be saying bad things about him?

Later, I told myself. I would hear about it, and probably discover that it was merely a misunderstanding. In the meantime I was going home. Rory still hadn't come out of the bathroom and might never. Maybe he was living in there. Or maybe he was avoiding someone. As interesting a thought as that was, I wasn't in the mood to dwell on it. Instead I headed outside, where I was almost blinded by the brilliance of the sunshine and by the heat it was generating.

"Hey, Mom, where've you been?"

Jeremy was lounging against my car. I might have felt sorry for him, standing out there in the heat, except that he was eating a jelly-filled doughnut and there was a carton of milk, as well as a white sack, on the hood of my car. Obviously, Jeremy had just arrived from the bakery.

"Why didn't you come in?" I asked as I walked toward him.

He looked down at the doughnut in his hand. "I haven't been here long."

"Lewis said you came by while I was doing rounds—that was almost two hours ago."

"I had some other things to do, and then I went to the bakery. It's no big deal. Are you ready to go home?"

I opened my car door and let a wave of heat escape. "Yeah. Is there anything else you need to do while we're in town?" I sat down in the car and rolled down the window. "And why are you in town? How did you get here?"

"Matt brought me in." He got in the car and held out the sack. "Want one?"

I looked inside the bag and saw two more jelly doughnuts with red filling already oozing out. IdaMae Dorfman at the bakery on Main makes some of the best doughnuts in the world. Her cream pies could get Richard Simmons off his diet. Not to mention the breads she makes, and my personal favorites, her shortbread cookies.

"No, thank you," I said firmly, handing everything back to Jeremy. "So, where is Matt?"

"Oh, he had a tennis match. That tournament thing."

And being the wonderful and attentive wife I was, not only was I not there cheering him on to victory, I had forgotten all about it. So, I'd just have to be wonderful and attentive another time.

I skirted the square and turned left toward the ranch.

"Hey, Mom, can we stop at the country club?"

"Sure. You want to watch Matt play?"

Jeremy hesitated while he looked out his window. I recognized the maneuver well—it was the prelude to a lie. But he didn't lie; instead he turned back and actually looked at me. "His match was at eight; I'll bet it was over a long time ago."

"Then why are we going to the club?" I hadn't turned off the highway, yet; we weren't committed.

"Because I want to talk to someone," he said. "And I'd like you to help. If you don't mind. But I really think it's important...."

I was tired and I didn't have a lot of patience left for his stalling. "Jeremy, would you, please, just tell me what this is about. Now. Before I die of old age."

"Okay," he said, probably not intending to sound huffy. He swallowed and started in slowly, "I still want to do something for Tim because he was my friend." His words came faster. "I know you don't want me going after Jorgenson, and I realize that it wouldn't matter if I did. We don't know for sure that he killed Tim. Mac says maybe he didn't. Anyway, so I want to do a memorial to Tim and I thought you could help me write it."

I glanced over at him. This was important. "Of course I'll help. Only I don't see why we have to go to the club to do it."

"Oh, well, I don't want to just put down my thoughts about Tim. It would be better if some other people got to tell a story about him, too. Or just say something about how important he was to them. Or how nice he was. You know."

"I think that's a wonderful idea. His mother will be so touched."

Jeremy squirmed, making it apparent that he wasn't doing this for Grace. I decided it didn't matter who he was doing it for; it was a gift that he was giving to Tim and Tim's family.

"I thought we could talk to Lurline first," Jeremy said. "Since he worked for her for a long time."

I turned down Sage Club Road with its manicured grass divider and flowering oleanders. The trees on either side of the road formed a canopy above us—it always reminded me of soldiers holding out their swords so royalty could pass through. "That's fine. We don't have a lot of time; isn't the funeral going to be on Monday?"

"This isn't for the funeral."

"Then what's it for?"

"The *Tribune*."

I took a breath. Rory is almost manic about KSGE and our coverage of the news, but I didn't have any idea what he thought about the newspaper or any competition between it and the station. Considering my already shaky relationship with Rory, it might be something to discuss with him first.

"Jeremy," I began slowly, "I'd like to help, but it could be a little problem for me. You know, Rory could consider it some kind of conflict for me to be writing for the paper."

"F. Rory Stone is a jerkbrain."

"Jeremy—"

"Besides, I already asked him about it. I talked to him first and he didn't want to do a memorial." Jeremy's words ground to a bitter halt. I glanced over at him and realized his jaw muscles were working hard.

"What exactly did he say?"

There was a pause, then Jeremy cleared his throat, an

angry flush moving over his skin. "He said he didn't want it on his radio station."

"Because?"

"Because it was emotional pabulum for sappy people."

TEN

HAD F. RORY STONE been standing at the side of the road I would have aimed the car at him and left Michelin marks across his body. I couldn't believe that any human being could be so cruel, especially when Jeremy's pain had to have been obvious. Now I knew exactly what the expression "Killing is too good for him" meant. I didn't want Rory dead—I wanted him suffering.

We pulled up in front of the country club and I stopped the car. I was so angry it was hard to speak. "So, what did you say to him?"

"Nothing. 'Thank you.' 'Good-bye.'" Jeremy turned to stare at me. "You know, if you don't want to help, you don't have to, but it wasn't my fault—"

"Jeremy! I know that! I'm on your side."

"Then why'd you ask me what I said?"

"Because if I'd been there I'd have punched in his fat face."

"Oh." He looked surprised. "Really?"

"Of course, really. Rory Stone had no right to talk to you like that. He doesn't even know what normal emotions are."

"It's okay, Mom, you don't have to get all riled up."

"I'm *already* all riled up, and this is not over. I intend to do something about it."

"And what about your job?"

I grabbed up my purse and the strap caught on the parking brake. "This has nothing to do with my job. Rory Stone was inexcusably rude and that's a piss-poor way to represent the radio station." I yanked the strap free. "And besides that, nobody—and I mean nobody—talks to my son like that.''

"Except you.''

"That's right. And don't you forget it.'' I swung open the door and got out. "Come on, let's go find Lurline, and then after I calm down a little, I'm going to track down Rory.''

As we started off, Jeremy pulled a micro cassette recorder from his back pocket, a gift from Matt for improving his geometry grade. "Take me home before you look for Rory; I don't want to get involved.''

"Don't go seventies on me, Jeremy; it doesn't become you.''

"I was kidding. Sort of.''

But he hadn't fought the idea of my defending him so maybe there was a bit of the little boy still left inside the rapidly maturing Jeremy. I hoped so. I hated for him to grow up completely and not need me for anything.

I STOPPED IN the wide glass and tile foyer and looked out into the huge dining area, instinctively searching for Tim. And for just a moment, I thought I saw him. There was the same young body with dark hair, wearing the long black shorts and turquoise shirt. But, of course, it wasn't Tim. After the first heart-stopping moment, I realized it was another young waiter. Sadness began to seep through me. I didn't know if Jeremy would feel it, too, but I slid my hand onto his shoulder, anyway.

Arielle Lambert, a high school girl who waited tables part time at the club, whizzed out of nowhere to appear in front of us. She was a little over average height and a little over average weight. She wore no makeup, and she might have appeared matronly if it hadn't been for her shiny, ash brown hair and bubbly personality. "Hi, y'all. Great skirt— I love that color!'' she said, pointing to my teal skirt.

"Thanks, Arielle.''

"A table for two?" she asked. "I think I can squeeze you in somewhere."

It was only a little after eleven, so there was no lunch crowd yet, in fact, no crowd at all. All the tables were set with their pink paper napkins and cut-glass goblets but there wasn't a single person at them.

"Arielle, do you know if my husband is around by any chance?" I asked.

She rested the empty tray she was holding against her hip and thought about it for a second. "He played one of the first matches in the tournament, didn't he? I think he whipped John Knight in straight sets and then went on home. About an hour ago, but I could be wrong. If someone isn't hollering for something to eat or drink, I don't pay them much attention."

"Is Lurline here?" Jeremy asked. "We'd like to talk to her."

"Sure. Why don't you sit down over here." She led us to a table against a side wall. "You want something to eat or drink while you're here? The special today is grilled shrimp in an orange and ginger sauce. You get six shrimps, cole slaw, french fries or baked potato, rolls and coffee or tea for six ninety-five. We also have our California burger with guacamole and sprouts, fries, and coffee or tea for five ninety-five. Any of those sound good?"

I was suddenly starved. "Sure, I'll have—"

"Uh, Mom, we're kind of in a hurry. Don't you think?"

I had no idea what his rush was, but I was being agreeable. "Okay, how about a bagel with cream cheese to go. And iced tea."

"And what about you, Jeremy?" she asked.

"I'll take a California burger to go. No sprouts, and a Pepsi to drink now," he said. "Oh, and can you tell Lurline we're here?"

"No prob." And then she whipped away.

I looked at Jeremy. "Why are we in a hurry?"

"I don't think I want to hang around here." His shoulders slumped and his sadness seemed as visible as a cloud of fog.

I reached out and touched his arm. "You don't have to do this if you don't want to. I could talk to Lurline for you."

"I want to do it." He straightened up in the chair. "Maybe you'd better go call Matt and tell him we'll be late."

It felt like a request for privacy; or maybe it was just a sensible suggestion. Whichever it was, I stood up. "Be right back." The three of us have this deal: if you're going to be late you call. It has saved a lot of worry, and a lot of useless waiting. And probably a lot of arguments, too.

I used the phone in the lobby, only I didn't get Matt. I got Jeremy's voice on the answering machine: *"You've reached the Wyatts at Double W Ranch. We can't come to the phone right now, but if you'll leave your name and number at the tone, someone will call you back. Thanks for calling."*

During the first month after our move to Purple Sage, Jeremy had gone all-out cowboy on us. He bought boots, wore bandannas and a felt Stetson hat that dwarfed his body. He'd started listening to country music, especially old Bob Wills songs, and had begun talking like something out of a Gabby Hayes movie. He'd even used that language on our outgoing phone message. Thankfully I've forgotten most of it, but I do remember the tape had begun with, "Howdy, buckaroos!"

One evening Matt had "accidentally" erased the tape and then had asked Jeremy to re-record the message. Only, as Matt had said, "How about this time making it a little more professional sounding? After all, you are part owner of a modern, working ranch—I think you should sound like it." Jeremy had loved the idea of being part owner of the ranch, so he took the hint and his Hollywood-cowboy stage ended.

As soon as I heard the tone I said, "Hi, Matt, it's me. It's a little after eleven and Jeremy and I are at the club. I'm sorry we missed you, but I heard you won your match in straight sets. Congratulations! Does this mean you play again tomorrow?

"Oh, and go ahead and eat lunch without us; Jeremy is involved in a project but we should be there in an hour or so. Love you. Bye." And then I hung up the phone.

I stopped in the turquoise and pink bathroom and by the time I got back to the table Lurline was seated across from Jeremy.

"Hi, Lurline," I said as I sat down. "How's it going?"

As she glanced up at me I couldn't help but think she looked more tired than I felt. "I'm fine."

"You must miss Tim. I'm sorry."

Her pale eyes searched my face, then she nodded. "Thanks."

Jeremy stood up. "I'll be right back. Thanks, Lurline."

She watched him retreat toward the rest rooms. "I've already given Jeremy something he could put in the memorial story," she said.

"That was quick."

She shrugged her shoulders. "I just had something right on the top of my brain that I wanted to say. If it doesn't sound okay, you'll call me, won't you? Help me make it right?"

"I'm sure it will be fine," I said. There was something I wanted to find out about Tim, and Lurline seemed like a safe person to ask. She didn't gossip; in fact, I'd never heard her say an unkind word about a single member of the club. That's an amazing attribute, considering that her position made her privy to many of the secrets people tried so hard to hide.

Arielle appeared and placed my tea in front of me as I

began. "Lurline, someone suggested to me that Tim might have, well, that some people might not have liked him. Do you know why that might have been?"

Lurline seemed to stiffen. "No. I don't."

Arielle grunted softly like a baby pig. "Like hell; we all knew about Tim and—"

"Arielle!" Lurline almost knocked the girl over as she jumped up. "That's enough. Not one more word."

"Uh, sorry." Arielle glanced at me and I was dying to ask a question or two, but Lurline was too quick.

"This was a private conversation," Lurline said, her voice low and angry, "and you are not supposed to be listening. Or don't you remember?"

"Right; I remember. 'We don't see, we don't hear, we don't tell.'" Arielle dropped her head a half inch to a subservient pose that didn't look sincere. To me she said, "I'll go get your food." And then she moved off.

I waited, watching Lurline. She sat back down, muttering, "Damn kid." Then she stared out the window while her tanned hands fidgeted with a paper napkin, smoothing it until the crease disappeared. Finally her head came up and she realized I was waiting for something. She looked off in the direction that Arielle had gone. "I'm sorry about that; Arielle just isn't too good with discretion."

"It's okay," I said. "I had asked about Tim."

"What kind of crap have you been hearing, Jolie?"

"Nothing specific at all, just that not everyone liked Tim. It struck me as odd. Jeremy thinks he hung the moon; I suppose I thought the same thing—I just couldn't imagine Tim doing anything wrong. And since Tim worked here, and you saw him with the rest of the kids, I assumed you'd know more about...well, whatever it was."

It was her turn to stare at me now. I couldn't read the expression on her aging pixie face. There was tension, and I supposed it covered the emotions she was holding back, but I wasn't sure what emotions those were. Even when she spoke I still couldn't tell. "Look, Tim was a good person. A nice kid. He worked hard, he was responsible, and the members liked him—that's what mattered to me."

"But what? He couldn't have been perfect—nobody is."

"I don't know anything to tell you." She stood up, put out her hand, and shook with me. Her grip was so firm it was almost painful. "Tell Jeremy good luck on that memorial story. That's really nice of him."

Jeremy was already on his way back to the table. He and Lurline said something in passing but they didn't shake hands because Jeremy's were full. He was holding two bags and two foam cups—no doubt our order along with extra drinks. That was typical of the club.

"I signed the charge slip already," he said as he got to the table. "Are you ready to go?"

"Sure." I dropped a dollar on the table for Arielle.

"I put the tip on the charge," Jeremy said.

"Oh." I picked up my money and started walking side by side with Jeremy toward the front door. Funny, I wasn't near as hungry as I had been.

Once we were outside and I was unlocking the car, I heard a soft "psst" from somewhere behind me. I turned around to find Arielle standing near the corner of the building behind Lurline's new white Saturn. She was waving frantically at us, her index finger at her lips to indicate that we should be quiet. "Jolie, pssst." Her voice was a stage whisper and she kept looking behind her. Probably to see if Lurline was lurking anywhere nearby.

"I'll go see," I said to Jeremy, and then I attempted to saunter casually across the parking lot, although I suddenly felt like 007 avoiding capture by enemy spies. When I got to the sidewalk I cut left past the big windows until I was safely out of sight of anyone in the club. Then I hurried. "Arielle, did you want something?"

She grabbed my arm and pulled me back around the building toward a door that presumably led to the kitchen.

"Jolie, listen. About Tim—you need to find out about his love life. The women he was dating—" The knob on the kitchen door behind her rattled and she jumped. "Oh, shit, I've got to go. Bye." And with that she swung around and practically ran back behind a six-foot Dumpster. She was pulling a pack of cigarettes and a lighter from the pocket of her black shorts as she went, as if she were just outside on a short cigarette break.

I didn't want to give her away so I stepped around the corner of the building where I couldn't be seen from the kitchen door, then hurried to the car.

"What'd she want?" Jeremy asked. He was already sitting in the passenger seat, munching his California burger.

"She said we should go see the girls Tim was dating."

"Why was she being so secretive?"

"I don't know," I said. I slid into the car and Jeremy handed me my tea as soon as I had my seat belt on. "So, who was Tim dating?"

"Sharon Jorgenson."

I took a sip of the tea, then wedged the cup in between my seat and the console. "Before that there had to have been others."

"He dated lots of girls."

"Like who?" I asked, starting the car.

"Well, I don't know really, but I saw him one time with Michelle Kleinsmith. Maybe a couple of times."

"Michelle from the radio station? That Michelle Kleinsmith? Are you serious?"

"Yeah. Why?"

"Because I never would have put them together."

"Why?"

"I don't know." Maybe because I thought Tim was the bulky, muscular All-American boy, and Michelle was hot and exotic, sexier than Madonna without an eighth of the effort. Not a match with Tim, at least not on the surface, but then what did I know?

I wondered how long ago they had dated, and what their relationship had been when he'd died. Despite the fact that we worked together, I hadn't talked with Michelle since I'd heard about Tim's death.

"Do you mind if we run by the radio station?" I asked as I pulled out of the parking lot. "It won't take but a minute."

"You want to talk to Michelle?"

"Maybe."

"Maybe I'll tag along."

ELEVEN

MICHELLE WAS NOT at the radio station, nor was anyone except the disc jockey, so we got back in the car. It was nearing noon and most of the stores that carried staples for the locals would be closing, although the ones with crafts and souvenirs would be open until at least five for the tourists. That meant that Sage-ites who liked to shop, like Michelle, usually went out of town or engaged in one of their other favorite activities. I had no idea what that might be for Michelle, but I did know where she lived. "Want to try her apartment?" I asked.

"Sure."

So, we drove to the Gramercy Place apartments. They were crowded into a residential area of what Jeremy called "granny houses" because of their wide wood porches and overblown pecan trees. There was lots of gingerbread trim on the houses and each one seemed to have something distinctive to set it off from its neighbors. One had a double-size swing on the porch, another a twig wreath with forget-me-nots and blue bows. The Gramercy Place apartment complex looked like an elephant that had wandered in among the delicate houses and died there. It was a two-story box painted an ugly shade that was somewhere between ocher and beige. The trim was rough-hewn wood in a brown so dark it was almost black. The only thing that saved it from being a total eyesore, as well as obtrusive, was the landscaping. The grass was a deep green and half-barrels overflowing with marigolds, white alyssum, and pink petunias were placed strategically on the porches and under the trees.

I parked on the street and we walked up the gravel path

to Michelle's apartment, which was on the ground floor directly in front of us.

"Have you ever been here before?" Jeremy asked.

"One time. I dropped her off when her car was in the shop."

"Oh."

I rang the bell and waited, wondering what I was going to say, or maybe what she was. When she opened the door it was a relief to be welcomed as if we were expected guests.

"Hey, Jolie, Jeremy, come on in." She stepped back and gestured us into the small, dark-paneled living room. It was almost claustrophobic, but we didn't stay there long. Apparently Michelle used it for nothing more than a hallway. "Back this way. I spend most of my time out here." She led the way in her white cotton gym socks, dark gray sweatpants, and man's white, V-neck T-shirt. On her the outfit was sexy looking and I thought I detected a subtle shift in Jeremy's breathing pattern as we followed her.

She took us through the kitchen and into a sunroom, with two small love seats in a powder pink stripe, a braided rug, and scads of artsy-craftsy decorative pieces in pink calico and french blue. A sliding glass door covered the back wall, letting in lots of sunshine.

"Oh, how pretty," I said, glancing around.

"Thanks. Have a seat," she said, as she ran a hand through her long dark hair. The word *tousled* came to mind, like something out of a romance novel. I sat on one of the love seats, and Jeremy took a spot on the floor gazing upward at Michelle as she curled up on the other love seat. "So what are you two up to?" Michelle asked. "Just cruising around?"

"If this is a bad time…" I began.

"No, it's okay."

Somehow I had justified the visit because I worked with Michelle, because I had seen her almost every day for three weeks. I knew what she ate for lunch and I was beginning to know her wardrobe and her sense of humor. I also knew a little of her history—and that was making me feel even worse for barging in when she could be grieving. Michelle had already had plenty of grief at her young age.

Someone had told me the story when I'd first moved to Purple Sage. Those first six months it was like I'd started class late and everyone was trying to get me up to speed. They told me stories about Purple Sage's history, about many of the buildings in town, and a lot about the inhabitants. I only remembered the bare facts I'd heard about Michelle, but they'd been enough to make a lasting impression. Michelle had married at seventeen and moved to Purple Sage when her young husband, Ronny, I think his name was, had gotten a job with a county road crew. Shortly after that, just two weeks before Christmas, there had been a heavy snowfall, something Purple Sage wasn't used to, and Ronny had been sent to clear some roads south of town. Apparently he went too far to the side and the wheels of his grader had slipped into a deep drainage ditch. Whatever he had done to try to rectify the situation hadn't worked, and the heavy machinery had ended up flipping onto its side at the bottom of the pit. Ronny had been crushed to death beneath it.

No one had ever said how Michelle coped during those first few months, but most people remembered that she went home to San Angelo in late January and came back with a lawyer who filed suit against the county. The attorneys then spent a great deal of time preparing their case, and had ended up haggling behind closed doors to work out a settlement without a trial. To support herself during that period, Michelle had taken a job as bookkeeper at the radio station. When the $150,000 settlement was awarded, no one talked about how much of it had actually gone to Michelle. But there was pride in many voices when they pointed to the way Michelle had settled down in Purple

Sage and made a life for herself. How she practically "ran that radio station." Hard work was something people in Wilmot County could identify with.

What if Michelle were, once again, grieving over the loss of a man she loved? And what if we were intruding on that grief?

"We can come back another time...." I began.

She gestured to a Spiegel catalog. "I was just reading. So, what's up?"

I looked at Jeremy. I had gotten us into this situation, and the least I could do was handle it. "Well, Jeremy is doing a special article for the paper," I said. "We wanted to talk to you about it."

"Oh, really?" She seemed flattered. "What kind of article, Jeremy?"

"It's a memorial for Tim Michelik."

Michelle's entire body stiffened. "So why come here?" She sat up, glaring at me.

"I'd heard you dated Tim," I said, "and I thought you might want to say something about him. For the memorial article."

"Oh, I'd like to say something about him, all right. So, what else did you hear? How stupid I was to believe what he said?"

No, she wasn't grieving, at least not in any way that I was familiar with. "Michelle, I'm sorry; I thought you and Tim were friends."

She sank back then, going from full fury to sadness in one heart-wrenching second. A giant tear slid down her cheek as she shook her head. "It's okay, Jolie. I shouldn't have jumped on you." She wiped away the tear and others popped out to take its place. "I guess you didn't know, but Tim Michelik and I were not on speaking terms. He just, just...oh, never mind." A small sob escaped.

"Just what?"

More tears? "Didn't care. Not about me. Not enough. I

wasn't enough.'' She glanced toward Jeremy and wiped at her face with the back of her hand.

I slipped into the kitchen and grabbed up a couple of napkins for her. ''You want to talk about it?'' I asked as I hurried back to give them to her.

She took the napkins, then glanced again at Jeremy and shook her head. ''No, I'm fine. Just a lot of those 'warring emotions' like you read about.'' She blew her nose and tucked the used napkin under a cushion. ''Let this be a lesson to you, Jeremy. You go around breaking women's hearts and they cry.''

He nodded but didn't speak.

We gave her a few minutes to regain her composure. Finally I asked, ''Are you sure you're okay?''

''I'm fine, now. Just a momentary thing. Tim always said I was whimsical.'' She laughed lightly, although it sounded as if she were off her stride. She jumped up. ''Can I get you anything to drink? Jolie?''

''No, thanks, I don't care for anything.''

''Jeremy, what about you?''

He was watching her intently and his concentration seemed to be broken by the question. After a moment he said, ''I just had a Pepsi. But thanks.''

''Oh, well, then...'' She sat back down.

My preference was to leave right then, but this was Purple Sage, the fringes of the Old South, and it wouldn't have been polite to walk out. We had to make a pretense of wanting to talk to Michelle and she had to make a pretense of being pleased about it. ''You've really done a lot with this apartment,'' I began. ''I didn't realize you collected country decorations.''

''Oh, I love them.''

Jeremy decided to help us out. ''Then you must like Miz Priddy's.'' A touristy shop owned by a man named Burt Apple.

"One of my favorite places," Michelle said. "But, Jeremy, I didn't know you were a writer like your mom."

"I'm not really. I don't do books or anything," he began. And then he started telling the story about his previous year's English term paper and how, halfway through the writing of it, he'd lost the book of Robert Frost's poems he was using. And how he'd faked the poetry and had still gotten an A. Michelle laughed out loud, then countered with a high school story of her own, but I wasn't paying attention. I was thinking about Jeremy.

Matt always kidded me about my "golden gift of gab," as he called it, and how I should have been an ambassador since I could sit down and visit with anyone. When I had taken the job at the radio station he told me he was going to write Barbara Walters to warn her that I'd be taking over her job very soon. According to Matt, Jeremy had the same gift, although we hadn't seen much of it when Jeremy was going through his early-teen "sullen years." Now I realized that Matt was right, Jeremy had literally charmed Michelle into a good mood.

She ruffled her hair. "I must be a mess."

"Actually, you look just like you always do," I said. "Beautiful. It's disgusting; very hard on the rest of us."

"Sure, I'm buying that, Jolie." She gave me a small smile, changed her mind about it, and reached again for the napkin. She didn't blow her nose or wipe her eyes, she just looked at it. I suspected that at the core, Michelle was a survivor, as tough as she needed to be for any situation.

I stood up. "Well, we'd better get out to the ranch. Matt will be wondering what's happened to us."

She stood, too. "I'm glad that you stopped by." She smiled at Jeremy, making the lie almost believable.

I put my purse strap over my shoulder and motioned for Jeremy to come on. He was up in a flash, leading the way to the front door. When we got there I turned around to

Michelle and touched her arm. "I really am sorry we upset you, Michelle."

"Don't be. I probably just needed a good cry from when Tim and I broke up."

Ten or so tears didn't exactly make a good cry in my book, but maybe Michelle had done her crying earlier. I had the feeling that there was a whole lot more to Tim Michelik than I had suspected, but Michelle obviously wasn't going to say anything at the moment, at least not with Jeremy around.

"Anything else we can do for you before we go?" I asked. "Pull leaves off your plants? Break a glass or two, maybe?"

"You could kick my neighbor's cat—it keeps peeing in my planter and digging up the marigolds."

"Sorry, cat-kicking is an extra charge," I said.

"Then forget it."

"Okay, see you Monday."

"Bye. Bye, Jeremy."

Once we were in the car and actually moving out of sight of the Gramercy Place apartments, I let out a long breath. "That was horrible. Poor Michelle."

"You don't know that," Jeremy said.

"What?"

"We don't know if it's poor Michelle. We don't know anything at all about what happened between Michelle and Tim."

I looked at his face. I had assumed Jeremy was the fatuous one, gazing up at Michelle in all her beauty, swapping stories with her and accepting everything she'd said. It appeared Jeremy had been far more critical than I had been. "What are you hinting at, Jeremy?"

"Maybe it's poor Tim. Maybe she did something terrible to him."

"Like what?" I asked.

He stared straight ahead and said, "Like killed him."

I started to tell him how utterly insane that was when I remembered that Tim *was* dead and someone *had* shot him. Someone who had known him and hated him. Or maybe loved him.

"I hope not," I finally said. "There was something she said about 'not being enough.' Did you catch that?"

Jeremy thought about it for a minute. "Yeah, but it sounded like some kind of self-righteous martyr stuff."

"I wish I understood," I said. Physically I was maneuvering the car around the square, but mentally I was peeking behind the little hints that had been dropped about Tim, hoping to get a glimpse of what had really been going on in his life. The impression I was getting was that Tim's love for all mankind might have gone a little too far when it came to womankind. Or maybe his intentions had just been misunderstood.

That sounded like something every womanizer said.

But Tim hadn't said it—I had. Or at least I'd thought it. I looked over at Jeremy. His eyes were closed now and his head was resting against the back of the seat. The sun cutting across his face turned the sweep of eyelashes on his cheek a golden color. It had been a long twenty-four hours for him, too, both physically and emotionally.

I thought about Jeremy's response to Michelle and how he'd covered it with charm.

"Jeremy, how could you have been so nice to Michelle when you thought she murdered Tim?"

He opened his eyes and looked at me. "I didn't think that until she told the story about stealing the term paper."

"I missed that. But you made up Robert Frost's poetry—isn't that the same thing?"

"I didn't hurt anyone," he said, his voice filled with indignation. "She stole the paper from someone else at another high school and she never got caught. Someone else probably got an *F* because of her and she thought it was funny. That's not funny."

Camus said that every man had a moral code of his own likes and dislikes, and I could see the wide chasm between Jeremy's moral code and Michelle's. I had to agree with Jeremy that hurting another person was worse than faking something, but stealing a term paper wasn't on par with murder. Or was it part and parcel of the same set of values?

"Jeremy," I said. "I was wondering how many people Tim was dating. Do you know?"

"No, but I can find out."

"How?"

"Give me ten minutes and a telephone."

"Done." I turned right onto the highway and headed for the ranch.

TWELVE

I DON'T KNOW who was more disappointed, Jeremy or me, when we drove up to the ranch and saw Trey Atwood's Jeep sitting in front of the house.

"Maybe Trey is just here to see Matt," I said, parking the car.

"No, it's all three of them—they called this morning. I was supposed to tell you they were coming by this afternoon, but I forgot."

"Oh, well, we'll save the phone calls for later." Just then the front door opened and Diane, Trey, and Matt came out onto the porch. I jumped out of the car and hurried up the walkway. "I understand I'm late," I said as I joined them.

"By a whole forty-eight seconds," Diane said. She waited until Jeremy was on the porch, then gave him a quick hug. "How are you doing?"

"I'm okay. Thanks," he said, not quite shrugging her off. "Where's Randy?"

"Oh, he got a new software program and the modem he's been wanting, so he stayed home to get it installed."

"Cool," Jeremy said as he went into the house.

Diane turned to me. "Is he really okay?"

"He's doing better. So, what's the occasion?"

Matt was holding open the door and he gave me a quick kiss as we all went inside. He glanced in the direction Jeremy had gone and said in a low voice, "We're going spelunking."

"Spelunking?" And then I got it. "The cave!"

"So why don't you get changed?" Diane said, shooing me toward the stairs.

"Okay. Come on up. You can talk to me. Hey, how

come you gave Randy his modem now? You said that was for his birthday.''

''Well, we thought it would be better.''

We were in my room now and I was already getting jeans and a Purple Sage Dragons T-shirt out of a drawer. ''What would be better about now?'' I asked.

She sat down on the edge of the bed and leaned back on her elbows. ''Jolie, it's nothing against Jeremy. I love that kid, and you know it—it's just that right now, I think it's smarter if the boys are apart.''

I let my skirt slip from my hands and onto the floor. ''Why would you say that?''

Diane leaned over and picked up the skirt. ''Because together they might do something crazy that they wouldn't do alone.''

Like Jeremy was the instigator. And as soon as I thought it, I knew Diane wasn't blaming Jeremy. On some level I recognized that I was being overly sensitive, but it had been a long twenty-four hours. Too many things had happened and I hadn't adjusted to any of them. I hadn't even been able to *absorb* some of them, so my emotions were riding just beneath a thin layer of skin.

''Please, don't look at me like that,'' Diane said. ''This isn't because Jeremy is bad or wrong.''

''But he is the one who wanted to go off after Jorgenson.'' I pulled jeans over my hips and yanked up the zipper.

''Jolie, stop that. We don't know whose brilliant idea that was and I'm not blaming either of them.'' She held out her hand. ''Give me a hanger—you don't want your skirt to wrinkle.''

I took a hanger from the closet and handed it to her. ''You know, maybe Jeremy and Randy should be together to help work out their grief.''

''Maybe they should, but if that's the case, then they can say so. Here,'' she said, giving me the carefully hung skirt. I dutifully put it away as she went on. ''Jolie, it's just human nature to be more impetuous when two people are together.''

I closed the closet door with a smart slap and whirled to face her. "Jeremy needs people around him who care. He needs his friends right now—he doesn't need to be isolated.''

"That isn't fair—''

"Oh, right, and keeping Randy away from him is?''

"Jolie—''

"This is bullshit, Diane.''

She was off the bed in a flash. "Even we've done things together that we wouldn't have done alone.''

"Like what?''

"Like that time we were shopping in Dallas and we both bought three-hundred-dollar beaded dresses! What possessed us to spend that kind of money on something we'll never wear in Purple Sage?''

"That was just silliness....''

"And like the time we broke into the *Tribune* offices at night and ended up in that crazy car chase—''

"That wasn't a big deal.''

"—and drove right over the ninth hole at the country club!''

I stared at her.

"Look, Jolie, maybe I was wrong, but I did it with the right intentions—to protect both the boys.''

"Fine.''

There was a soft knock at the door. "Jolie, Diane, what are you two doing? I thought we were going to go.'' It was Matt.

I opened the door. "Sorry, we got to talking...''

"And she wouldn't let me leave,'' Diane finished.

"We'd like to do this in daylight,'' he said. As if darkness were imminent. It was only a little after one.

"You two go down and I'll check on Jeremy,'' I said, trying not to sound as angry as I still felt. As soon as they started down the stairs I knocked softly on Jeremy's door, and when I got no answer, cracked it open. Jeremy was sound asleep on the bed. I tiptoed over and kissed him on the forehead. He was so defenseless that Diane's actions seemed barbarous.

Gently I touched Jeremy's brow, then tiptoed out.

I hadn't even cleared the doorway into the den before Trey was leaping out of the recliner. "About time, Jolie! So, we're off to see the Wizard?"

They were all set for an adventure, and it was Diane who answered, her voice low and vibrant. "Better than the Wizard—the Rom Cursed Cave."

WE TOOK MATT'S BRONCO and traveled along the wide, two-lane Farm to Market Road that I drove every day on my way to Purple Sage. You couldn't see much beyond the barbed wire-and-cedar-post fence because of a line of mesquite trees with fluffy green branches that blocked the view. Below the trees was algerita, a squatty, spreading, prickly-leaved bush that reminded me of a pale blue-white holly. After almost six miles, we turned off the Farm to Market Road and traveled for another half a mile along a bumpy ribbon of caliche that sent up a white cloud of dust behind us.

I watched the fence line, trying to see beyond it, without success. The Hammonds had moved into a pretty little house in town just over a month ago and I was curious about the house they'd left behind. The house that we now owned. And despite my residual anger with Diane it was impossible not to feel some anticipation. Especially when Matt and Trey were radiating excitement like an electrical charge.

"So where is this Rom Cursed Cave?" Diane asked from the backseat.

"Not even a mile from here." Matt slowed and turned right, stopping in front of a metal gate that covered a cattle guard. I could see a heavy chain held in place with a fist-sized lock.

"Do you have a key?" Trey asked.

Matt held it up. "Right here."

Trey's hand came from the backseat and took it. "I'll unlock the gate." He jumped out of the Bronco, fumbled with the lock for just a moment, then pushed back the gate so we could drive through. It was a short but bumpy ride over the cattle guard.

"You can leave it open," Matt said to Trey through his open window. "We'll lock up on the way out."

So Trey climbed back in and we went bouncing along on the neglected dirt road.

I had never been on the Hammond land before. Matt had merely come home one night and said that it was for sale and we should buy it. It made perfect sense to me—he'd been wanting to expand the size of the ranching operation, and this land adjoined ours. I hadn't needed to see it. Matt, on the other hand, had ridden most of the place on horseback with Arthur Hammond. He knew where the pens and barns were, and what kind of condition they were in. He also knew what portion of the land was suitable for grazing, and what needed work. If asked he could probably even say how many of the cedar fence posts needed replacing and which ones they were—Matt has that kind of mind. Personally, I care more about other things.

"Where's the house?" I asked.

Matt pointed to our left. "It's up that way. Do you want to see it?"

"Another trip," Diane said. "I want to see the infamous cave with a curse. Besides, if you've seen one old house, you've seen them all."

I had to force myself to sound civil. "How can you say that?" I asked.

"Crystal ball. Let me guess, it's an old wooden shotgun-style house with two front doors; one goes directly into the living room, one goes into the hall that has two bedrooms and a bath. The kitchen is behind the living room. Well, am I close?''

"Hit it exactly," Matt said.

Trey laughed. "Diane cheated—she's been in the Hammond house."

"You don't have to tell everything you know," Diane said, slapping Trey on the wrist. Or she would have, but the Bronco was almost bucking now as the road got rougher and started climbing. "How much farther?" she asked.

"It should be right up here," Matt said. "I haven't actually been there, but Art mentioned it was off the saddle."

The saddle was the low sloping spot between two large rises of land. You couldn't call them mountains, not compared to those anywhere else, but they were the tallest landmarks around.

"We can't drive all the way there," Trey added. "If I remember correctly the road stops and we have to walk some."

I frowned. "How much is 'some'?"

"We'll go up behind the pass," Matt said. "We can get closer that way."

We bumped up the road as it wound between mesquite and live oak trees. It was what Matt had called good ranch land. The ground had been pushed in the not too distant past, clearing away the bulk of the scrub, weeds, and cactus. The road we were on was dirt and only used to get around to check on the livestock. I still spotted a few cows—or maybe they were bulls. We didn't get close enough to see.

"Whose animals are these?" I asked.

"Art Hammond's. He's shipping them off to auction next week. I told him he could keep them here 'til then." We crossed a small, dry streambed, then made a quick left and we were practically on top of the hill. The road ended, leaving us nowhere to go but out. "This looks like it's the end of the line," he said, putting on the parking brake and turning off the engine.

It looked more like the back of nowhere to me, even though it had taken only a few minutes to get there from the road.

Trey grabbed some flashlights he and Matt had rounded up, and started walking off through the brush, down toward what I hoped was the cave. Matt was right behind him.

"Are we sure we know what we're doing?" I asked as I trotted after them.

Trey looked over his shoulder long enough to shake his head at me. "You sound just like Diane. And yes, I know where I'm going."

Diane wasn't impressed. "Well, it's been at least seventeen years," she said, stepping over a cow patty. "Unless you've been sneaking out when I was asleep."

We were weaving through brush: prickly pear, algerita, tall blooming yuccas, and a million kinds of weeds. Little burrs stuck to my socks and tennis shoes. The air was hot and muggy, making the going even rougher. The sun kept popping in and out from behind dark, swollen clouds. I wondered if they were going to rain on us, or just push the humidity even higher.

"It's down here," Trey said, not even stopping to point. The land sloped to a barren spot below. "That's it; I'm sure of it." He sounded slightly winded, although it could have been from excitement. He was moving faster, too, and so was Matt. They were both about ten feet in front of Diane and me. They skirted around to the left while we followed. And there it was: the Rom Cursed Cave.

The opening was like a gash in the rock in front of us, about twelve feet long and, nearest us, not more than three feet high.

"This way," Trey was saying as he walked a little farther. I would have sworn there was a swagger to his gait.

The top of the entrance slanted upward until, eventually,

it was high enough that Trey could enter without ducking. "I'll be first," he said.

"It's my cave," Matt said, only half jokingly. He went in right behind Trey.

I lowered my head, and slipped inside the cool darkness, too. There was a soft musty smell and I had to blink a couple of times to let my eyes adjust to the dimness.

"This is it?" I asked. My voice echoed hollowly around the room that seemed to fade into shadows just a few feet beyond us. Diane nudged us aside to get in the cave.

"This is it," Matt said.

Trey handed us flashlights.

"I feel like a kid on a school trip," Diane said. "Thanks, Teach."

"Yeah, well, just stay close together and don't get lost," he said.

We all began shining our lights around the interior. The first "room" of the cave was probably fifteen feet across and thirty feet deep. The roof sloped upwards like a natural cathedral ceiling. I flashed my light along the ground and noticed animal tracks in the soft and dusty ground. When a crack of thunder came from outside I jumped and almost landed on Trey. "Sorry," I said, realizing that I'd dropped my voice automatically and the others weren't speaking at all.

Trey and Matt moved forward and began poking into every crevice, shining their lights in obscure places so that we could all see.

"Look at this," Trey said. He pulled an old Coke bottle from a crack in the cave wall. It was one of the little ones that were standard so many years before.

Matt reached out for the bottle and held it in his hand. His light was dimming quickly. "Should have changed the batteries," he said. The rest of us added our light beams and looked at the bottle. Matt's voice held a touch of wonder as he said, "This must have been left here in the sixties.

Probably by kids exploring. Probably by you, Trey." Matt hefted the bottle up and down a few times. "Amazing how heavy they were."

Diane moved in for a closer look. "Check the bottom. They always had the name of the town where the bottling company was." Matt turned the bottle over and Diane read aloud, "Cleburne. Isn't that fun! Good ole Cleburne, Texas."

"You can probably get more for it now than Coca-Cola did when it was full," Trey said.

"I'll let you have that honor," Matt said, holding it out to Trey.

Trey shook his head. "Let's give the bottle to Jeremy...."

"But then," Diane said, "we'd have to tell him where we found it and we're not talking about the Rom Cursed Cave. I don't want Randy and Jeremy sneaking out here."

"I think," Matt interjected, "there's a better way to handle that. Why not just let them plan to spend the night in the cave? Maybe with some other friends."

In the past it always seemed that Matt gave Jeremy more credit for being mature than I did, which, I suppose, is the natural tendency of an adoptive parent. In this instance, though, I agreed with him totally. "I think that's an excellent idea," I said.

Matt was nodding. "We could take all the mystique out of the cave and the curse."

"You're right, honey," I said.

"Maybe we should just think about that one for a while," Diane said. "Discuss it later."

Matt exchanged a look with me, but he smiled at Diane as he said, "We don't have to make a decision now." He put the bottle down near the entrance and we continued to explore.

I had been thinking about creatures who usually live in caves, besides Coke bottles, and decided it was time to check for them. I ran my light across the ceiling and discovered to my relief that there were no bats. I flashed my light around the floor. There was another hole just a few feet away. It was in the wall, less than two feet off the cave floor, and about a foot or so in diameter.

"Look," I said.

Matt got down on his knees and shined his light in. I bent down, too, and even in the dimness of his fading beam, I could see two small beady eyes glaring back at us.

"Holy shit!" I jumped up.

Matt was on his feet instantly. "I can't tell what it is."

"Did you bring a gun?" Trey asked. Ranching out here is rough work and guns are just part of the equipment.

In this day and age environmentalists believe that all creatures great and small, even poisonous ones, should be left to thrive and propagate. After all, those creatures were born to the wild and deserve to live there. That's fine if you're talking about pandas or lions or even bobcats. It's especially easy to say if you live in an apartment in a city. However, I live in the country, and I'm not a country person by birth, only by marriage, so if there's a poisonous creature on my land, it better have burial insurance.

"There's a rifle in the Bronco," Matt said. "Let's find out what it is first." He stepped out of the cave while the rest of us stood back from the hole, aiming our flashlight beams on the opening, just in case whatever it was decided to come out and be sociable. Or unsociable.

Within a minute Matt was back carrying a long stick with a natural crook close to one end. "Here, let me get in there." He stepped to the side of the hole. "Everyone get back; I'm going to bring him out." We did as he suggested. Then Matt slid the stick in the opening. "I've got him," he said. He used the stick to inch the creature forward until we could see it.

A rattler.

THIRTEEN

IT HIT THE GROUND with a plop, then reared its head, and threw its diamond patterned body toward me. I let out a noise and jumped back, hitting Diane.

Matt brought the stick down, gently but quickly, and caught the snake in the middle. I think he was trying to lift it, which would render it harmless since they can't strike from that position. Unfortunately, the snake slipped off the stick and it was mad now.

It lunged toward me again. I pushed Diane out of the way and raced for the back of the cave. I was in the second room, in the darkness broken only by my skittering light, when I heard Trey yell, "Jolie, it's a bull snake. It can't hurt you!"

Before I could respond, my foot hit a hole and I felt myself slipping. I yelped. Gravity wrenched me downward; my butt hit the cave floor. The flashlight flew out of my hands and shattered on impact.

"Honey, it's okay," Matt was saying. "I'm putting it outside. It's gone."

So was my leg. And it was dark where I was. "I think I need some help here," I yelled.

I couldn't tell how big the hole that had captured my leg was, or how deep; I only knew that I wasn't going any farther down without a struggle. I threw myself forward on the safety of the dirt floor and tried to crawl. I didn't know what was down that hole, if anything, but I had visions of creatures that would do bad things to my innocent body.

I was scrabbling hard and making no headway when the beams from three flashlights hit me at once. "What in the hell—" That was Trey. Sometimes that man is not quick.

"Good Lord!" That was Diane.

Matt didn't say anything until he had both arms under mine and he was pulling me up. "Don't squirm—just let me get you." He literally lifted me out of the hole, then set me gently back down on my own two feet. "Are you okay?"

I nodded. "Is that the infamous drop-off?"

They turned their lights on it and we all got a good look. "Must be," Matt said.

My vision of a massive drop-off altered radically. Obviously this hole, which was only big enough to swallow a child, had grown in size with the telling of the story. It had also gained a few inches from my fall, since I had knocked some dirt off the sides. I reached down and brushed off my jeans and shirt.

"Are you okay?" Matt asked again.

"I'm fine," I said. "Mad. Stupid hole. Stupid snake." Bull snakes look almost identical to diamondback rattlers, except that their heads are less pointed and they can't bite you. Instead they have been known to throw themselves at unsuspecting people. I guess they think they can scare their victims to death. They probably can.

Matt put an arm around me and kissed me firmly and quickly on the lips. "What are we going to do with you?" he asked when he was done.

"Keep me away from snakes," I said.

A huge crack of thunder seemed to shake the very ground under our feet. Everyone else ignored it, but goose bumps slithered over my body.

"Actually," Diane was saying as she leaned over and peered down the hole, "I don't think you could have fallen all the way through." She glanced up to look me over, then turned back to the hole again. "Maybe, but it's doubtful. I know the rest of us couldn't have gone down."

"How comforting," I said. They were all gathered around it now and I moved forward to join them for another look. I'd swear I saw some light down there, as if the hole went someplace, but I couldn't tell for sure. "How deep is it?" I asked. Again I brushed off my rear end and realized I was going to have a major bruise. I already had a major sore spot.

"Who knows," Diane said. "Maybe it goes to the center of the earth."

"Where large bull snakes wait for unsuspecting humans," Trey said, with what he probably thought was a humorous leer.

I straightened up and looked around. This was a much smaller room than the first and I couldn't see any passages leading off it, nor any secret hiding places.

"Just for seeing this we're going to be visited by evil spirits?" I said. "Seems like a gyp."

"You pays your money and you takes your chances," Diane said.

"Shall we go?" I asked. "There's nothing else here, and unless there's going to be a quiz..." I glanced at Trey. "Besides, I'd like to see the house before the rain hits."

We all took one last look around and then moved toward the mouth of the cave. The clouds were closer together now, making the sky a dark mottled gray. Trey led the way back to the Bronco and a few drops splattered on the windshield as Matt started it up.

"Are you sure you want to do this?" he asked me.

Diane had gotten what she wanted and now it was my turn. "I'm sure. We won't stay long."

THE HAMMONDS' HOUSE WAS tucked back among mesquites and live oaks. We had followed the road straight to reach the cave. Had we turned left we would have come to the house, although we wouldn't have seen it because of all the trees and the shrubbery. There were blowzy oleanders with flowers ranging from brilliant pink to a deep fuchsia. Two lilac bushes, both at least six feet tall, cut off our view from the corner of the house. There was even a picket fence across the front of the yard, although the Hammonds had settled for chain link along the sides and back. Those portions were covered with climbing roses, a deep vibrant scarlet that really set off the white frame house. I could already picture it with a fresh coat of paint and some dark green shutters. Maybe paint the trim green, too...

"Looks like the lawn could use cutting," Matt said after he had parked the Bronco out front and was holding the picket gate open for us.

"This is wonderful," I said. "We ought to be renting it, so it doesn't get run down."

"I think so, too," Diane offered. She stopped to stare at the front of the house. "Maybe paint the trim a dark green."

"Women come up with too much work," Trey said.

Diane ignored him as she turned to Matt. "Mind if I pick some flowers? They smell heavenly."

"Help yourself," he said. "No one's enjoying them out here."

While she headed for the fence line and the roses, Trey glanced around, still appraising. "What you're not figuring is that you can't get much for rent and the people you do get will be those who want to live off the land. Recyclers and leftover hippies who think mud is healthier than green grass and flowers. The kind of people who think that having two goats and three broken bikes on the front porch is a sign of environmental consciousness."

"You're Mr. Optimistic," I said. "Maybe a nice retired couple."

Trey shook his head. "They have to be in town so they're close to their doctors. And the pharmacies and other necessities of old age. It's a losing proposition; trust me, Jolie." He started for the back of the yard. "I'm going to take a look at the barns."

"I was kind of thinking of having this place for a guest

Deal Yourself In and Play
The Mystery Library's
ACTION POKER

Peel off this card and complete the hand on the next page

It can get you:

♠ Free books

♠ PLUS a free surprise gift

PLAY "ACTION POKER" AND GET...

★ 3 first time in paperback, mystery books just like the one you're reading — FREE
★ PLUS a surprise gift — FREE

Peel off the card on the front of this brochure and stick it in the hand opposite. Then check the claim chart to see what we have for you — FREE BOOKS and a gift — ALL YOURS! ALL FREE! They're yours to keep even if you never buy another Mystery Library book.

THEN DEAL YOURSELF IN FOR MORE MYSTERY

1. Play Action Poker as instructed on the opposite page.
2. Send back the card and you'll receive brand-new, first-time-in-paperback Mystery Library novels. These books have a cover price of $4.99 each, but they are yours to keep absolutely free.
3. There's no catch. You're under no obligation to buy anything. We charge nothing — ZERO — for your first shipment. And you don't have to make any minimum number of purchases — not even one!
4. The fact is thousands of readers enjoy receiving books by mail from the Mystery Library Reader Service. They like the convenience of home delivery...they like getting the best in mystery novels before they're available in stores...and they love our discount prices!
5. We hope that after receiving your free books you'll want to remain a subscriber. But the choice is yours — to continue or cancel, anytime at all! So why not take us up on our invitation, with no risk of any kind. You'll be glad you did!

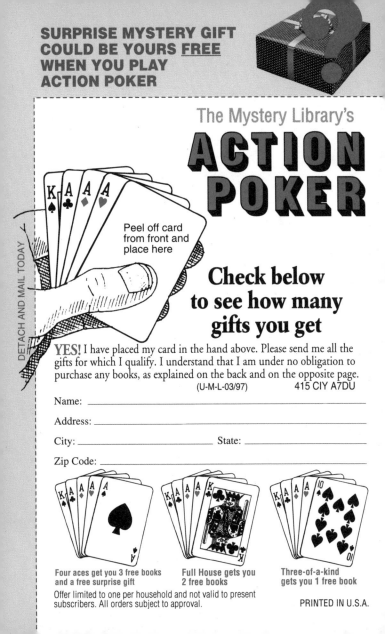

SURPRISE MYSTERY GIFT COULD BE YOURS <u>FREE</u> WHEN YOU PLAY ACTION POKER

DETACH AND MAIL TODAY

The Mystery Library's

ACTION POKER

Peel off card from front and place here

Check below to see how many gifts you get

YES! I have placed my card in the hand above. Please send me all the gifts for which I qualify. I understand that I am under no obligation to purchase any books, as explained on the back and on the opposite page.

(U-M-L-03/97)　　　　415 CIY A7DU

Name: _____

Address: _____

City: _____ State: _____

Zip Code: _____

Four aces get you 3 free books and a free surprise gift

Full House gets you 2 free books

Three-of-a-kind gets you 1 free book

Offer limited to one per household and not valid to present subscribers. All orders subject to approval.

PRINTED IN U.S.A.

THE MYSTERY LIBRARY READER SERVICE: HERE'S HOW IT WORKS

Accepting free books places you under no obligation to buy anything. You may keep the books and gift and return the shipping statement marked "cancel". If you do not cancel, about a month later we will send you three additional novels and bill you just $4.19 each, plus 25¢ delivery per book and applicable sales tax, if any. You may cancel at any time, but if you choose to continue, then every month we'll send you three more books, which you may either purchase at our great low price…or return to us and cancel your subscription.

*Terms and prices subject to change without notice. Sales tax applicable in N.Y.

house," Matt said. Something in his voice wasn't right and I turned to look at him as he finished. "I know it's not exactly in our backyard, but it's nice enough for a guest house. And it wouldn't take much to furnish it, if, say, my folks wanted to come and stay a month or so. They wouldn't have to stay with us and they wouldn't be in anybody's way. You know."

Matt can hide things from me forever if he doesn't talk, but once he starts talking, I catch him. He doesn't realize it, but when he's prevaricating he falls back into the Texas drawl that he tried to leave behind, when he studied at Harvard.

"When are your parents coming to stay for a month?" I asked.

"Well, it's not for sure yet," he began. "Remember we talked to them a couple of weeks ago, and they were thinking about coming back for the Centennial Celebration this summer? Then they called this morning and they're coming for sure."

"So, what's the big deal?" I asked. I remembered the conversation, or what I'd heard of it, since I hadn't been on the phone the whole time. We'd all agreed it would be great to have his parents come out for the Celebration. It was still a couple of months off and not something I really had in the forefront of my mind. Now that we had the Hammond place, of course his parents could stay there. They could stay for the rest of their lives for all I cared. They were nice people with only a few irritating flaws, no worse than mine, and not nearly as bad as my mom's. They weren't as loud and noisy as my brother, Win, and his family, nor as grating as my sister, Elise, and her husband and kids. All in all, they were the best possible choice to come visit for a month. "I think it would be great to have them stay here."

"Super." He held the door open for me, but he wouldn't look at me.

Trey had wandered off and Diane was going around the yard carefully selecting the flowers she was going to take home. We were alone as I turned to Matt. "Okay, what's up?"

He let out a long breath. "I don't think now is the time...."

"It's the time," I said.

He waited a few beats and then looked me square in the eye and said, "When Mom called this morning, she said that Cecily might be coming, too."

Cecily. Cecily Wyatt. Cecily Wyatt, Matt's first wife.

Shit.

"She's coming here?"

"Well, not here to this house. She'd stay in town—we aren't all that civilized."

"Who isn't?" I asked. "Her or you?"

Now that the whole story was out, Matt was back to his real self with his voice and his humor intact. He put his hand under my chin and lifted my face to his. "You aren't that civilized."

Of course Cecily was civilized—she was British. Proper. Only the ranch wasn't, and after a few years of living there she'd started drinking. After five years she had run back to England. But that's not what most people remembered. Every once in a while someone will still comment on how delightful her accent was, and how much fun it was to listen to her talk. And Matt's mother still corresponded with her. Diane, on the other hand, told me straight out that she thought Cecily was a lazy alcoholic who expected Matt to compensate for all her own inadequacies.

Matt put his arms around me, drawing me into the here and now. "Look, the Centennial Celebration is still two months off. A lot can happen in that time. This is all just talk from my mother, so let's forget it, okay?" His dark eyes watched me for signs of something, but the only signal I was sending was not friendly. It was a mask for fear and, please don't ask why, I was frightened. I know Matt loves me. We have a great relationship, now that I have my act at least somewhat together, and we work at that relationship. Maybe I was afraid because I'd had one husband inexplicably walk out on me, and I was never sure it wouldn't happen again. Admittedly that was fifteen years before, but it left a scar that hasn't completely healed, and one I can't always hide. I suspect it's the cause of my periodic, although unintentional, man-bashing, as Jeremy calls it.

"Jolie," Matt went on, "we don't know for sure that she's coming and, even if she does, it has nothing to do with us. We probably won't even see her. And she's bringing her new boyfriend with her."

"She probably wants to show *you* off to keep him in line."

Matt started laughing. "I love you. Totally and completely. And sometimes I think you are straight off your nut."

"Is that an English expression?"

He pulled me close to him. "This is an American expression." With that he kissed me. Firmly. Seriously.

When he was done I said, "I think that's French."

Diane pounded up onto the wood porch, making a lot more noise than was necessary. Probably to stop us from kissing again. "I thought you wanted to see the house?" she asked me.

"I got sidetracked."

"Well, it's starting to drizzle and I'd like to stay dry." Diane was carrying an armload of roses, and they gave off a heady scent as she moved past us into the house. "Not much here."

I pushed all thoughts of Matt's mother and dear Cecily out of my mind as we entered the bare living room/dining room combination. We all stopped and looked around a moment. I had expected dust and that smell that comes from lack of use, but it wasn't musty at all. Maybe because we'd had the door open, I don't know.

There were windows with wood sashes, three along the front wall and two wider ones along the far side, as well as a fireplace. It seemed a little dark because of the clouds outside and, without thinking, I clicked on the light switch. An overhead light came on.

"Hey, the electricity is still on!" I said.

"The water pump at the well runs electrically, so I told the Hammonds to leave it on but put it in our name," Matt said. "I completely forgot about it."

"We'd have remembered when we got a bill." There were hardwood floors and pull-down shades on the windows that were rolled up to let in the maximum amount of light. That didn't seem quite the way to leave a house, but I didn't think any more about it. Instead I followed Diane into the kitchen. It was a small room that had been remodeled but not very recently. There was white-and-beige-patterned linoleum on the floor and lots of wood cabinets with glass fronts on the walls.

"Did they leave any glasses?" Diane asked. "Something I could put these roses in?"

I looked and found nothing. "Nope. Here." I gestured toward the brushed aluminum sink. "Why not put them in here, just to let them get a little water?" I started to reach for the tap, then stopped. "Diane, look at this."

She stepped closer and peered down. One side of the sink still had a little water in the bottom. And suds. As if someone had just been doing dishes.

We exchanged a quick look and she reached down into the sink and brought up some soap bubbles. "The metal is still warm."

"Matt," I called. "Come here a second."

He walked in and I told him about the sink. He reached down, too. "That's really strange." He turned to Diane. "You didn't do that as a joke, did you?"

"I was out front picking flowers. You saw me."

"I was busy," Matt said.

"Yes, well, I saw you. And no, I didn't do this." She frowned. "Someone has been here. Recently."

I opened the cupboard below the sink and found an almost full bottle of liquid dishwashing detergent. I also discovered that the newspapers Mrs. Hammond had used to line the bottom of the cupboard were wet. A chill was beginning to crawl along my spine. "I don't think we should touch anything," I said.

Neither Diane nor Matt disagreed. Diane said, "Let's keep looking."

We eyeballed the kitchen as best we could then stepped back, toward an old-fashioned pantry. I used the bottom of my T-shirt to pull the door open. There were a few food items on the shelves: crackers, animal cookies, and some cans of soup. "These aren't old," I said.

The refrigerator clicked on and the three of us turned toward it. It was an old one with rounded edges and a noisy motor. No doubt the Hammonds hadn't thought it was worth moving. "It's got to be empty," Matt said.

"Here, let me." I used my shirttail again to open the refrigerator door. Inside we found a half gallon of milk. The expiration date was still a week away. I looked at Matt and Diane and said, "Someone's been living in my house."

Diane nodded. "You're right, Mama Bear. And I bet I know who."

FOURTEEN

MATT AND DIANE spoke together. "Jorgenson."

"And his sister, Sharon," I added. "I don't see James Jorgenson doing dishes."

Diane began to look around more seriously. "So where are the dishes?"

Obviously not in the glass-fronted cupboards. "I'll try the other rooms," I said.

While Diane and I covered separate areas of the house and yard, Matt went out to the Bronco and called the sheriff's department on his cellular. It took a good twenty minutes, but finally Wiley Pierce arrived. By this time the soap bubbles were gone, but we had other things to show him. I had found a trash bag at the back of the house and it had the wrappers from packages of plastic cups, plastic plates, and plastic silverware. I didn't find any of those items in the trash, though. Obviously, Sharon had washed them and taken them along. That one simple act on her part brought Sharon to life for me in a way I never would have thought possible. I could almost hear her thinking, Waste not, want not, a country homily that lived on in Wilmot County. Probably one that her grandmother had repeated to her often while she was growing up.

Wiley poked around the house and yard for a while, then he radioed in for Mac to come out. He didn't talk much to us, didn't ask many questions, so Trey and Matt went to look over the livestock and Diane and I sat on the steps of the big wooden porch. I couldn't get over the fact that James Elliott Jorgenson and his sister, Sharon, two fugitives from the law, had been here in a house I owned. It gave me a shivery feeling to realize that they must have left while we were at the cave. If we'd come straight to the house—

It had stopped misting now and the sun was attempting to break through the clouds, although it only succeeded for a few seconds before it was hidden again. Still, it was a beautiful spot. Peaceful and protected, just like a front yard in the country should be. It must have been hard for the Hammonds to decide to leave, but as Trey had pointed out, when you reach a certain age you need to be near the necessities, like doctors.

A light breeze started up, and it seemed to be clearing the worst of the humidity away. It also brought with it the scent of roses. Matt's mom, Edith, would love this place. She would start entertaining the minute she got here.

And then I remembered that Cecily might be here, too.

I jumped up and began to pace around the porch, anything to get rid of that thought. Instead I tried to imagine what Jorgenson did in this wonderful little hideaway. I couldn't begin to visualize it. Part of the reason may have been that I didn't know what James looked like. Or Sharon, for that matter, and somehow I had this great need to know them. Especially her. I looked at my watch; it was after two-thirty. Too late to go to the *Tribune* office and get Rhonda to help me dig out an old newspaper with the Jorgensons' pictures in it. I did know how to get into the *Trib* office through a back door, but that was something probably better left undone. Surely there were other places to find pictures. Then I remembered that Sharon was still in high school—her picture was probably in Jeremy's yearbook.

I might have headed out right then, but Matt had taken the Bronco. I paced some more and another thought struck me. What would Jorgenson have done if we'd driven up to the house? What would have happened if we had innocently pulled in behind that light green pickup, not thinking, not realizing—

I caught my breath. If it hadn't been for Diane's insistence that we skip the house, we might have had a face-to-face confrontation with James Elliott Jorgenson.

Diane was still sitting silently on the steps and I went over and sat down next to her. "I'm not mad at you anymore," I said.

"That's good. Why not?"

"Because you may have saved all our lives by insisting that we go to the cave first. If we'd driven straight to the house—"

"I thought about that. Scary, huh? We don't know if he had guns, or if he would have tried to make a break for it or what, but still…"

"We'd probably have blocked him in with the Bronco, you know, before we realized whose pickup it was." I put my arm around her. "Thanks."

She hugged me back. "It was pure D luck, but you're welcome." Then she wrapped her arms around her knees. "I was just excited about seeing the cave, and I was still being a little pissy because you were mad at me." She took a breath. "I'm sorry, too. You were right, that was shitty of me to give Randy the modem so he'd stay in town. It's just that when I got home yesterday I started thinking about how Randy is growing up; in a couple of years he'll be gone. My baby will be gone and I'll never have him back again. I don't know if I can take that, so I want to keep a part of him as my little boy. Does that sound crazy?"

"Yeah," I said slowly. "Really nuts." I pulled a slender stalk of clover from the grass. "And it's exactly how I've been feeling about Jeremy. I'm getting more protective just at the time when he's got to grow up. No wonder teenagers rebel."

She leaned her body over and nudged me. "At least now I know that if I go crazy I'll have company along the way."

"Not always very good company, though…"

BY THE TIME Mac arrived and had poked in every corner of the house and yard, and done some fingerprinting, it was almost three-thirty. Trey and Matt had returned and we were all gathered on the porch. I was starved, but we couldn't leave just yet. Mac had questions for us, and even though our answers weren't very helpful, he had to hear them.

No, we hadn't seen the pickup at all. No, we hadn't heard a pickup. No, we hadn't heard any voices. Yes, the gate had been locked, and no, we hadn't been on the Hammond place since James Jorgenson had broken out of jail. As to how he'd found this particular house, we didn't know. Mac agreed with us that it was probably luck, although Sharon might have heard about the Hammonds moving to town and assumed the house would be empty. Word travels fast.

When Mac was done asking questions, we got a few in. The first was obvious: Was he sure it had been James and Sharon Jorgenson in the house?

"Pretty sure," Mac said. He pointed to the trash sack he had set beside his car. "You maybe didn't notice, but there were cigarette butts in there and an empty Marlboro pack. That's the brand James has been smoking since he was thirteen." He pointed to the gravel. "I looked for tire marks, thought those might help, but there's too much rock in the soil. Just couldn't find a clean print. I did get a couple of fingerprints from the house, though, and if those aren't one of yours, or the Hammonds', then maybe we can tell."

"But in your own mind you're positive," Matt said.

"Sure am, Matt. Off the record, I'm positive."

Diane was next. "But, how did James and Sharon get the pickup through the gate?"

"That's easy," Mac said. "The kid's been trained as a locksmith and he's a real good one. I wouldn't be surprised to find out he was kin to Houdini."

"So why would they relock it after they drove in?"

"My guess is to keep Matt or Jolie from bein' suspicious

if they happened by. Besides, it would keep other people out.''

He and Wiley packed things up and we were all starting toward our cars when I stopped Mac one more time. ''Mac, I'm going to need to do a story on this—can I quote you about it probably being Jorgenson?''

''Long as you say it's just supposition on my part; but why don't you let Rory do the story? You look beat, kid. Like you could use some rest.''

I smiled at the ''kid.'' When you're thirty-nine it's nice when someone regards you as young. Besides, Mac said it with affection. ''I'm not really tired,'' I said. ''But I wouldn't mind a real meal. Unfortunately I don't know where Rory is.''

''Ten bucks says he's already called my office,'' Mac said as he leaned in the open window of his car and picked up the mike from the radio. ''Unit One to Base.'' He paused and the dispatcher came on, telling him to go ahead. He did. ''Yeah, Loretta, I was just checking to see if I'd had any calls while I was out.''

The answer came quickly. *''Yes, sir, you did. That reporter from the radio station called and wanted you to call him. He bugged me to death about telling him where you were, but I figured I'd better not.''*

Mac was grinning. ''You just insured yourself another paycheck from the county. I'll call that reporter as soon as I get in. Unit One clear.''

''Base clear.''

''Well,'' Mac said, still smiling as he turned to me, ''what'd I tell you?''

''I'll let Rory handle it.'' But there was one more question I had for Mac, one that had been bothering me for two days. ''Mac,'' I began, ''do you think that James Jorgenson killed Tim?''

He took his time and thought about it before he looked at me squarely and said, ''I don't know, Jolie. He's never hurt anyone before. I'd like to think he never would, but I just can't say for sure.'' With that he got in his car and gave me one last wave before he drove off.

THE NEXT DAY WAS Sunday and Matt likes it when the three of us go to church together. I don't know that it has so much to do with religion as it does with family. That's what families do. And this is Purple Sage, on the fringes of the Bible Belt, so it's socially important. Matt prefers, but doesn't insist on, the Presbyterian church because that's the one he went to as a child. Jeremy would rather we all attend the Baptist church, which is where most of the high school kids go. I like the Episcopalian church because I like the service and because Father Kerrigan gives inspiring sermons, but it isn't crucial to me. I figure God shows up at all the churches.

I'm not religious, but I do consider myself spiritual. I grew up believing in God and I still believe in him. I trust him not to give me more than I can handle at one time and to take care of the people I love, when it's at all possible. When your father has lung cancer and still won't quit smoking, I figure God has to move on. Most important, I think God loves us all equally and he doesn't give a flip where we spend our Sunday mornings. It's more *how* we spend our lives. But then, as I said, I'm not religious, so what do I know.

That Sunday morning Jeremy was more insistent than usual on going to the First Baptist Church at the top of the hill on Main, and Matt and I deferred to his wants. We took both cars since Matt had a tennis match at one-thirty. Jeremy rode with Matt, and by the time I got to the gracious old white limestone church, Jeremy was sitting with his friends, several rows away from where Matt was saving me a place. Togetherness teenage style.

Brother Pilstow must have sensed the way the kids were feeling, what with one of their idols dead and another of their contemporaries on the run from the law, because he outdid himself in the sermon department. He captured not only their attention, but mine as well, speaking on choices and how our choices affect our lives.

"In your own life, think of a time when you did something you were really proud of. It could have been anything: a business success, setting a goal and achieving it, winning a track meet, whatever it is, think back to that victorious moment. You can probably tell me what you did to have that success. Can't you?" Brother Pilstow, a short man with a rotund figure and a clean-shaven kind of jolly face, looked around at the congregation expectantly. We didn't disappoint. Most of us nodded our heads in agreement. "But," he went on, "if you talk to people who are constantly in trouble, they will very often tell you whose fault it is." He paused dramatically. "You see the difference? Some take responsibility for their choices. God gave us free will and the intelligence to use it. We are supposed to think about our lives and make choices. Oh, we'll make some mistakes, too, but that's why forgiveness is so handy." He chuckled and twinkled, like a jolly elf in the heat of early June. "Now, there's another little catch to this free-will thing—your choices also affect the other people around you. If you choose to rob a store and end up in prison, you're not the only one who suffers. All the people who love you will also be afflicted with the pain and the punishment as well."

I assumed that was a nice way of telling the kids not to do what James Elliott Jorgenson had done. I kept glancing over at Jeremy, hoping he was getting it. I wanted to make sure he saw that his decisions had a direct result in my life. And then I realized that the sermon was meant for me, too, and I should be listening for myself instead of worrying about him. I finally did just that.

Afterward Matt and I had to stand around the front of the church in the hot sun waiting for Jeremy, who didn't appear with the first wave of teenagers, nor the second, and not the third either. When he did show up he was hurrying.

"Sorry," he said. "I wanted to talk to some guys. You know." He practically ran past us and went straight for the Mazda.

"Guess he's riding with me," I said to Matt.

"Guess so." Matt waved at Jeremy and turned to me. "I'd better run. I'll just grab something light at the club and then it will be time for my match. Unless you'd like to come along and cheer me on?"

"When you read one of my books, I'll sit in the stands and cheer." It's an old bone of contention. Matt reads techno-thrillers and golden age detectives; I write cozies with a female protagonist. Once, not long after we were married, Matt read a hundred pages of one of my mysteries and then took two weeks to slog through another ten pages. Finally he just let the manuscript collect dust on an end table until I called him on it. He said he felt terrible about putting the manuscript aside, but it just wasn't "his type of book." Then he babbled for a while about how well I set a scene, and how the images I'd created were so vivid, and the like. Fine, but the bottom line is that he hasn't read any of my books. Sometimes I don't care at all, and sometimes it bugs the hell out of me, and sometimes I use it as an excuse not to do something I don't want to do anyway. This time I was using it. And it rankled a little, too.

Matt leaned over and kissed me quickly. "I still love you."

"And I still love you. Have a good game."

We went our separate ways and I joined Jeremy in the Mazda. "Okay," I said as I started the car. "What's up?"

Jeremy had his pocket recorder out and apparently had been making notes to himself. "Well, I talked to some of the guys and found out that Tim has been dating a lot of girls. At least three, and all the girls might have thought it was, you know, exclusive."

"Did it cause him any problems?"

"I don't know. But I thought we could find out," he said, buckling his seat belt. "You want to?"

I didn't even have to think about it. "Sure, and maybe we can get another quote for that article."

"I have a bunch. I've got Lurline, and this morning I called the Boys' Ranch and got one from Harold Blinn, he's the director. And I got one from Mrs. Fisher at the high school, and Mac gave me one that night we were driving around."

"Sounds like you've been doing a great job. So, Kemo Sabe, where are we headed now?"

"North on Main to the other side of the square. We're going to go see Ashley Draper."

The name sounded like it should be familiar but I couldn't seem to place it. "Who is Ashley Draper?"

"You know. She graduated last year—her dad is the deputy sheriff. Linc Draper."

FIFTEEN

NORTH OF THE SQUARE lie several diverse neighborhoods separated by the highway. To the west, behind tractor and implement dealers, are many old homes, some three stories tall with frou-frou and gingerbread, cupolas and towers. At one time many of the houses also had termites, mold, and peeling paint. Up until about five years ago, most of them had been purchased by people with large families and small incomes; apparently even the most basic repair work wasn't affordable, let alone the massive restoration that would return the homes to their former glory. It wasn't uncommon to see a cheap, homemade, unpainted screen door in front of a genuine leaded-glass antique door. It was also not uncommon to see a rusted and battle-scarred old junker parked under a three-story portico with stately Doric columns. Matt had once remarked that some of the homes were held erect by nothing more than the sheer force of will of their owners.

The first time I drove through the neighborhood some little yuppie part of me screamed out that here were bargains ready to be snatched up and restored. Obviously I wasn't the only one, because in the last few years one whole street has been converted to something resembling the past. Two other streets are in transition. Diane keeps saying that as the real estate values go up the homes will change hands more quickly and the improvements will happen faster. I think she's right, but I'm not interested in being part of it anymore.

On the other side of the highway, to the northeast of the square, is Wilmot International Airport. The "International" part was added because a plane from Mexico had landed there—once. It was said to be carrying drugs, but that's another story.

Between the airport and the highway is Oak Ridge Estates. Billy Jack Kemper developed the estates, and although there never was a ridge, Billy Jack kept every oak he possibly could, so that now, the small, unimaginative three-bedroom houses are nestled in among clumps of trees, making the whole area much more inviting than it might have been otherwise. Even the proximity to the airport isn't a drawback—air traffic in Purple Sage is about par with ground traffic.

I had assumed we were heading for Oak Ridge, but Jeremy corrected me on that. "Turn left on Palmetto. Then right on Pomegranate," he said. I glanced at him and he added, "Randy gave me directions."

He guided me to a two-story home that was in the midst of what appeared to be some heavy restoration. All of the window frames had been replaced and there was fresh paint on the entire house, except for about half of the trim, which hadn't been finished yet. The color was a blue-gray, accented with a deeper gray and a dusky mauve. It was obvious that a great deal of work had gone into the house, and just as obvious that it was a labor of love.

The house sat about three feet above street level and, after I parked, Jeremy and I went up uneven cement steps to a small gate set in the low chain-link fence. Beyond that was a tiled fountain, old and cracked in the baking sun. Still, if what had already been done was any measure, this home was going to be a showcase someday.

I glanced to the street and over to the driveway. There was only one car parked in the drive, an older-model dark green Volvo. It had a Purple Sage Dragons sticker on the rear bumper and a troll doll hanging from the rearview mirror. Obviously this was Ashley's car, and there weren't any others around. I considered that a very good sign. I didn't want to have to talk with Linc. I wasn't even all that positive about talking with Ashley Draper.

I turned to Jeremy. "What are you going to ask her?"

"For a quote."

He rang the bell and we waited on the wood porch. He was just about to ring the bell a second time when the door opened and a young woman stepped forward. She stopped, framed in the doorway, looking like a captured ray of sunshine. Her long, strawberry blond hair hung straight around her face and her skin was a radiant, soft golden color. She had long legs that were bare beneath wheat-colored cutoffs and a baggy top of some homespun material.

She glanced at Jeremy, then at me, with eyes that were the color of grapefruit dotted with tiny flecks of brown and gold. When she smiled, she showed the most beautiful, even white teeth I had ever seen in my life. I literally had to catch my breath before I said, "Hello. Are you Ashley?"

"Yes." She seemed delighted to see us. "And you're Jolie Wyatt. I hear you on the radio all the time." She turned her magnificence on Jeremy. "And you're Jeremy. I think we met at a football game last fall."

Jeremy nodded. "Yeah, we did."

"Come in, okay?" She stepped out of the way so that I could see the interior of the house. It was sparsely decorated yet almost elegant in its simplicity. There was a pine armoire against the far wall and a simple pine rocker beside it. Next to the rocker sat a huge wooden bowl filled to overflowing with magazines and catalogs. On top was a catalog for firearms, and beside it was the latest *Glamour*. There was a braided rag rug on the wooden floor and a couch in gray blue with at least a dozen pillows scattered on it. The window shades were drawn halfway, probably to keep out the worst of the sun.

"Is your mother a decorator?" I asked.

Ashley shook her head. "My mother was killed two years ago." Even though she didn't explain, I got the feeling that her mother's death was still very near the surface. With an effort Ashley looked directly at me and forced a smile that didn't convince me otherwise. "We only moved here last summer. Daddy and I did all this. In fact, Daddy made most of the furniture. He's good, huh?"

"Very good," I agreed.

"You can sit down." She gestured to the couch, and Jeremy and I sat at either end while she moved to another doorway, one that led into the back portion of the house. "Would you like something to drink? I've got tea. And juice..."

"I don't care for anything, thanks."

"Me, neither," Jeremy said. "Are we interrupting you?"

Ashley smiled. "No. I was getting kind of bored. Daddy had to work today, and I didn't have any plans." Suddenly her face changed, and her eyes and nose began to turn that telltale red you see right before someone starts to cry. She gave us a startled look as if the emotion had surprised even her. Then she swallowed. "It's a pretty day outside, huh?" She looked out the window, keeping her face averted as she moved to the rocker and perched on the edge of it.

"A very nice day," I said, wondering what had brought on the sudden tears. It couldn't have been the fact that her dad was at work. "It's pretty hot, too, but then that's what you have to expect in June."

"Uh-huh."

Jeremy cleared his throat and looked at Ashley. "Uh, Ashley, I'm doing a memorial article on Tim Michelik for the *Tribune*. Since you knew him, or were dating him, I was wondering if you'd give me a quote for the article. On Tim."

"What?" She turned back to us, but the sun was behind her and I couldn't see the expression on her face. "I wasn't dating him."

"You weren't? Randy said you were."

"Well, not anymore."

"Oh..."

She got up and sat on the floor just in front of Jeremy. "We broke up. I wasn't seeing him anymore. I haven't seen him in a long time. Didn't see him before he, ah, died." She was staring up into Jeremy's face as if entreating him to understand.

"I guess we shouldn't have bothered you, but I didn't know that," he said, looking at the carpet beside Ashley. I can't say that I blamed him. It was disconcerting to see this sunshine of a young woman putting herself in such a sub-servient position. It must have been even more difficult for Jeremy when she was literally sitting at his feet.

Jeremy brought his eyes back to Ashley. I had expected some note of sympathy; instead he asked, "When did you two break up?"

She looked at Jeremy, then at me, and finally back to Jeremy. "It was in March. March fourteenth." Another wound, and this one even more raw. Her face began to redden again.

Jeremy said, "I guess it still hurts, huh?"

He was speaking Ashley's language. Her eyes filled with tears, she nodded her head and the tears began to spill. "It hurts a lot. And then Daddy made it even worse." She glanced at me, this time sniffing hard as if trying to draw the tears back up. "It's over now."

Only for Ashley it obviously wasn't over and she wasn't going to let her guard down with both of us there. I got the impression that she was dying to talk and might have if Jeremy had been alone, or if I had been. It's kind of like being undressed: You can be undressed in front of your mother and you can be undressed in front of your husband, but you can't be undressed in front of both of them at the same time. I stood up.

"Ashley, I'm really sorry about your loss." I took my purse and edged toward the door. "And it must be hard to think up a quote with me staring at you. I hate it when I'm trying to compose something and there are other people in the room. Makes me not able to think at all.'' I had my hand on the doorknob. ''Take your time and I'll just wait in the car for Jeremy.''

With that I stepped outside and left him to it. In truth, I was grateful to be outside. Jeremy had an excuse to be talking with Ashley, but I didn't, and I didn't think Linc would appreciate my presence one bit. In my brief acquaintance with the two Drapers I had gotten the impression that Deputy Linc Draper was very protective of his little girl, as well as of his investigation of Tim's death, and he wouldn't take kindly to my interference with either one.

I sat in the car with the front door open, hoping to catch a breeze while I waited.

IT TOOK ALMOST forty minutes, and I gave some thought to charging the house to see if Ashley had taken Jeremy hostage. Not that I didn't think he could handle himself, and Ashley, but I was hot, hungry, and getting cranky. When Jeremy finally came out his face and body seemed closed off, as if he had taken in whatever Ashley had said and he was either guarding or digesting it. Like Matt does.

Jeremy got in the car without saying a word. I started the engine while he stared out the window.

''Well?'' I said.

''Well, what?''

''How did it go?''

''Fine.''

I brought up the next most important thing on my list. ''How about getting some lunch? I'm starved.''

He didn't look at me. ''I guess so.''

''Want to try Athini, that new bed-and-breakfast? They have brunch.''

''Better not,'' he said with a quick shake of his head. ''It's too small. We'd be conspicuous.''

Conspicuous? As if we could be anything else in Purple Sage.

"Buckle up, buddy," I said as I pulled the car away from the curb. It was one of those things we'd told each other ever since Jeremy had seen a film in second grade on wearing your seat belt. Usually the words made him smile, but this time Jeremy merely nodded silently, as if he hadn't really heard.

I could have pushed to find out what Ashley had said and why he was so quiet, but I thought better of it. "Want to eat at the country club? Oh, no, there's a tennis tournament. Okay, we could drive over to Fredericksburg. Or maybe to Llano." Both were within an hour's drive.

"How about the cafe?" he said.

That was a three-minute drive. "Sure."

After that neither of us spoke until we were seated in one of the faded, red plastic booths at the Sage Cafe. Above us was a dusty and moth-eaten deer head with glaring, glassy eyes. All the tabletops, ours included, looked as if they'd been covered in somebody's old linoleum, and the walls were a faded knotty pine.

Hanging out at the Sage Cafe is a tradition among the local people, and in my three years in Purple Sage, I'd begun to feel right at home there. Since the after-church crowd was finishing lunch, it was clearing out.

Jeremy shifted and I could hear the plastic seat crackle. He heaved a sigh, shifted again, swallowed some water, and looked at me. He didn't say anything.

I waited a few more seconds; he looked as frustrated as I felt. "Did Ashley kill Tim?" I asked.

"What? Mom!" He looked around quickly, then dropped his voice. "You shouldn't say that so loud—people could think you're serious."

I leaned forward. "Should I be serious about that?"

"No. Of course not."

LouAnn, a waitress who once told me she'd worked in

the cafe since it opened in "nineteen and forty-eight," came over to the booth and took our orders. I requested the chef's salad, dressing on the side, with a diet Coke. Jeremy nodded that he'd have the same. LouAnn gave him a surprised look, but she wrote it down carefully, then slipped her pencil behind her ear. "Be out in a jiffy," she said as she swung off toward the kitchen.

"Mom," Jeremy began, "you have to promise that you won't repeat any of this, or judge anybody, okay? It's kind of a weird story."

"Okay."

"Some people did some things that were kind of rotten, but I don't need a lecture, okay?"

"Fine," I said. "I'll just listen."

"I didn't mean that you'd—" He saw my look, took a breath, and started over, his voice low so no one else could hear. "See, Tim was dating a lot of girls. A lot. And he told all of them that he was in love with them. He even talked about marriage to all of them."

"All of them? Whoa! And how do you know this?"

"Ashley told me," he said.

"Ah."

He shifted around for a second as if looking for a comfortable position, didn't find one, and began. "Well, it's like this. Ashley said that Tim told her he wanted to marry her. That was in March and she was really happy about it. When Tim said he was going out of town for a weekend to visit his mom, Ashley said fine. She kind of thought he should have invited her to meet his mom, you know, officially, but Tim said he wanted to keep the engagement secret. Just until he could afford a ring. That was fine with Ashley, too; at least, now she says it was." Jeremy made a face. "Tim was supposed to be back Sunday night and she was going to go out with him, only her dad told her no. Seems he saw Tim leaving that weekend and Tim wasn't alone in the car. Michelle Kleinsmith was with him.

Deputy Draper pulled them over about eight miles out of town and gave Tim a speeding ticket, just to get a better look. They had two suitcases in the backseat. He didn't tell Ashley until Sunday night, because he didn't want her to be thinking about it all weekend.''

"That seems considerate."

"Except then he told her that she couldn't date Tim anymore.''

"She's over eighteen, how could he stop her?"

"He said that as long as she lived in his house and he was paying the bills, she had to do what he said. She said he was only trying to protect her. So she went to Tim and broke up with him. When he asked why, she told him the whole story and Tim said her dad was lying, that he was alone in the car when her dad stopped him."

For just a moment I was on Tim's side, and then I remembered that Jeremy already knew the end of this story, and as a matter of fact, I was pretty sure I did, too. "Did she believe Tim?"

"Why wouldn't she? Tim's... Tim was a nice guy. She thought her dad was just being overprotective—she said he'd been like that ever since her mom was killed. So then she started sneaking around behind her dad's back to see Tim.''

Our salads arrived. I poured dressing on mine while we waited impatiently for LouAnn to bring us a basket of crackers and little plastic cubes with butter in them, and then fuss over us a minute to make sure we had everything. Finally, she left. "Okay, so what else?" I asked.

Jeremy was staring at the deer head as if he'd never seen it before. "This is the part Ashley isn't too proud of. I guess nobody would be," he said. He shifted his focus to his salad for a moment, frowning at it. Finally he looked at me. "See, Ashley snuck out one night to visit Tim, only she was going to surprise him. And she did, all right. When she got to his apartment he was with someone else. They were…'' He looked down as if groping for the right term.

"Having sex?''

"Yeah. It was Michelle.''

"I guess Ashley's dad was telling the truth all along.''

Jeremy nodded and picked up his fork. "I guess. Ashley thought she had to know the whole truth, everything, so she started following Tim around. At night, she'd sit in her car outside his apartment and then see where he'd go, or who came over. Sometimes she'd follow him after work.''

I firmly believe that there are times when we don't need to know the whole truth and this had certainly been one of them. Too bad Ashley hadn't had a mother around to tell her that.

I just shook my head as Jeremy went on. "Sometimes she'd sneak up to his balcony window so she could hear what they were saying.''

Dear God. This was the worst kind of masochism I could think of.

"She found out about every one,'' Jeremy added. "And he was lying to them all.''

Jeremy's hero was not only dead, he was crumbling as well. Jeremy's reaction to it seemed to swing between depression and belligerence. I couldn't blame him. It was obviously something we'd have to talk about, but I wasn't up for it just then; these revelations were shocking to me, too. Not what Tim had done. Obviously millions of men have done the same things in the past, even some married men, so it wasn't his actions that shocked me. It was the fact that it was Tim. The nicest kid in town. The kid every mother hoped their son would grow up to be like.

This was something better tackled when Matt was around to offer his special brand of evenness. Especially since I wasn't willing to look at my own feelings on it, yet.

"First things first,'' I said, taking out a small notebook and my pen. "Who else had Tim been seeing?''

"You want the whole list?"

"The whole list."

"There was Michelle Kleinsmith, but you know about her."

"Right."

"And then he broke up with Michelle about three weeks after he started dating Paige Beaman. She was head cheerleader this year."

I knew her mother, Linda, and I can't say that I particularly liked the woman. She had treated me like a leper at the ballpark a few months back when I was being accused, wrongly, of having committed a murder in Purple Sage. She was heavy, almost beefy, the way some women get after many years of hard labor on a ranch. Paige Beaman, however, didn't look like her mother, or at least not the way her mother looked now. Paige had bright red hair, creamy skin, and deep brown eyes. No freckles that I've ever noticed. She drove the biggest pickup in town, a dark blue Chevy that the kids called the Street Eater. It was completely unexpected for the very feminine, very gorgeous Paige.

"Tim had good taste in women," I said. Every one of the females he'd dated was almost stunningly beautiful, intelligent and, at least in my brief acquaintance with each of them, a very nice person. "Too bad he couldn't have been a little more honest with them," I said. Jeremy scowled and I added, "I'm sorry, I didn't mean to be judgmental. He had a lot of good qualities, too."

"I know."

"But wasn't Paige a little young for him? She wasn't even out of high school."

"She was eighteen. They held her back a year when she had scarlet fever." He ate a slice of egg and a cherry tomato from the top of his salad before he put his fork down. "He dated older women, too."

Older? "How much older?"

"A lot older."

I waited, hoping against hope that Jeremy wasn't going to mention one of my friends. I didn't want this to be a Mrs. Robinson kind of thing. When he ate instead of talking I said, "Okay, so who was the older woman?"

Carefully he finished chewing and swallowed twice before he said, "Lurline Batson."

I heard a fork clatter on the table, but I didn't realize it was mine until Jeremy picked it up and handed it to me. "She's at least twenty years older than Tim!" I said.

"Mom, not so loud!" We both looked around and discovered that ours was the only occupied table on this side of the restaurant.

"Sorry."

He rolled his eyes before he went on. "Ashley says that Lurline was thirty-six and Tim was twenty-one. Fifteen years. He only dated her about a month, anyway, and then he started going with Sharon Jorgenson."

"Wait—he told all of them that he loved them, but did he tell all of them that he wanted to marry them?" I asked.

"Ashley said he did. And I guess she'd know."

"Did they all overlap? I mean, like Ashley and Michelle did?"

"Yeah. Sometimes three of them overlapped."

I was still shaking my head, partly in amazement that Tim could get away with this in such a small town, when I realized something else. "Jeremy, we've got to talk to Ashley!"

"Why? I just did."

"Don't you see? She was following Tim around. She might have been following Tim when he was killed. She might have seen something. Maybe something she doesn't even realize is important."

SIXTEEN

"I ALREADY THOUGHT about that. I asked her, even," Jeremy said, poking some more at his salad. "The night that Tim was killed she was at home. With her dad. She kind of feels bad that she wasn't following him, so she could have saved him."

My conviction that Ashley Draper needed therapy in the worst way was being confirmed right and left, but at the moment there were other things to be taken into consideration. "Jeremy, has Ashley talked to her dad about this?"

"No, and she's not going to." Flat statement; no nonsense and an added "don't push it" in his tone of voice.

I ignored it. "Look, Jeremy, I realize that this is potentially embarrassing for Ashley, but her father is investigating a murder and she could know a lot more than she realizes."

"She doesn't, she said so. Besides, her dad came home Saturday and told Ashley that she should be glad that he wouldn't let her date Tim, now that he was finding out about him." Jeremy pinned me with a solemn stare. "And you can't talk to Deputy Draper, either. You promised that you wouldn't say anything."

"I didn't—"

"Mo-ther!" It was primal indignation, presumably the same as children have been letting loose at their parents since caveman days.

"Well, maybe if we said something to Mac—"

"Oh, right. And he'd go straight to Deputy Draper, so it's the same thing. Ashley doesn't want her dad to know." He stopped talking, then after a moment's thought, added, "If you tell him I can never trust you again."

It was a blow aimed straight at a mother's heart and he knew it. I put my fork down and pushed my salad away in disgust. "Okay, you win. I will not tell Mac or Deputy Draper or anyone else official that Ashley was following Tim. But," I added in what I hoped was a suitably ominous tone, "if Tim's murderer is never caught, you have to live with the knowledge that you held back evidence."

"It's not my evidence to give."

"Fine." I signaled to LouAnn that I wanted the check, then glanced at Jeremy's almost full salad bowl. He isn't a salad eater, and he'd hardly touched it. He had to be starving. "You want to go get a hamburger?"

"Yes."

I was already reaching for my purse. "Where do you want to go?"

"The country club? Maybe we could watch the end of Matt's match."

I was behind him as he hurried out of the booth and charged off for the front door of the cafe. It seemed that he was done finding out about Tim's life and didn't want to go any further. Besides being disillusioned, I wondered if he was afraid of what else we might discover if we dug any deeper.

When I reached the car, Jeremy had his door open and he was swinging it back and forth as if he were trying to get the heat out of the car.

"Let me turn on the air conditioner," I said. He waited until it was going full blast before he climbed into his seat. "I'll drop you off," I said. "I have another errand."

Jeremy gave me a suspicious look, but he didn't say anything else.

Actually, Jeremy had a right to be suspicious—it's hard to do errands in a town that pretty much closes down on Sundays.

As I PULLED UP to the club I remembered what Ashley, via Jeremy, had said about Lurline and her relationship with

Tim. There was a momentary hesitation on my part. I would have loved to talk to Lurline. I was even tempted to dash into the club on some pretense, just to look at her. I wanted to see this woman who, at thirty-six, had been having an affair with a twenty-one-year-old.

However, I didn't go into the club at all. The tennis tournament wasn't a major event in the Western Hemisphere, but it was enough to keep Lurline busy. Besides, she hadn't been keen on talking with me before; I couldn't imagine that she'd changed her mind.

"Sure you don't want to come in?" Jeremy asked.

"No, I have other things to do." I glanced around the lot. "Can you get a ride home with Matt? Do you see the Bronco?"

Jeremy nodded to a row of vehicles on our right and said, "It's over there."

"Okay, see you later." I waved as Jeremy loped off, then I aimed the Mazda back toward town. I'm a strong believer in hunches; I think they have something to do with our subconscious that sees all and hears all. At that moment I wanted to talk with IdaMae Dorfman. A kind of hunch, if you will.

IdaMae owns the bakery on Main Street and it's an institution in Purple Sage. Come to think of it, so is IdaMae. She was born here some seventy, or eighty, or ninety years ago in the little rock house where she still lives. No one is sure of her real age, and when I asked her once she gave me a long stare and told me it was none of my damned business. Then she lit a cigarette and blew a couple of smoke rings in the air before she looked back at me and started laughing.

Every time I drive by her house I've wanted to get some big shears and start clipping things. Two massive bushes flank the steps that go up to the front porch, only the bushes are now higher than the roof, and you have to turn sideways to get between them. There are climbing roses, heavy with small brilliant red flowers, that have taken over the entire west side of the house. They cover the wall, the ground, and most of the chimney as well. What isn't thick with roses is thick with honeysuckle. What I assume was once a chain-link fence is now a symmetrical mound of tangled vine that, in the spring, is a mass of fragrant honeysuckle blossoms. The flower beds around the porch are a billow of hydrangea, impatiens, and monkey grass, or, as IdaMae once told me, anything that survived that year's winter. It's a once domestic garden that rioted into a decadence of green. So far we haven't lost anybody in it, but I'm still waiting.

I parked the car and pushed open the gate, calling as I went, "IdaMae, are you home?" There was no response so I edged up the steps to the porch. It was dark and cool, shaded by all the vegetation. I tapped on the faded, black screen door and said again, "IdaMae? It's me, Jolie."

I heard a sound before IdaMae's diminutive figure appeared wearing a shirt with narrow pink, white, and baby blue stripes over baby blue polyester double-knit pants. On her feet were bedroom slippers—the big fuzzy kind. "Hey, Jolie, what're you doing out there?" she said.

"I wanted to talk to you, if you have a minute. Am I interrupting anything?"

"Not a thing," she said, opening the screen door and urging me in. "I was jest settin' on my behind on the screen porch, communin' with nature. Come on back."

I followed her down a narrow hall, past a parlor with heavy antique furniture, past a door that led to a small bathroom, and then to the screened porch. It was more like a sunroom, with jalousie windows on three sides and lots of old wicker furniture that had been spray-painted bright yellow. The cushions on the wicker were calico with just a touch of the same yellow as the furniture. And, of course, there were plants. Zillions of them in everything from expensive imported ceramic pots to old coffee cans. Here the plant-of-choice seemed to be the geranium, in every color possible. There were also more than a half dozen hanging airplane plants in white and green stripes.

"Have a seat," IdaMae said, gesturing to a wicker love seat. Obviously she had been in the rocker—the pillow was crushed and the table beside it was overflowing with books. IdaMae reads everything, although her favorites are what she calls "peppy mysteries."

"Thanks." I pushed a pillow to the side and sank down on the wicker.

"So, what can I do you for?" IdaMae asked.

"Oh, nothing really. I just thought I'd stop by and say hi."

IdaMae cackled. "That's the biggest whopper I've heard you tell, Jolie Wyatt! And you didn't tell it very well, so if I was you, I wouldn't go tryin' it again."

"Honest to God, IdaMae, you are something. What I said was a 'social nicety'; couldn't you have just let it pass?"

She laughed again. "Oh, you can be social, and mosta the time you're nice, but I'm not, so you don't have to be at my house." She reached under a cushion and pulled out a battered pack of cigarettes with a purple plastic lighter stuck in the cellophane wrapper. She held it out toward me. "Want one?"

"No thanks."

"You worried about cancer?"

"Actually, IdaMae, when I quit smoking eight years ago I was, a little. And I was worried that I'd pass on my bad habit to Jeremy. But these days, I don't think I could smoke because it's just not politically correct. People snarl at you."

"And don't I know it!" She stopped long enough to light a cigarette and take a deep draw before she said, "Hell, I feel guilty lightin' up in my own house. Might be a down-wind that'd choke out one of the neighbors!"

I laughed. "If they come to the house, I'll hold them off at the front door so you can sneak out the back."

She grinned, took another puff of her cigarette, and said, "You still ain't told me why you come here."

"To talk to you," I said. IdaMae watched me carefully; her bright little eyes narrowed. She doesn't let you get away with much. "I wanted to ask you about Paige Beaman," I said. "You know, Linda's daughter? I think Paige worked for you at the bakery for a while."

"I knew it," IdaMae said with a wicked grin. "When I saw you comin' up the front walk I said to myself, 'IdaMae, there's Jolie Wyatt and she's detectin' again.' I was right!"

"I'm not detecting anything," I protested.

"So, what're you callin' it these days? *Investigative journalism?*" She said the two words slowly, enunciating every syllable.

"Actually, Jeremy just mentioned that Tim Michelik had dated Paige and I was curious what she was like."

IdaMae hadn't stopped grinning. "I hope you don't play poker, cuz you don't lie for beans." She got an ashtray from the drawer of the small wicker table beside her and carefully tapped her ash in it. Then she became serious. "Do you know Paige?"

"I think I've seen her a couple of times; I do know her mother." With IdaMae you very often have to go back a generation or two to bring her up to what you want to know. That's not a complaint on my part; usually the information is fascinating, even if it's not relevant. It's only a problem when you're in a hurry and I wasn't.

She let out a big puff of smoke. "Now, that Linda's a piece of work, I'll tell you that for sure. It's funny, too, cuz when she was a girl she was real pretty—had all the boys chasin' after her. She was syrupy sweet; kinda talked baby talk about half the time 'til you wanted to smack her. Then she married Travis and they was hardly outa the church before she started changin'. First thing she did was started gaining weight, and after the kids come along she got downright fat and complained she just couldn't lose it. Well I guess not! If I ate me a couple dozen doughnuts a week and a pie and a cake, I guess I'd be fat, too. And she ain't sweet dispositioned despite all that. She's kinda bitter, don't you think?" IdaMae stopped and shook her head. "Would you just listen to me goin' on about Linda Beaman as if it's any a my business! Oh, well, if you tell anyone I said it, I'll just say you was lyin'. Still, if I was Travis I'd plunk her out on a road somewheres and hope she couldn't find her way home."

"That's the Linda I know, and not one I particularly love, either," I said. "But, what's Paige like? She's really nice, isn't she?"

IdaMae was leaning back in her chair, thinking. "Paige Beaman is a real sweet thing. Doesn't have that mean streak her mama does."

"But what?" I asked. "You're hiding something. And you're no better at it than I am."

IdaMae shook her head. "I don't know, Jolie, I have what you might call a *moral dilemma* when you start talkin' about Paige Beaman. I don't like to speak ill of that child, but I had to let her go—jus' couldn't have her workin' at the bakery with the problems comin' up all the time."

I felt like a missile put on full alert. "What problems?"

"Shortfall. The cash drawer was always comin' up short when Paige closed up. It wasn't a bunch of money, just five here and two there, and ten thataways. But it added up, you know? In one month I lost pert near a hundred dollars. Next month it was around eighty."

"And you think that Paige was stealing it?"

"I don't know," IdaMae said. "I sure didn't want to accuse her wrongly, nobody needs that, so I worked with her on how to make change. I told her to be real careful countin' cash, but nothing helped. She was either real smart, or dumb as a post. Either way, when she had to take off two times in a row, I let her go. Told her I just couldn't work out a schedule with her off shakin' her pom-poms at some regional cheerleadin' conference.''

"Hmm." I sat up and swung around to face out the back windows. IdaMae's backyard was as overgrown as her front, creating a humid domestic jungle that almost reached into the cool of the house. But I wasn't thinking about plants; I was thinking about Paige Beaman.

I knew she was beautiful, but then so did anyone who'd ever seen her. She had seemed pretty straightforward, too. And nice. But, most kids in Purple Sage are nice. We don't have much of an attitude problem with our teens—it's hard to cop an attitude with people who have seen you grow up and who've baked brownies and pies so your class could go on a field trip to visit Shamu.

So Paige was pretty, nice, and maybe smart. Or maybe not. But was she smart about men?

"IdaMae," I said, as I turned back around to face her, "did you know she had dated Tim Michelik?"

IdaMae put out her cigarette. "That was right before I let her go. That girl was starry-eyed. Coulda walked on clouds after she started datin' that boy. You know, I think she did walk on clouds."

"And then what happened? Did Tim feel the same way about her? Did he dump her?"

"I don't have the least idea. Sorry, but that's right when I let her go. Didn't see her after that except when she come in to pick up her last paycheck."

"Oh." I could feel the tension in my shoulders let go. I had been expecting more. "When was that?"

"Just after the fifteenth of April—I always call that day a federal holiday, is why I remember. Not for us, of course, just for them rats in the federal government what get our tax money." She grinned.

"Right."

"You know," IdaMae said, "I thought you was comin' to talk about them Jorgenson kids. I thought maybe you was trying to track them down."

"You did? Why would I talk to you?"

"Because I knowed their grandmama real well and I might could tell you a thing or two."

SEVENTEEN

IDAMAE BROUGHT OUT two old albums, the kind with black pages and little stickers on every corner of the pictures to hold them in place. The glue had dried out with age so that some of the pictures were in danger of falling out, but IdaMae didn't treat the books as if they were treasured relics.

"Emma Toffler, their grandmama, was a real nice person." IdaMae plopped down on the wicker love seat beside me and began flipping pages. "Kinda shy at first, but once you got to know her she was a real sweet person. Always willin' to go along with the crowd and have some fun." She stopped and pointed to an old black-and-white photo. It showed a group of five people on the bank of a river. Judging by the clothes, it must have been in the early forties. The two men wore baggy trousers, two-toned shoes, and short-sleeved shirts. One of the women was also in trousers topped with a thin sweater that tied at the neck. Her pant legs were rolled up almost to her knees; she was wading in the water, waving at the others as if daring them to come in. The other two women wore dresses; one was sitting demurely on the bank, the other dipped just a toe in the water near the shore. Everyone was smiling or laughing, and it looked like they were having a wonderful time.

"That's you in the trousers, right?" I said.

"I shoulda guessed you'd figger it out," IdaMae said, fingering the edge of the picture. "How'd you know?"

IdaMae today has white hair that forms wisps around a face filled with character and the wrinkles that come from it. The young woman in the picture appeared to have a flawlessly smooth complexion and shiny, dark hair that was cut short and waved softly. It framed a face radiating an impish joy. Not a beautiful face, but the face of someone who'd be fun to have around. Had I seen the picture in another context, I probably couldn't have figured it out at all, but here in IdaMae's house, it was hard not to get it right. The spirit was the same. "I think the trousers were the biggest clue," I said. "This was the forties, right?" She nodded and I went on. "And this was somewhere near Purple Sage, so I suspect that you were pretty daring to be out in public dressed like that. Besides, there's an attitude. Who else but you, IdaMae, would be the first in the water?"

She looked at me with her bright eyes for a moment longer than was comfortable. Then she broke the mood by leaning forward to look at the picture. "This here is Emma," she said, pointing to the woman with just a toe in the water. Emma Toffler's expression made her look as if she were doing something really risqué and delighting in it. "You cain't see her face real clear—oh, but this here is Toff. Weren't he somethin'?"

"Her husband?" I asked.

"Yep. Harold Toffler, but we all called him Toff. He was the best-lookin' thing in three counties, and didn't he know it!"

He had dark eyes and dark brown hair and a kind of poet's wistful look that some women find so appealing. Apparently IdaMae was one of those women, which I wouldn't have expected.

She flipped some pages quickly then pointed to another picture. "This was taken out at their farm 'bout two months after they got married. He died when he was just thirty-five. Their daughter Corinne was just eight. Got hit by lightning when he was out plowing." IdaMae sighed and she studied the photo some more. The memories must have been strong. "They was a striking couple. She was just flat beautiful. Polish, did I tell you? You could see it in her bones.''

And you could. Emma Toffler had cheekbones that were high and wide in her heart-shaped face. It was a dramatic face, especially with the wide-set, almost almond-shaped eyes. Very European.

"I'm Polish, too," I said. "Too bad I didn't get that kind of cheekbones. What color were her eyes?"

"Hazel. James has eyes just like her, too. Sharon's are more like her grandaddy's. Pansy eyes. But almost black."

I could see that even in the old photo. "Do you have any pictures of James or Sharon? Or their mother?"

"Sure do." She pulled out the second album, this one newer—the photos toward the back were in color. "This here is when Sharon was christened." She pulled out a picture that showed Emma Toffler and half a dozen other people on the steps of the old Christian Church. Emma Toffler was older, but her face was still beautiful. A young woman standing in front of her held a baby in a white blanket. It must have been cold because everyone was bundled up. The woman holding the baby bore a slight resemblance to Emma. "This is Corinne Jorgenson?" I guessed.

"Uh-huh."

Beside her was a man who was obviously her husband. He was smiling down, beaming as only a proud father can. His hands were resting on the shoulders of the two small boys in front of him, both with soft blond hair and wide smiles. They must have been about two and four, although it was hard to tell.

"Which one is James?" I asked.

IdaMae looked carefully, then pointed to the smaller of the two boys. "That's James. And that's Franky," she said, her gnarled finger on the taller boy.

"A relative?" I asked.

"Nope. There was three kids. Only after the car wreck, Emma couldn't keep all three—she just couldn't afford to—so she let Franky go to some cousins' up north some-wheres. 'Bout broke her heart but there wasn't no way she could feed all three of them kids and he was the oldest and the most self-sufficient.'' IdaMae shook her head. ''The real sad part is that the cousins became missionaries and moved off and Emma didn't even get to keep up with them. She just lost that boy forever.'' IdaMae sighed. ''Emma had one of them real tragic lives.''

''And now she has her two grandchildren on the run from the law.''

''She's probably spinnin' in her grave.''

''Her grave?'' I said. ''I thought she was alive.''

''Not lately. She died, oh, 'bout six months ago. It was during that hard freeze right after Christmas. She got pneu-monia and died.''

''So what about Sharon? Where has she been living?''

''She's eighteen—she was just keepin' on in her grand-mama's home, I expect. Leastways until last Friday when James busted out of prison.'' IdaMae flipped more pages. ''And I'll tell you one thing—if Emma Toffler were alive today, Sharon wouldn'ta pulled a dumb, damn stunt like helpin' James. Her grandmama woulda tanned her hiney but good for even thinking about doing any such thing.'' She almost ripped a page in her agitation. ''Here. This here is James.''

There were two children standing in front of a big oak tree. James must have been in about first or second grade, all skinny arms and legs with plenty of scratches. His T-shirt was a little tight and his hair looked like it had been cut at home, but he seemed very pleased with himself. He was looking straight into the camera with a practically toothless grin that would melt any mother's heart. Beside him was his younger sister, who couldn't have been over three or four. She was partially turned away, looking off into the distance, with a very serious and slightly puzzled frown on her delicate face.

"What was going on when this was taken?" I asked.

IdaMae looked at the picture. "I don't have no idea," she said. "But that's about as typical a pose for them two as I've ever seen. James just cocky as hell, like he always was, and Sharon sorta away in her own world."

I still couldn't seem to get a handle on the two Jorgensons. I knew so many of the facts about them, and yes, they were tragic, but the two had been cared for. It seemed obvious from the pictures that before the fatal accident their parents had been loving and caring. James and Sharon had been loved very much by their grandmother, too, at least that's what I had inferred from IdaMae's conversation. So why had James taken to a life of such bizarre crime? The whole thing was like a big overblown game of cops and robbers, only James was much too old for that, and certainly too old to be dragging Sharon into it. Didn't he understand how high the stakes were now? And how dangerous?

I asked IdaMae that very question, and she puzzled over it for a while. Finally she just shook her head. "I don't reckon I ever understood what was inside James's head. I don't imagine anybody has."

Then I asked the final question, the one that plagued me the most. "Do you think James killed Tim Michelik?"

IdaMae took her time closing up the albums, then she shrugged her shoulders. "Cain't say, Jolie," she offered without looking at me. "I just cain't say."

I COULDN'T HELP remembering Tim's remark that last time I'd seen him at the club. Something about how life had gotten out of hand. I guess so. Tim had dated so many girls, women, whatever they were, I wondered how he had kept his dates straight. I certainly couldn't.

I knew that some of the time frames had to overlap and I couldn't be sure who was when. I needed paper and pencil, and the nearest place I could think of to get that, and a little peace and quiet, was the radio station. I headed in that direction, my brain in overtime. I didn't even look at the parking lot, just pulled into a space and jumped out of the car. I kept thinking that if I could only get Tim's string of females in some kind of time sequence I could figure out who killed him.

Once inside I discovered the cool quiet I had been seeking. I didn't make my presence known to the jock, and while that was a courtesy—rather than scaring the poor kid half to death when he bumped into me in the hall or discovered me on his own—I wasn't thinking about courtesy. I could only think about Tim and my proposed dating timeline.

At my desk I pulled out pen and paper and drew a line vertically. First I knew that Paige Beaman had started dating Tim around April 15, so I marked a spot midway down the paper with a short horizontal line and wrote the date along with Paige's name. Ashley Draper had mentioned a date, too, but I couldn't remember exactly when it was. Jeremy had said something about Tim going out of town, but when? I wracked my brain. February? No, that wasn't right. I jumped up and paced the room, sat down and closed my eyes, then paced some more.

Finally it came to me. Ashley had told us that she'd broken up with Tim on March 14. My sister's birthday, which is why I finally remembered.

So I drew another short line about two inches below the first with Paige's name and wrote *March 14th, Ashley*. That's when I remembered that Michelle had gone out of town with Tim while he was dating Ashley. And he had also slept with Michelle after that. It put Michelle at early March to mid-April. Which is when he took up with Paige Beaman, probably mid-April to around the first of May. And it was now mid-June.

I sat back and looked at the sheet. He had taken up with some of the most attractive single women in town, promised marriage, reneged, and then moved on. Knowing what I did now, I wasn't a bit surprised that Tim had been shot—the only surprising thing was that it hadn't happened sooner.

And he'd been such a nice kid.

I leaned forward, my chin resting in my hands as I stared at the sheet some more. Michelle had been pretty open about her dislike of Tim, and I had to wonder if someone who had murdered would be quite so vocal about their dislike. And then there was Paige, an unknown to me. Of course, her mother wasn't.

Without even hesitating I reached for the phone and the phone book at the same time. You can do that in Purple Sage. The phone book is about as thick as a yellow tablet and still has room for the numbers of everyone in the county. I looked up Travis Beaman, and dialed the last five digits. That's another convenience of Purple Sage: It's so small we don't even have to dial the whole number.

The phone was answered by a teenager, naturally. "Hi, Travis, is that you?" Travis Jr. was on Jeremy's baseball team.

"Yeah. Who's this?"

"Jolie Wyatt. Is your mom around?"

"Just a minute." He set the phone down on something hard so the clunk reverberated in my ear for a minute, and then Linda came on the line.

"Jolie. How are you?"

"Oh, just fine, Linda. How are you doing?"

"I am just beat. I mean frazzled. We just got in from Austin and I can't wait to take a cool shower and relax. I'll tell you what, Austin seems to be getting bigger by the minute. I mean *the minute!* I drove down there through Dripping Springs and Wimberly, thinking, Now there won't be any traffic until we get right downtown, but I'll tell you, we weren't even past the Y in Oak Hill before it was bumper to bumper. Luckily we were going *into* Austin, not *coming out,* or it would have been even worse. And lucky that was on Thursday instead of on Friday, because they tell me that Fridays are just unbearable! Of course, I think traffic in that town is unbearable all the time.''

She sounded like she was just getting wound up, with a lot more she wanted to say. I didn't mind, since there was a lot more I wanted to hear. She had said she'd driven in Thursday—the night Tim was killed here in Purple Sage.

"Did the whole family go to Austin?" I asked. "A mini-vacation?"

"Hardly!" Linda snorted. "Just Paige and me. We were finding her a place to stay for the summer. And next year, of course. This fall she'll be a freshman at the University."

The University. That's the way it's referred to in this part of Texas. Kind of the way people in New York refer to Manhattan as the City. Or the way people in the Bay Area refer to San Francisco as the City. As if there were only one in the whole world, even though we all know better.

"Well, that's great," I said. "And Paige is going to summer school in Austin too?"

The smugness in Linda's response was as thick as the meringue on IdaMae's cream pies. "Cheerleading camp. We've been told, confidentially, of course, that she is practically a shoo-in for cheerleader." The smugness turned to a complaint. "But, my Lord, I can't believe how big that campus is. And naturally there is no parking unless you have a permit, so we trudged up this way, and down that-away, and all through some area that was just like a big park with squirrels and such, until I thought I was going to drop! You cannot imagine how they ran us around from one place to another. And then we had to go off campus to look for a room for the summer because the dorm she'll be in is being renovated. It was just run, run, run!"

"It sounds exhausting." Especially when you were carrying an extra hundred or so pounds. Even as I had the thought I realized how uncharitable it was. I offered a silent *mea culpa* and went on. "So you were there for three days?"

"A little over. We got in about four-thirty Thursday and then came on home this afternoon." She paused for a breath and said, "And then we found out about Tim Michelik and I'll tell you, Paige like to died! That child was more upset than I would have believed, especially since they broke up just ages ago. I mean, he was a nice enough boy, but let's face it, Tim wasn't going no place, if you know what I mean. Paige can do a whole lot better and she will, I guarantee it. She don't need someone who's just hanging around Purple Sage, being a waiter at the country club."

She waited, apparently wanting me to support her opinions. I did in one respect: Tim's behavior toward women had been cavalier and I didn't wish that kind of treatment on anyone. Still, I didn't like branding him less than the rest of the world just because he wasn't in college. Oh, to hell with it, I thought. Aloud I said, "Paige has years ahead of her before it's time to get into a serious relationship, besides, she needs to be concentrating on her college. And her cheerleading." The last had just slipped out and it didn't sound sympathetic.

Linda noticed. "Oh, you can use that tone of voice, Jolie, but you're raising a boy so you maybe don't realize how it is out there in the real world. Sure, there's women's lib and all that, but you just go look at the statistics and then you'll see what I mean. Women still don't make near as much money as men, even when they're doin' the exact same job. If a woman really wants to have a nice lifestyle she's still got to find her a man who can make some powerful money."

I had been a single mother for over twelve years, supporting Jeremy and myself in a style that was hardly extravagant. I knew all about sexism, and I knew what it was like to make less money just because you weren't a male, but Linda didn't give me a chance to say anything.

"Paige is gonna do great," she said. "Just you wait and see. As a cheerleader she can pick and choose the boys she goes out with. Then when she marries, she's gonna do real well—she don't have to settle for no poor dirt farmer."

The last phrase seemed to echo on the phone line. Linda's bitterness had a source and, maybe for the first time, I began to understand her. As for what she wanted for Paige, that was the same as parents had always wanted for their children—a better life.

"Paige is a beautiful and intelligent young woman," I said. "And I'm sure she can have whatever she wants." I caught myself thinking of how young she was. "Tim's death has been hard for Jeremy to take; I guess it's pretty much the same for Paige. I'm sorry she has to go through it."

Linda's voice lost its belligerence. "I expect you're right. It's just the shock, but she'll get over it soon enough. Shoot, she's got to be packed and out of here by next weekend." She took a breath and became businesslike. "So, now, I suppose you're calling about the party."

"Party?"

"The end-of-school party that you and Matt are having for the kids. Now I know I said we'd help, and we will, but I really can't do more than just show up. I just don't have the energy for any cooking or such, but the two of us will chaperone, since I promised. What time do you want us there?"

My mind began to reel. Matt and I were giving the kids an after-school party the day school got out—this coming Tuesday. We had agreed to do that a month before at the sophomore parents' meeting and now it was time. Almost time. Just two days away. Two short days!

"Uh, I'm really not sure what time we'll need you," I stammered. "Probably midafternoon. Uh, maybe four-thirty. Let me call you. I, really, um, just needed to know that you'll still be coming.''

''I don't go back on my word. Me and Trav will be there. And Trav Junior, of course.''

''Thanks, Linda. Great. See you then.'' I hung up the phone, my breathing escalating rapidly. Having sixty-odd people at your house is not a small feat, at least I didn't think it was—I'd never had a party that size. First I had to find out exactly how many kids and parents were coming and then I had to go home and round up Matt and Jeremy so we could get things done.

Except that I felt totally overwhelmed by the whole thing and I wasn't moving at all. The phone under my hand rang twice before I noticed it and then I just stared at the blinking light before I realized it needed to be answered. By the time I snatched up the receiver, someone else had gotten the call.

''Hey, man—I finally tracked you down.'' There was a little static and a hollowness as if the call were coming from a cellular phone.

The next voice was Rory's. ''I can't believe you! You've got to be the dumbest—''

His words got lost in the other man's laughter. ''You're gonna have a heart attack; don't be such a pompous asshole!'' More laughter.

I didn't have a clue where Rory was in the building and I didn't much care. Someone was calling him the names I'd wanted to call him for weeks. I'd just leave the guy to it. I gently hung up the receiver and picked up my purse. I had more important things to do.

EIGHTEEN

PLANNING A PARTY for fifty-seven people, which was the final count including chaperones, was a whole lot more work than I had imagined. First of all, where were fifty-seven people going to sit? There certainly wasn't room for them in the living room, or even the living room and den combined. If we used the living room, den, kitchen, and the downstairs closets it was still going to be standing room only. So we decided to concentrate the party on the deck and in the backyard, both of which are, luckily, large. In case of rain we'd move everything to a barn, spread straw around, and try to convince the kids it was the latest in chic, as opposed to an emergency measure.

By that night we had the major items worked out. We'd also called the high school principal and had the promise of the loan of several long tables as well as thirty chairs— everyone else would sit on hay bales. Matt and Bart, the foreman of the ranch, would pick the things up at the school Tuesday morning. Then we planned food.

A number of places in Austin advertise that one phone call would get sufficient amounts of edibles delivered on short notice. However, Matt is a firm believer in taking care of the people who take care of you. In other words, shop in Purple Sage when at all possible. With only two days before the party I had to call three barbecue places to get a commitment for enough food to feed our guests. Drinks were easy. We could buy them at the grocery store along with paper plates, napkins, plastic cutlery, etc. Henshaw's Hardware had blue-speckled iron pots and pans, and I was commissioned to purchase sufficient amounts of them to hold all the food, coffee, and condiments. Perry Brothers would have purple plastic cups somewhere in the storeroom (after all it was the school color), plus they would have purple bandannas, which I would tie on anything that didn't match in order to make it look like it did.

Dessert would be a huge cake that I would get IdaMae to bake. It would no doubt take some begging due to the lack of planning time, but if I couldn't talk her into it, Matt would give it a try. If he failed, we knew Jeremy could sweet-talk her, no pun intended. We would also serve watermelon for the chaperones who were on diets. And, of course, there were all the munchies, since teenagers seem to make eating a marathon event.

The biggest problem was finding sufficient storage to keep the cold things cold and the hot things hot immediately before and during the party. We delegated that task to Matt, while Jeremy was assigned the job of creating and distributing flyers with the particulars of the party and a map to the ranch.

That filled up the daylight Sunday and my dreams Sunday night. I spent a lot of time wandering around and worrying instead of sleeping. As it turned out, I wasn't the only one who'd been prowling around during the midnight hours.

"HE DID WHAT?"

It was early Monday and I was sitting in Mac's office on the second floor of the courthouse; the sun blazed in the window and Mac was shaking his head sadly. Since the light was behind him I couldn't see his face all that clearly, but I suspected he was more amused than distressed, and trying not to show it.

"Well, first," Mac said, "he broke into the Colonial Convenience Store out by the lake. According to what I've been hearing"—he picked up a piece of paper with some nice neat printing on it—"our friend Jorgenson stole cigarettes, same brand he's always smoked, the whole display of lighters, and a couple of cases of those fire logs. Oh, and some tools. Screwdrivers, hammers, just the basic stuff they carried. They know that some food is missing, too; all the fresh fruits that were in the cooler are gone, but they can't tell about much else until they do a complete inventory.''

''Just picking up a few staples,'' I said.

Mac nodded. ''Oh, but that was just the start of our boy's shopping spree. Next he went on over to Henshaw's Hardware—''

I made a sound, thinking that if Jorgenson had stolen all the blue iron containers I was going to shoot him myself.

''What?'' Max asked.

''Oh, nothing. What did he get there?'' I began taking notes.

Mac read off the list. ''Cleaned out the whole front window display. Two sleeping bags, two air mattresses, a small hibachi, a lantern, bug spray…well, you get the picture.''

''So you know for sure that Jorgenson is camping out somewhere.''

''Or that he wants us to *think* he's camping out somewhere.'' I groaned and Mac grinned. ''Luckily all these break-ins aren't my problem. Bill Tieman over to the police department is handling the paperwork on them, since they occurred inside the city limits. Lucky break for me.''

''And for Andy Sawyer,'' I said. Andy was the senior deputy at the police department and I always believed he did the bulk of the work. However, Andy was on vacation somewhere in the Rockies and wasn't expected back for another week. ''Of course you still have to find Mr. Jorgenson,'' I added.

The phone rang and Mac picked it up. ''Sheriff Donelly here.'' While he talked I looked over my notes on the break-ins and pretended not to listen. ''Okay, go ahead,'' he said. ''Oh. Are you sure? How many guns?'' A pause while he listened. ''Damn kid. I know, Joan, I know. Well, I don't want him to get himself killed, either. Or Sharon.

Yeah, I agree. That's okay, I don't need the registration numbers—Bill Tieman will—but I'd better have the basics, just so I'm prepared.'' He listened and wrote for a few minutes then finished with, ''I don't know that there's much we can do 'cept step up the search. Let me know if you find anything else missing. Thanks.'' And with that he hung up the phone and looked at me. ''We got us a problem, Jolie.''

''What problem?''

''I know you heard part of that conversation and I presume you're going to ask about the rest and I don't want it on the news. What do you figure we can do about that?''

I thought about it for a minute. I am not Connie Chung, and I'm not Diane Sawyer. I will never be a hard-bitten reporter who pushes a microphone into the face of people who've just been through a tragedy. While I know all about First Amendment rights, and the public's ''right to know,'' there are times when I think it's none of the public's business. There are laws higher than the Constitution and certainly higher than those of our broken justice system. I remember once when a defense lawyer refused to reveal the location of a kidnapped baby because she had gotten the information from her client, making it ''privileged.'' As far as I'm concerned, what she did to the family of that child was unconscionable, and there isn't a law anywhere that should be used in such a way. At least that's how I believe, so if Mac had a good reason for me to withhold information from the public, then I would, and I told him so.

''For me it's never come to the point where I had to choose between the law and what I think is right, and I hope to God it never does.'' Then he became businesslike. ''That was Joan Henshaw on the phone. She and Wade have been doing a quick inventory because of the break-in and they've noticed a couple more things missing. A thirty-ought-six, and a nine millimeter automatic Beretta.'' I sucked in some air as he went on. "A real expensive scope for the rifle is missing, too, and plenty of ammunition. Even an extra clip for the Beretta."

I'm not a gun expert, but I did know that the .30-06 was a deer rifle, bolt action, that could hold several bullets in an internal clip. I know this because my first year in Purple Sage Matt had tried to introduce me to the joys of deer hunting and he had a .30-06. I had been an excellent student of the intricacies of guns—after all, I am a mystery writer, and that was pertinent information to my chosen profession.

The hunting itself was an entirely different matter. I had spent our one "hunting" morning mentally screaming "Run, Bambi!" and once I may even have said it out loud. But I didn't yell it, the way Matt says I did when he tells the story. And I don't go deer hunting anymore. Guns still make me a little nervous and the fact that James Elliott Jorgenson was building an arsenal made me *very* nervous.

"Mac, why do you think he wanted the guns? And why don't you want me to mention it on the air?"

"Personally, I think he just wanted the weapons for show. Maybe to feel good. Or tough or something. I don't think he intends to use them." He looked down at his desk, his face suddenly older and more tired. "And I hope I'm right. I don't want anything on the radio because, as you know, the general population of Wilmot County is armed to the teeth—always has been—and I don't want anyone reachin' for their guns when there's no need. Right now everybody believes that James and Sharon are real colorful and not too dangerous. I'd like it to stay that way."

"And what if James Jorgenson is dangerous?"

"Like I said, Jolie, I can only hope I'm right."

Loretta, the dispatcher, came in and handed some mail to Mac. "I think you'll like the postcard," she said with a grin as she left. Mac thumbed through the envelopes and advertising flyers, then came up with a full-color postcard. He held it up and I could see that it showed the Wilmot

County courthouse on the front. Mac was frowning as he turned it over and read the back of the card. He swore, and said, "I'll be damned—" then "That kid—" He'd pull up short every time he realized I was listening.

"What?" I asked.

Mac flung his hand out toward me as if he didn't want to be associated with the card anymore. "Here."

I took it from him and turned it over. The writing on the back was big and flashy. All it said was *Having a wonderful time*. It was signed *James*.

My head popped up and I looked at Mac. "James? As in James Jorgenson?"

"I expect," He said through gritted teeth.

I looked at the card more carefully. "It was mailed yesterday here in Purple Sage."

Mac stood up and reached out for the card, but he didn't look at it—he just threw it in his top drawer. "That's one more thing I wouldn't like to hear about on the news."

I was fighting hard not to smile. "Sure. Got it."

"I'd better see what we can do about expanding the size of the search party. We have a young man who seems to be in need of the kind of hospitality only the sheriff's office can provide. If you'll excuse me..."

He was reaching for his hat when I remembered there was another reason for my visit. "Mac, I know you're in a hurry, but could you spare just another minute?"

He looked surprised as he turned around to face me. "Sounds real serious," he said.

"It could be." I stood up and took a deep breath. "You may already know all this, but I thought I'd better mention it just in case you hadn't heard. Your deputy, Linc Draper...is he pretty good?"

"I think he's a real fine law-enforcement man and a real fine person, as well."

"Oh..."

"What's on your mind, Jolie? Spit it out."

Before I thought any more about it, I said, "Did you know his daughter used to date Tim Michelik? And that Linc broke it up?" I licked my lips. Mac was giving me no encouragement at all. "He saw Tim out with another girl—woman—when he was supposed to be going with Ashley, so he told her she couldn't date Tim anymore." I stopped completely this time. Under other circumstances I might have been tempted to mention how Ashley had begun playing detective, following Tim, and how she might have seen something the night Tim was murdered, except I didn't believe that anymore. What I did believe was that she might have seen things leading up to the murder that would be helpful to the investigation. "At any rate, Mac, I didn't know if you knew that, but I think Ashley could tell somebody a lot about Tim. If she would."

"All right." He stopped and looked squarely at me. "Are you thinking Linc might be a suspect, too?"

I nodded, but I didn't say anything. Mac looked somber. "Jolie, if I remember rightly, you thought this same thing about Andy Sawyer during the investigation of Judge Osler's murder. Wasn't more than three months ago."

"I know, but it seems like deputies and the police shouldn't have a personal involvement in their cases. Isn't that true?"

"It'd be real nice, but Jolie, we got us a small force of officers in a small town. In a big town it might could be different."

"Mac, this is Linc's daughter. And she told Jeremy she'd been following Tim around after they broke up. There's no telling what she saw."

"Okay, you've convinced me," he said as he put on his hat. "I'll do something about it, Jolie. Just give me some time to figure out what."

I followed him out, belatedly remembering I'd promised Jeremy I wouldn't say anything. "Uh, Mac—" We were halfway down the wooden staircase that went from the third story to the second. Mac turned to look at me. "Uh, Mac," I went on, "one favor deserves another, don't you think?"

"In some cases. What did you have in mind?"

"I wasn't supposed to tell you Ashley dated Tim. Or followed him."

"Jeremy ask you not to say anything?" he asked. I nodded, and after a moment he said, "My memory is the damndest thing. I hear somethin', but I swear I can't tell you who I heard it from. Kind of like the grapevine. Just can't trace a thing to its source..."

It only assuaged a little of my guilt.

"HAVE YOU GOT a minute?" Michelle was standing in the doorway of the news office, one hand on the frame, an anxious look on her face.

"Sure." I turned away from the computer and the story I was just finishing.

Michelle came into the office and sat her jean-clad bottom on the edge of Rory's desk. "Is that more about Jorgenson?" she asked, pointing to the computer.

"The ongoing adventures of James Elliott Jorgenson. Someone should write a book."

"Maybe you."

I smiled. "I don't do true crime, but this is quite a story. So what's on your mind?"

"Oh." She ran her fingers through her long hair, pulling it off her forehead. I could see the start of a wrinkle on her otherwise perfect face. She took a breath and let it out with a quick puff. Her eyes were square on mine as she said, "I feel bad about the other day and I needed to say something. You know, the day you and Jeremy came over."

"We were the rude ones—we dropped in uninvited."

"That's just being neighborly. Besides, you wanted to find out about Tim."

"Okay," I said, "So what did you do that was so terrible?"

"I never should have told Jeremy that story about the term papers." She said it quickly, took a breath, and continued just as fast. "I've felt like crap about that ever since I did it. It's like the sin in my closet and I hate that I did it. And then to tell Jeremy—But it was like at a party where people are getting drunker and drunker and revealing more and more…you know what I mean?"

"I know."

"That's how I felt. Besides, I was embarrassed that I'd cried in front of Jeremy." She flipped a big lock of hair back from her face and stood up. "I shouldn't have told that story and I needed to apologize to you. That's a lousy example for a kid. I'm sorry."

"It's okay," I said. "You didn't mean—" I stopped speaking as Rory came.

Michelle headed for the door. "Anyhow, sorry," she said, passing Rory as she left.

Rory stopped long enough to watch her leave, his attention focused on the back of her jeans. When she was out of sight he turned to me. "Is she okay? What's she got to be sorry about?"

"Oh, nothing," I said, reaching for my notes to show him. I figured news would serve to distract Rory from Michelle and the odd conversation she'd just had with me. One that I intended to think about first chance I had. "I've got some new information on Jorgenson. They're expanding the search party, since they're sure it was Jorgenson who robbed Henshaw's Hardware and the convenience store out by the lake." I didn't mention the postcard Mac had received. "Mac is calling in more law-enforcement people."

"I guess I'd better get out there, then." He dangled the keys that were still in his hand, while I glanced at the big clock on the wall.

It was eleven-forty and I had miles to go before I slept and mountains to conquer before I could relax. "What about the noon news?'' I asked. ''I'm leaving just as soon as I finish this story.''

''You'll have to do the newscast. You can have a little overtime—work the whole afternoon.''

''You don't understand; I can't. I have to leave. Tomorrow I'm giving a party for fifty-seven people and I have a lot to do.''

The look on his face was one of pained patience. ''Jolie, this is news—it isn't about little parties.''

''A party for fifty-seven people is not little—''

''It's a party. And this is news,'' he said, his tone condescending. ''Can you see the difference in importance?''

''Yes.'' I jumped up. My adrenaline was pumping so fiercely I had to hold my voice in check or it would have knocked down walls. ''The party is more important.''

''Oh, brother—''

''You see, every year on the day that school gets out, some of the kids decide to celebrate. Some of them drink too much and some of them drive too fast, and too often they do both at once. Two years ago a very nice young man named Christopher Grayer died from the combination of alcohol and automobiles. Last year there was a wreck and Betsy Oberbeck was crippled. Well, it's not going to happen this year because there is going to be supervised celebrating. Parties, with bus transportation, for every kid in Purple Sage high school. And fifty-seven of them are going to be at my house. It would be nice if I could offer them food and nonalcoholic beverages, which I can do *if* I'm not working on news.'' I stopped to breathe. ''Now do you understand?''

''Look, what you're doing is really nice, Jolie. Just do the newscast and then you can leave. You'll be out of here by one. I'll come back in time for the five o'clock news.''

''Wow, thanks, Rory. What a swell guy you are.'' I gave him a sweet smile as I pulled open a drawer and retrieved my purse. ''But see, it doesn't work that way. This morning

I got here fifteen minutes early, like I do every morning, and so now I'm *leaving* fifteen minutes early." I swung around and started for the door.

"Wait a minute—"

I turned back and pointed to the desk where my notes were. "Oh, and you'll have to type your own story, but it will be better that way—since you're so good at recognizing what's important and what's not."

NINETEEN

"I THINK IT'S going to work out fine," Matt said. He has a way of saying things like that just when I'm ready to head for the nearest tall buildings so I can practice my jumping. The most amazing thing is that he's right almost all of the time. I hate it.

"And what if it doesn't work out fine?" We were sitting at the kitchen table, Matt, Jeremy, Diane, and myself. It was nearly nine-thirty and we'd gone over the next day's chores at least three times. We even had yellow tablets in front of us with a kind of timetable, and despite having added a number of additional chores, including moving stereo equipment and adding more food for later in the evening, things appeared to be under control. This was our final push before the party and it was all too easy—I knew that something was going to go wrong.

"What if the barbecue isn't ready?" I demanded. "What if I can't get the cups? What if we have bad weather?"

Diane started shaking her head and said in a high, sweet voice that she uses to mimic the head of the PTA, "You're not going to be elected Miss Optimism with this kind of talk."

"That's good, because I didn't want the job. 'If nominated I will not run, if elected I will not serve.' And what if the kids trash the house? Do some real damage?"

"We'll repair it or remodel," Matt said, with a glance at me. "You've been wanting to remodel, anyway. This will just give you an excuse."

"Besides, that's not going to happen, Mom," said my son, the defender of teen rights.

Diane reached over and patted my hand. "You can relax, Jolie; this will be a snap."

"Easy for you to say." I'd never given a large party. As a single mother I'd never had the house, the time, the money, or the inclination. Diane, on the other hand, had all of those things, plus the temperament and the silverware. Hell, she couldn't miss.

I was about to expound on that when I noticed that Matt was tapping his pen against the table and glaring at me at the same time. It appeared that my even-tempered husband had heard enough of my skepticism. Matt only explodes about once every six months, but when it happens it could be measured on the Richter scale. I once saw him take on a bull barehanded, all because it wouldn't go in the pen like it was supposed to. I decided it was time to back off.

"You're right, I'm sure. Things will work out perfectly—we'll all follow the timetable and it will be as smooth as a space launch."

Of course, the only space launch I could think of was the *Challenger.*

"THE STORM FRONT that's been moving down from the Pacific has picked up speed overnight and has now reached the Texas Panhandle. When the cold air collides with the warm stationary front that's already in place there is the potential for severe thunderstorms, high winds, hail, and even tornadoes. According to radar, that front should continue moving to the southeast and could reach our area sometime before dawn tomorrow." I took a long breath and glanced at the clock.

"For complete weather updates on the hour stay tuned to KSGE. If the weather breaks, you'll be the first to know with K-SAGE news and weather bulletins."

Doing newscasts, and even bulletins, was becoming easy, especially when I had other things on my mind.

"Recapping our top story, law-enforcement officers from

Mason, McCulloch, San Saba, and Llano Counties joined the Wilmot County Sheriff's Department yesterday afternoon and spent the daylight hours searching for prison escapee James Elliott Jorgenson and his sister, Sharon Alice Jorgenson. The manhunt will continue this morning and county residents are reminded to lock their doors and to inform the sheriff's department if they see anything unusual.

"That's KSGE news, a service of Western Trails Bank, and I'm Jolie Wyatt."

I turned off my mike, started the commercial, and looked up through the glass window to find Dan in the control room waving the phone receiver in my direction. As soon as I got my headphones off I picked up the phone and said, "News, Jolie speaking."

"Jolie, I wanted to catch you right away." It was Fred Elgin, the manager of Perry Brothers. "I just got done going through the storage room and I found a case of the purple bandannas. I've already set them up by the cash register so Helen will know right where to look."

"Terrific—"

"Now, the bad news, I'm real sorry, but, Jolie, I just cannot find those purple cups. I know we had them, I remember ordering them, but I don't know where they're hidden."

"Rats." I'd wanted to say more, or worse, but it wasn't Fred's fault. Or maybe it was, but it was going to be a long day and I knew better than to panic this early. I needed to pace myself.

"You might want to call Lurline," Fred went on. "She's usually got plenty of cups saved up for parties."

"Great thought. Thanks, Fred." I said thanks at least three more times, assured him I would be by soon to get the bandannas, and finally Fred said good-bye so we could hang up. He's a *very* nice man.

I carefully picked up the news copy, and headed out into

the hall. Dan was standing there, his long, lean body casually propped up against the wall. I could hear network news coming through the control room door. "Sounds like they're getting serious about catching Jorgenson," he said, then frowned. "I keep wondering why he hasn't taken off for some other part of the country."

I thought about the postcard, again. "I think he's just having some fun. Taunting Mac and playing like it's a life-size game of hide-and-seek."

"Kid needs a brain transplant."

"Isn't that the truth." I heard the phone in the news office. "'Scuse me." I dashed into my office and picked up the receiver on the second ring. After I'd said hello I heard the high, nasal voice of Lloyd Longmier. Lloyd is the high school principal.

"Jolie, I'm just checking with all the sponsoring parents this morning. Your party starts at four-thirty, is that right? And lasts until eleven?"

As if there hadn't been a million flyers around the high school that Lloyd could have looked at. "That's right. And the kids are all arriving by school bus, right?" I said.

"Yes, and after the party the kids are to get back on the buses—they may *not* ride home with friends who come to pick them up. I want to stress that."

"Got it," I said. "Actually I'll probably let Matt handle all that."

"Excellent idea—he's very good with people." Like I'm not. "Just don't spend any time worrying about it."

"I won't—I have other things that are higher up on the list." Like cups. I didn't want our guests drinking out of the horse troughs. I also had to worry about the chips, queso, and salsa that I had decided the kids would be hungry for around eight-thirty or nine, which I still had to purchase or prepare, depending on which you were talking about. "Anything else?" I asked.

"No, I think that covers it all. I'll see you tonight."

I hardly had the phone back on the hook before it rang again. It was going to be one of those days.

BY QUARTER OF ELEVEN I had the trunk of my car loaded with additional food, bandannas, and thirty large bottles of various soft drinks. I still didn't have cups to pour the liquid in, but I had left a message for Lurline at the country club and I was just waiting for a return call. I had also spoken to at least half a dozen parents who were double-checking that the party would be at our house and that school buses would be bringing the kids home. And, in between, I had written three news stories and answered over a dozen calls about the weather in the Panhandle and the search for Jorgenson.

Back at my desk I pulled out my timetable for the party preparation, checking off the completed tasks. Matt should have picked up the tables and chairs, so we were on schedule, except for those damn cups. I growled in my throat and heard the bell go off on the news-wire machine. It meant big news.

I dashed off to the corner of the office and discovered that the storm front had made it as far as Amarillo, which was several hundred miles from us, but it had spawned a tornado. The tornado had hit a trailer park and destroyed several homes. So far reports were that there had been no deaths and only a few minor injuries. They'd gotten lucky on that one.

Without thinking I ripped off the story, then checked the weather wire as well, before I dashed down the hall. Dan was in the middle of a commercial set; I waited impatiently until the music had started up again, then I pushed open the door.

"There's been a tornado in the Amarillo area," I said. "I need to do a bulletin."

It no longer mattered to me what Rory might think of as "important" enough for a bulletin. Purple Sage-ites were

Texans, a wonderful breed of people who came from pioneer stock, and they had relatives, more Texans, all over the state. When there was a problem in the Panhandle, you could bet it involved family and friends of our listeners. Besides, the front was coming our way.

Dan looked at the weather-wire story in my hand. "Bad news on the storm?"

"Unfortunately, yes."

"Rory loves this kind of thing," he said, pulling tape cartridges, the ones that had the bulletin intro and the commercial. "I'm surprised he hasn't come charging in here to take over."

"He probably will as soon as he hears me on the air."

"Lucky us." When he had the cart machines loaded he looked at me. "Just wave when you're ready and I'll fade the song."

"Gotcha." I hurried into the news booth and took a breath, reading over the copy as I did. As soon as I was done and had my headphones on, I looked up at Dan and nodded. I kept my eyes on him until he pointed at me.

"This is a KSGE News Bulletin, a service of Jackson's Funeral Home and Ambulance Service. A tornado has hit the Amarillo area, destroying several mobile homes at the Westside Trailer Park." I gave all the details I had, then added, *"The Pacific storm front that spawned the tornado has been on the move for the last several hours and weather watchers now say it has stalled near Amarillo. While it is not expected to reach our area until the early morning hours, you should stay tuned to KSGE for the latest weather developments.*

"That's a K-SAGE news bulletin and I'm Jolie Wyatt."

Dan started the commercial; I went next door and stuck my head in the control room. "If Rory calls, let me know, okay? I have to talk to him," I said.

"Sure. If you need some help, Wade just got here, so I'll be available in a few minutes."

Wade is the disc jockey who takes over after Dan gets off the air. He should have been on the air at ten, but Wade was new and, so far, habitually late.

"Thanks, but I think everything's under control," I said and went toward the front office. When I got there I found Michelle working away, her thick hair falling over her face as she concentrated on reconciling the bank statement. We hadn't really talked since her apology and I chose not to mention it. "Michelle?"

She looked up and stretched. "Hey, Jolie. What's up?"

"Have you heard from Rory?"

"Oh, damn." She began to shuffle the papers on her desk. "Sorry, he called in about ten and said that he was out with the manhunt. Hold on, I'll find the message somewhere." She lifted and moved things around until she finally located a square pink sheet of paper with my name at the top. "Here it is. He said he'll be back by twelve-thirty or one at the latest. He wants you to go ahead and do the news."

"He what? But I can't!"

"You have plans?"

"No shit! Fifty-seven high school kids and their chaperones will be at my house for a party that starts at four-thirty. This afternoon. Damn it!" I gulped in some air. "I'm sorry, I don't know why I'm yelling at you."

"That's okay. The bearer of bad news gets her head cut off, I guess."

"I still shouldn't have yelled. Damn, damn, damn." I wanted to start running in circles, screaming things about the sky falling. "Who else is here?" I asked.

"Lewis left for the airport a half hour ago—he wanted to beat the weather out. This is his big fishing trip somewhere outside of Albuquerque and he wouldn't miss it for anything." She ticked the names off her fingertips. "Dan's on the air, Wade just got here, Jack is calling on his clients in Llano and won't be back until four or so, and Gloria is out with her daughter, who's sick. That leaves just you and me."

In a pinch I'd been told that Lewis could read news—in fact did it pretty well—but he wasn't going to be any help in an airplane halfway to New Mexico. Michelle didn't do anything on the air, ever. Gloria and Jack were our sales-people and they both did commercials, so I assumed they could have helped had they been available. Apparently they weren't.

"Thanks," I said. I could have asked Wade to read the news, but with the weather likely to create some problems I didn't want to chance it. Wade was new and still fumbling over the everyday things a jock had to handle; I could iden-tify with that. He certainly didn't need any additional du-ties. "I'll ask Dan to cover for me."

I whipped around just as the front door opened. Matt stepped inside. "Hi," he said, closing the door.

He wasn't supposed to be there. He was supposed to be doing things for the party, and I could only hope the feeling of doom in the pit of my stomach was just too much adren-aline and too little food. "Is anything wrong?" I asked.

"Oh, not much. Bart and I brought the half-ton in to get the tables and it seems that Lloyd has already loaned out every table he can until after lunch. Unless the kids sit on the floor in the cafeteria." Matt sounded thoroughly an-noyed, something I don't hear often.

"What about the library tables?"

"The Bozells have those for the seniors. Ours won't be available until two o'clock."

And why the hell couldn't our dear anal-retentive school principal have mentioned that before Matt made the trip out? Matt wouldn't say anything like that, so I didn't either. "What are you going to do?"

Matt cleared his throat. "We're heading back to the ranch, but I thought I'd see if there was anything I could do for you while we're in town."

I didn't have to think about it—the list was emblazoned on my brain like a burning brand. "You could get the soft drinks out of my car and put them on ice." I mentally checked off one line. "The cake won't be ready until after twelve, so I'll get that. Oh, you could take the chips and stuff, too. I'll make the dip when I get home."

Michelle had been watching us and she picked that moment to stretch again, which set her large breasts to undulating. Then she flipped her hair over her shoulder. "Hi, Matt."

He turned toward her and said, "Hi, how are you doing, Michelle?" As if he didn't even notice that her gorgeous brown eyes had been taking him in carefully. The man is a saint.

She shrugged, something it should not be legal for her to do. "Oh, fine. Better than Jolie."

Matt turned to me with a puzzled look. "Is something wrong?"

"Come on back and I'll explain." He nodded at Michelle and I led him through the door and back to my office. As we moved down the hallway with its ugly shag carpet I told him about Rory's defection.

Matt slid his arm around me. "Don't worry, everything will get done. And what doesn't get done probably didn't matter in the first place."

More of his easy way of looking at life. "I know," I said, trying to believe it.

We stopped outside the control room and I automatically did a quick check through the glass window before stepping inside. Only it wasn't Dan at the board, it was Wade.

"Where's Dan?" I asked as I pushed open the door.

Wade pulled off his headphones. "He left."

"Already? He's already gone?"

"Yeah. Why?" Wade said. "Can I help?"

"I don't think so." I sank against the door as I closed it.

Matt looked at me. "You don't look happy—is everything okay?"

"I don't think so," I said. I took a breath and stood up. "Come on, I'll help with the stuff in my car. You'll need my keys." Normally we don't lock our cars, or our houses, in Purple Sage but with James Elliott Jorgenson on the loose I wasn't taking any chances.

Outside Bart was waiting by the truck for Matt. "Hi, Bart," I said, unlocking the Mazda.

"Howdy." We began hauling sacks out of the car. It didn't take long to empty it.

"I'll be home as soon as I can," I said to Matt, slamming the lid of the trunk. "By the time I get the cake it should be one. One-thirty at the latest."

"I'll see you when you get home," Matt said, giving me a quick kiss. "Love you." It was the last thing I heard as he climbed up in the cab of the truck and started the engine.

"Love you, too," I said, but he was already driving off.

TWENTY

I HURRIED BACK into the station to prepare for the noon news. During the next hour the news line rang seventeen times. Eight calls were requests for information on the manhunt. Six of the eight wanted to volunteer to help. Another six wanted to know about the weather, and three needed information on the party. I was almost late getting into the newscast because of the phone. It was for me and it was Rory.

"Look, just put me on the air first thing," he said, cutting off my questions about where he was and why the hell he wasn't at the station. "I've got an update on the manhunt," he added.

I did the intro and Wade put the phone on the air, and we were off.

"This is F. Rory Stone and I'm reporting from the southwest sector of Wilmot County near what DPS troopers call the 'Old Water Mill Road' where it connects with County Road 812. The manhunt for James Elliott Jorgenson is continuing and over twelve officers from neighboring counties have pitched in to help. The officers are from all branches of law enforcement, including police and sheriff's departments, the Department of Public Safety, and even the U.S. Fish and Wildlife Service. Texas Rangers are planning to join this afternoon, when the search will be expanded to cover a much wider area.

"In the meantime, every abandoned house, barn, or shed which might be sheltering the escapee is being checked. A request has been made for horses, and officials intend to ride the fields and pastures well into the night if that's what it takes to find Jorgenson and his sister. At this time no one

has spotted the pair and there is some speculation that they may have left the county. It would seem that's the only way they'll be able to elude the determined band of law-enforcement officers who are diligently hunting for them.

"I'll have additional updates on the manhunt as news develops. I'm F. Rory Stone in Southwest Wilmot for KSGE News."

I went into the next story, and by the time I came to a commercial break Rory had hung up. I had nothing left to do but go on with the weather. In the middle of it, Wade handed me an update from the wire. The storm front had moved again, this time wreaking havoc on a little town named Branton that didn't deserve that kind of punishment. I gave what information we had, and out of the corner of my eye I saw that the phone lines were lighting up even before I had finished.

I signed off the newscast and started answering calls. Wade and I stayed with it almost half an hour, and even Michelle came back and helped. It was after one-thirty before I could take the time to make a call of my own. I phoned the country club and got Arielle.

"Lurline isn't here," she said gleefully. "She called in and said she had a sinus headache; she won't be in 'til six."

"Well, hell—"

"She must have the worst sinuses in the world; she calls in all the time with sinus headaches. Personally, I think she just likes to sleep late."

Gossiping with the help wasn't something I had time for. I explained about the party and then asked about cups.

"There's scads of those cups. A whole cupboard full, you know, in one of the big storage cupboards. Oh, but it's locked and Lurline keeps the key."

"Doesn't the manager on duty have one?"

"Only Lurline, because she gets all pissed when things disappear. The extra liquor is in there, too."

Great. "Just give me her number and I'll call her. Maybe she'll let me come out and get the key."

Arielle gave me the number and I tried it immediately, except that I kept reaching a recorded message: *I'm sorry your call cannot go through as dialed. If you think you reached this recording in error,"* etcetera etcetera. I tried again, four times. Finally I looked up the number in the phone book and discovered it was a different exchange. Lurline lived south off Fisher Road so I had to dial all the numbers. When I finally got through, Lurline sounded fine. Actually she sounded slightly winded, as if she'd been running. She said to save myself the trip of coming out to her house. "I'll be at the club in half an hour, will that work?" she asked.

"Sure." What choice did I have? "I'll meet you there at…" I looked at my watch and my heart sank. I hadn't realized it was that late. "At two-thirty. And thanks, Lurline."

"No problem. Oh, and Jolie, I won't be at the club long—I've been helping with the manhunt—but if I'm not there I'll leave the cups for you at the front desk. Arielle will know where they are."

Manhunt? Arielle had said a sinus headache had kept Lurline home. I didn't have time to think about it. There were still things to be done and there was no sign of Rory. I dashed out and picked up the cake, then ran back to the station to check the weather wire. The front was advancing steadily, tearing up the countryside as it made its way through Texas. The temperature in Abilene had hit ninety-eight before the cold front blew in. Now it was around fifty, and the collision of the two air masses had caused high winds and golf-ball size hail. A funnel cloud had been spotted, but it hadn't touched down. Flash flood warnings for their entire region had been issued as well. I put it all together in another weather bulletin. I'd wanted real news and I certainly had it.

I was only halfway back to my office when the phone rang again. I took off at a run and got it on the third ring. "This is Jolie," I said, panting.

"This is Mac." He sounded as if he were a million miles away and his voice was filled with an emotion I hadn't heard in him before. "Look, I don't know what you've been saying on the air, but I don't want another word about the manhunt until I've got Jorgenson in a cell."

I swallowed hard. "I beg your pardon?"

"I'm sorry, Jolie, but this is serious. Nothing. Not a thing on the air. I don't care what you hear, or what your news-guy hears, I don't want anything on the air until I give the okay."

"Why? I don't get it."

"James..."

"What? What did he do?"

"He left a note—on the door of an old farmhouse. To me, saying 'Sorry I couldn't wait.'" The fury caused him to bite off the end of his words. "Just don't put another word on the air." And he hung up.

As if in collusion, the police monitor became silent, leaving me with only the clatter of the news machine and the chicken-screeching sound of the weather wire.

I called the house and got Diane.

"What are you doing there?" I asked. "Not that I'm not glad—"

"I came early. I'm cutting up the watermelon and tying purple bandannas on everything."

"Bless you! Is Matt around?"

"No, he was late leaving, something about the truck, so he's at the school getting the tables. Should I have him call you when he gets back?"

"Just tell him I'm going to be late. Probably three-thirty, maybe even four. Tell him not to worry."

"We'll hold down the fort."

I said thanks, then hung up. Next I called Dan to see if he could come relieve me. No one was home.

Four bells rang on the wire machine. The front had stalled over Abilene and it was spewing rain and high winds up to sixty miles an hour.

I did another weather bulletin and tried to call Dan again, but got no answer. It was almost four when I got two calls in succession. The first was Diane. "Matt just got back with the tables and said to let you know—the kids are already on their way. They were so keyed up with the end of school that Lloyd just started loading the buses. We've got everything under control but he wanted you to know."

"I don't like that—not with this front coming in."

"What front?"

Didn't anyone listen to the radio? "Never mind—I'll hurry," I promised.

"The food's arrived, but bring cups."

I agreed and grabbed the next call. It was Rory.

"Where the hell are you?" I demanded.

"I'm on my way in," he said, "Or I was, but I had a flat."

I could feel the muscles in my tense shoulders begin throbbing. "I have to leave," I said. "Now. It's almost four."

"Just do another bulletin and I'll be there." Then he hung up.

I kept running between the news room, the wire machines, and the telephones, doing bulletins, calling Dan, and all the time trying to visualize Rory into hurrying. At four-fifteen I called the house again. The kids were there and Diane had plundered the kitchen cupboards but was already out of glasses.

"I'm hurrying," I promised.

I checked the weather wire one more time—the front was on the move and we were on the outer edge of a new severe thunderstorm and tornado watch. The conditions existed for both to occur, but nothing was actually threatening us. Yet. I ripped off the information and read it on the air. Then I dashed into the control room. "It's all yours," I told Wade. "Rory should be here any minute. I'll wait for him in the parking lot." I snatched up my purse and keys and headed out the back door.

The air outside was still and the sky in the northwest was tinged with yellow. On the very edge of the horizon I could see a blackness, but it was hard to define what it was. I didn't like knowing that fifty-seven people were at my house with this kind of a front coming in. Damn, why hadn't Lloyd Longmier bothered to check the weather? But then who would on the last day of school, when the sky had appeared deceptively calm?

It wasn't calm now. The blackness was moving ominously closer even as I watched. As it drew nearer I began to see outlines of dark, heavy clouds. The yellow was like a watercolor wash blending toward us. The stillness felt eerie. I waited, mesmerized. Finally, Rory's Volkswagen pulled into the parking lot. I didn't wave or acknowledge him in any way; I was too busy getting the car started.

IT TOOK SEVEN MINUTES to drive to the country club, six more minutes for them to find Lurline, and five more to get all the cups loaded into my car. By that time I was running on frantic. The stillness of the air had given way to wind; the black clouds boiled halfway across the sky. I jumped into the Mazda and had to fight the wind to close the door. Fifteen more minutes, twenty if it started raining, and I would be at the house.

I was driving like a demon, battling the gusts to keep the little car on the road, watching both the sky and the highway. The noise of the wind had reached the level of a roar. Every few minutes I glanced in the rearview mirror, checking to see that no cops were coming up behind me. On the fourth or fifth look my eyes froze on the mirror. There was something new on the horizon and it was coming at me fast.

It was a full-blown funnel cloud.

TWENTY-ONE

I TORE MY ATTENTION from the whirling madness to look at the road in front of me. I knew the drill—drive at right angles to the path of the storm. But how? There was fenced pasture on either side of the highway. I stomped down on the gas pedal and the Mazda shot up to eighty-five. At the last minute, if I had to, I would pull over in the barrow ditch and lie flat on the ground. And pray the tornado didn't hit me. I shivered at the thought of getting out of the car.

When I looked into the mirror I saw the funnel cloud dip toward the earth. It must have hit the lake because a stark white swirled up through the mass. If it kept on in that direction it would hit the country club. I took a breath and searched the sides of the highway. Still no roads coming up. In the mirror the tornado slid upward. It never fully disappeared into the clouds; the dangling, whipping tail remained in sight. Before I could even breathe a sigh of relief, it slipped down again, bounced, and turned brown with the dirt and debris being sucked up into it.

It appeared to be past the country club and heading straight down the highway toward me.

And then I had it: the Hammond place. I punched the accelerator again until the car was doing a bone-shattering ninety-five. In the rearview mirror I watched the funnel cloud, sometimes veering off slightly, but always ending up a little closer. My only hope was to get to the Hammonds'. It wasn't far—couldn't be more than a half mile. I slowed a little. The winds were a howling nightmare now; trash and dead branches were grabbed up in the maelstrom and flung across the highway. Through the debris I spotted the caliche road and pumped the brakes. The Mazda took

the corner sideways, slamming against a cedar fence post.
I swore several times while the wheels spun in the caliche.
Finally they got traction and the car lurched forward. I
ripped along the caliche, anticipating the gate. If it was
locked I'd ram it.

The gate was closed. I slowed the car, turned for a better
angle, and floored the accelerator. The little car almost
bucked as if anticipating the crash, but there was none, just
a clang as the metal gate popped open and swung wide. I
drove through as fast as I dared. The house wasn't going
to be protection. I was headed for the Rom Cursed Cave.

Part of a cactus hit the windshield and I jumped, but kept
going. Up around the saddle and to the right. I barely jerked
the keys out of the ignition before I was running up the
short incline toward the mouth of the cave. There was a
terrible roaring sound as the wind tore at my clothes and
pulled my hair straight out behind me. I clutched the side
of the cave and the whole world seemed to become a
screaming, swirling mass of gray. There was too much dirt
to see—there was almost too much dirt to breathe. Something hit my shoulder blade and knocked me to the ground.
My head slammed against a rock, and a pain shot through
my leg. For just a moment I thought I was going to throw
up. Flying debris battered my body—my hand, my left
shoulder, my head. I struggled to my knees and crawled
forward until my head bumped the crumbly rock of the
outside of the cave. I grabbed at it with my hands and
pulled myself forward, then around the edge. Crouched, I
made it into the entrance.

Inside the cave, I was protected from the worst of the
wind, but it was black as night and I knew I still wasn't
safe. I brushed at my stinging eyes and stumbled forward
toward the second room. I found the opening, staying well
to the left to avoid the hole. When I came to the back wall,
I fell against it in relief and exhaustion. My head was
screaming with pain and even sharper jolts shot through

my shoulder. The only sound was my own wracked breathing and a small whimpering sound that must have been coming from me as well. Outside the storm roared, but it was muted now by the thick walls of the Rom Cursed Cave.

The panic was beginning to seep out of my body when I heard another noise. A soft rustling. Something brushed against my arm. Something soft, fleshy. Fingers—a human hand. I screamed and wanted to run but my body wouldn't move.

A light came on, some kind of electric lantern, and in its shadowy glow I saw a young woman in front of me. With one hand she held the lantern; with the other she reached out to pat my arm again.

"It's okay," she said. Her voice was gentle and she had to say the words several times, adding volume each time, to be heard above the storm that still raged outside. "You're safe now." Her pansy eyes watched my face with great concern.

I gulped. For a moment I thought I was facing the ghost of a long-dead Gypsy. Then she turned her head to look at someone beyond me and I turned, too. When I saw him I knew who they were. He was shorter than I would have guessed, only about five-eight, but the eyes were just as I expected them to be. They were almost almond-shaped and a clear hazel that glittered in the light. His high, wide cheekbones had obviously been inherited from his grandmother.

"Who are you?" he asked.

Sharon Jorgenson gave her brother a look of disgust while she pulled me down to the ground. I winced as my knees buckled and my shoulder hit the wall of the cave. "You're bleeding," she explained, her voice still gentle even though it was loud enough to be heard over the tornado. "Your forehead."

I put my hand up and discovered she was right. There

was a lot of blood, but I couldn't think what to do about it. Through a ragged rip in my pants, my knee looked terrible and my head continued to pound. I heard their voices through a roar that was inside of me, as well as outside the cave.

"The first aid kit," Sharon mouthed at James. He motioned toward the outer room and shook his head. Sharon frowned at him, but said nothing. We waited, all of us, listening to the wind and the crashing of things hitting the mouth of the cave. I had a stab of fear for Matt and Jeremy, but there was nothing I could do but offer a prayer for us all.

"SO, WHO ARE YOU?" James asked.

The wind and the tornado had eventually gone, leaving us with the sound of rain beating against the roof of the cave. We had moved to the outer room, Sharon letting me put my weight on her to walk. In the lantern light I saw that the cave was well stocked, although dusty from the swirling dirt that had passed through. Before any of us had spoken, Sharon had located the first aid kit and begun cleaning my knee, putting salve on it and fashioning a butterfly bandage.

"Are you from Purple Sage?" James asked me. "Can you talk?"

I tried to nod, hitting my head against Sharon's hand, but I didn't speak. Eventually he would know who I was simply by looking in my purse, which was still in my car somewhere behind the cave. At least I thought it was, but I wasn't quite clear on that. I didn't seem to be clear on a great deal, although I knew my name.

"I'm Jolie Wyatt," I said.

The same devilish grin I'd seen in IdaMae's picture flashed across James's face. He looked at Sharon and grinned again. "You know who she is?"

"Jeremy's mom?" Sharon asked me.

"Uh-huh," I said. She was working to clean my forehead now and I was afraid to move my head for fear that the throbbing would get worse.

"I don't know who Jeremy is," James said to Sharon, then he turned to me. "But I know that you're on the air with KSGE."

Sharon was looking at me critically. "I think you're going to have a scar, but it won't be a bad one. How are you feeling?"

"I have a terrible headache and my shoulder hurts, but mostly I'm okay. Thank you."

She began digging through the first aid kit. "Here's some aspirin. But I don't think you're supposed to take it if you have a head injury. Or is it internal bleeding? Do you have those?"

I shook my head, winced, and caught myself starting to laugh. "I'm okay. Tired, hungry, late…there are fifty-seven kids at my house. For the end-of-the-year party."

Sharon nodded as she dusted off a jug and poured some water into a paper cup for me. "I know about those end-of-the-year parties." There was a wistful note in her voice, but it was gone when she said, "Here, take the aspirin." She held out the cup to me.

"The party cups are in my car. If people want to drink they'll have to use their hands." I laughed before I swallowed the aspirin. It sounded silly and I laughed again. Then another thought hit me and there was nothing funny left in the world. "If everyone is alive. The tornado could have hit the kids. And Jeremy and Matt." I took a gulp of air that sounded like a sob. "Do you have a phone? I need to call home." It had been a crazy question—who would have a phone in a cave?

But then Sharon gave James a questioning look and I realized it wasn't so crazy after all. They did have a phone. James had moved his head the tiniest amount, but I recognized it for a no. I was betting it was a lie, and that tucked away in one of the piles of things that edged the room was some kind of phone. Cellular, no doubt. Rory had a cellular phone, too. No. His was broken, but someone had called him at the station on a cellular phone. The thought seemed to bounce through my head and I remembered the voice of the male caller. It had been James; I was sure I recognized his voice. Almost sure.

Was that possible? That James Elliott Jorgenson had called Rory?

"We don't have a phone," Sharon said.

Liars. "Then I'd better go. My family—you know." I tried to stand. The earth seemed to lurch and my head started to spin. I fell back against the rock; my legs were as shaky as a new colt's. Instinctively I put my hand over my mouth, hoping I wouldn't throw up.

"Are you okay?" Sharon asked, reaching out to steady me. "Your color is terrible. Maybe you should sit down for a while."

"I haven't eaten," I said, but I wasn't thinking at all, now. I was trying to function. I slid down to a sitting position, holding my head rigidly straight.

Sharon was already digging in some sacks. She pulled out a peach and wiped it thoroughly before she handed it to me. "Here, see if you can chew this. If not, I think I have some soup somewhere. We don't have a fire, so we can't warm it...."

"It's okay...." I took a bite and it caused a sound that reverberated through my head, but it seemed to clear it. I was suddenly very hungry. I took another bite and discovered I could chew if I didn't move anything but my jaw. There was no pain, and I didn't even feel lightheaded. The smell of the peach enveloped me.

James squatted down in front of me, watching me eat. "How did you get here? Is your car out there somewhere?"

When I'd swallowed I said, "It's behind the cave. If it

didn't get blown away, or smashed.'' I sounded almost normal.

James had already popped up. "I'm going to look outside," he said over his shoulder to Sharon as he left the cave.

For just a moment I was worried about my car and then I remembered that I had the keys in my pocket. I'd brought them with me, so he couldn't drive away. Not that he would, or would he? I couldn't seem to focus my thoughts.

In the meantime, Sharon had drifted to the mouth of the cave and was looking outside.

"Did the tornado do much damage? Did it hit outside?" I heard the words in my head, but they didn't come out of my mouth. I was so tired I couldn't even speak. The remains of the peach rolled from my hand and my body began to slump sideways. It was okay; the first aid kit was beside me and I could use it for a pillow.

WHEN I AWOKE there seemed to be a lot of hissing and it took me a minute to recognize it for what it was: whispering.

"What if she dies?"

"She's not going to die."

For just a moment I wasn't sure where I was. I opened my eyes and looked. I was in the back room of the cave; it was very dark and only a faint lantern light was coming from the front area. Even that little bit of light hurt my eyes so I closed them again and lay still.

"Her color looked bad—she needs to go to a hospital. Jeez, James, you don't want a murder charge on your hands! For once in your life use your head—"

"You say that again and I'll knock the shit out of you!"

Both voices were male, angry, belligerent, but they were fading in and out like a radio station with a weak signal. At times the words would slip away before I could catch them. For a moment I thought I recognized both the voices, but I couldn't hold on to the thought. Eventually a softer voice broke in and that one I did know—it was Sharon's. "We really shouldn't move her again, it could just make her worse."

"You see? Sharon, why don't you go stand watch outside?"

"You have to be quiet—"

"We will." I knew him now; it was James.

I heard a tiny creak, like a knee or something, and then soft footfalls that faded. Finally there was silence. The second male spoke—the one who wasn't James—and I was sure that if the voices would just be still I could say who it was. "So what are you going to do with her?"

Silence again.

"Jesus, James! You're not going to kill her!"

"Oh, of course not." But he said it very quickly.

"I thought you were going away? Just leave her behind."

"I can't do that; besides, it's none of your business. Got that?"

I felt my stomach heave and my brain flashed an image of Jeremy and Matt. Where were they right now? Were they safe at home, wondering where I was? Or had the tornado gotten them, too?

I pushed away every thought of them and summoned up my courage and my strength. I had to get out and I couldn't do that unless I was mobile.

Carefully I rolled over onto my side and a wave of nausea hit me. I breathed deeply, holding myself perfectly still until it passed. I'd moved a little too fast. I would simply go slower. I flexed my shoulder in anticipation of getting to my knees and this time there was pain, sharp and crisp. I told myself the pain was cleansing. I pulled up my knees and rolled onto them. Nothing terrible happened and that encouraged me. The progress was slow, but even my head remained clear as long as I was careful. Using one arm to push, I tried to stand up. Again my stomach heaved, but I was halfway up and I wouldn't quit. Instead, I used the wall for support and I slid the rest of the way upward.

It worked. I was standing. My head was also pounding and a sweat had broken out on my body. I felt sick and dizzy, but I knew how to take care of that: I lowered my head slowly, bending my back, hugging myself with cold arms.

The whispering faded out so that I only caught snatches and phrases. Something about a car, "her car," and something else about a search. I knew about the search for James and Sharon, but the officials had been in the southeast quadrant of the county last I'd heard. We were in the northwest, so I couldn't bank any hope on that. I focused my attention on the conversation, hoping to hear something that would help.

"I need a police scanner—it's the only thing I've asked you for."

"And I've told you before, the one at the station isn't portable, so it wouldn't do you any good. And Lewis Hilger bought the last one in town."

"So give me yours."

"James, I can't. It belongs to the station and I need it for my work. I've told you that before." I knew that superior tone and finally I knew who was out there with James.

"Don't use that voice on me, you cocky asshole," James was saying. "I can't leave for Mexico without more money and a police scanner—it's the only way we'll make it. Maybe I'll just steal yours."

Mexico. James and Sharon were going to Mexico.

"Oh, now that's a nice repayment, stealing from me. All you have to do is listen to me on the air—I'm feeding you every bit of information I can—"

The cocky asshole was F. Rory Stone.

Even as muddled as my head was, I began to understand

what had been going on for the last several days. Rory had been giving James information on the air and that was how James had been able to stay one step ahead of the manhunt.

And I knew why, too. It was simple when I remembered IdaMae's story about the third child, Frankie, the one who'd gone off with missionary relatives. Frankie Jorgenson. Frankie, who'd tried to come home only to discover that his beloved grandmother was dead and his brother was in prison. That couldn't be good for a career. And then after the escape, he was protecting everyone as best he could, including himself—Frankie Jorgenson. F. Rory Stone.

And he was here, in the cave, now.

Not only that, he was going to get me out of the cave—now.

TWENTY-TWO

My INTENTION WAS to charge into the middle of their whispered argument and confront Rory with his duplicity. And stupidity. And demand that someone help me to my car so that I could go home.

Instead I stumbled into the main room of the cave and fell forward in a heap at their feet. I remember two things very clearly before I passed out: the startled look on Rory's face, and that I threw up on the dirt floor.

When I woke again it was still dark and I had a blanket over me. It was hot and I pushed it down off my shoulders.

A voice soothed and pulled it back up. "You have to stay warm. I don't want you to get sicker." As my eyes focused I saw that Sharon was beside me, sitting, as if she'd spent the past hours in vigilance, watching over me.

"Was Rory here? I thought..." My voice cracked and no more words came out. There was a terrible taste in my mouth.

"Don't talk," she said, gently rubbing her hand across my forehead. She kept her voice low, I assumed because her brother was sleeping somewhere nearby. "I made you some soup. Here, it's in this Thermos. I made James start a little fire, so it's even warm. Are you hungry?"

"Some."

"Should you sit up?"

"I guess. What about Rory? Was Rory Stone here?"

"Shhh...we're going to need to concentrate to get you sitting." It took some time but she got me up enough so that I was leaning against her. Then she fed me soup and patted my hand or felt my forehead in between sips, making sure that I wasn't getting any worse. When I'd had my fill

I said thank you and she put the Thermos away without even acknowledging my gratitude.

"Why are you doing this?" I asked quietly.

She sat back next to me on the hard floor and eased me down into a lying position. I discovered that there was a sleeping bag under me.

When she didn't respond to my question I asked again. This time I felt her shrug. "Everyone needs someone to take care of them. Especially when they're hurt or sick. And I'm the only one here to do it."

It was some kind of country credo that I'd heard before in Purple Sage.

"Is that why you helped James escape? Why you're still with him?"

She made a sound of protest, then finally said, "I didn't help James. He wasn't supposed to escape—we were just supposed to talk. Oh, it's so confusing." She put her head down on her knees for a moment, then raised it up and let out a long sigh.

Maybe it was the dark, or maybe it was the intimacy that comes after going through something like the tornado together, or maybe Sharon Jorgenson just needed someone to understand her side of all of this. Whatever it was, she let go. Slowly at first, more easily as she went on. "See, James can do anything. I mean anything. He's smarter than anyone I've ever met. And when I went to the prison to see him it was always just, well, pretty terrible. I mean, you couldn't really talk, and it was cold and I hated it... so after Grams died, I'd go to the prison, but it just wasn't the same as having a real talk with him. And that's what I needed. So, James devised a way to get out. Just so we could visit. It was a big game for him—everything's a big game for James. We'd meet in the middle of the night a couple of blocks away from the prison and we'd just talk."

"He escaped."

"No, he just left, but only for a couple of hours. Then he'd always sneak back inside." I could hear a smile in her voice. "One time we played Scrabble and he beat me so bad I wouldn't bring the game back."

I was beyond doubting. In the other room I could hear rhythmic breathing. I assumed it was the wonder, James. "How many times did you do this?"

"Just three times. He said he knew the security system better than the guards."

"So, why did he escape? And why did you help him?"

"That's just it. Don't you see, Mrs. Wyatt? It wasn't planned. He was just out and then all these lights came on, and he said someone had figured out he was gone. He said we had to leave—" She sighed again. "I hate thinking about that night; that's when life started downhill fast. And keeps getting worse."

I remembered she had been dating Tim Michelik. I made my voice as soft as I could. "I'm sorry about Tim."

She took a long shaky breath. "We were going to get married, did you know? He loved me so much. He didn't even care that I had a brother in prison."

I wondered how many of his other women thought Tim had loved them so much. I said, "He was a friend of Jeremy's, too."

"I know. He liked kids. He liked everyone." Her voice, still soft, took on a dreamy quality. "That night I met James I was telling him about Tim and how we were going to be married. I said that maybe Tim and I would have to get married in the pickup in the middle of the night so James could be there. Only that's when the lights came on." She jerked around. "But see, it wasn't supposed to be like that. The very next night I was supposed to have a date with Tim. A late date because he said he had to talk to someone, explain about us. It was some girl, I think. I think maybe it was Ashley Draper. Then we were going to get married."

I remained focused on the name. "Why did you think he had to talk to Ashley?"

"She had a big crush on Tim. They went out a couple

of times way back in February, but it wasn't anything serious. She was nuts, kind of like that movie, *Fatal Attraction*. She followed Tim all the time. Sometimes it was spooky, we'd see her car lights pull up or we'd hear her on the patio." She shivered. "One night at Grams's house, gosh, it was just last Tuesday." She stopped to marvel at that before she went on. "Tim and I were making pizza and Ashley was out front with her lights off; we'd seen her drive up. Can you imagine? Just watching from out there?" We were sitting so close I could feel the shiver slide through her.

"It must have made you feel funny."

"Yeah, but there was something else—I almost forgot that...." Her voice trailed off.

I waited and when she didn't speak, I said, "What else? You saw something?"

"It was real odd. In a little bit we saw another car pull up behind Ashley's. It kept its lights on. They were on high, too, just kind of glaring into Ashley's car. I guess it scared her because she tore out of there. It was creepy. It even spooked Tim."

"What did the other car look like?"

"It was white. I don't know what kind. Not too big, not too small. Foreign, I think."

"Did Tim know who was in the car?"

"He didn't say so, but, well, I think maybe he did. He said there wasn't anything he could do about it, yet."

I had a sneaking suspicion that I knew. "Sharon, James didn't kill Tim, did he?"

She jerked away from me. "No. Of course not. James was with me the whole time since he left the prison. We never saw Tim." She settled back and I could feel her shoulders slump. "I didn't see Tim after Tuesday night."

Her pain triggered mine. I wanted Matt and Jeremy with an ache that was physical. I knew I couldn't run, but the soup had helped me gain some strength and I could at least talk.

"Sharon, you have to help me," I said as quietly as I could. "You know what it's like to love someone. I have to get home. I have to know that Matt and Jeremy are okay."

"I can't do that, Mrs. Wyatt."

"Please, just help me to my car. You can say that you fell asleep and I escaped. I can drive myself."

"James wouldn't believe that. He knows how sick you are."

"Then get me the phone, let me call and talk to them." Suddenly I was begging and I was willing to do even more if that's what it took. "I have to know if they're all right."

"I can't—"

"Please, you can hold the phone, say it's a wrong number, anything, just so I can hear their voices."

"But it's the middle of the night—"

"Then we know they'll be there. Please."

She sat and thought about it. Finally her head came up and she looked at me. Her face and voice were solemn. "I'll do it, but don't yell out or anything because James would get real mad at us. He has a pretty bad temper."

"I won't, I promise."

She got up carefully and moved across the cave looking over her shoulder several times to make sure I hadn't moved. I hadn't. Finally she opened something that looked like a duffel bag and pulled out the phone. When she was sitting beside me again she turned slightly so that her body was shielding the phone from the back room.

"I'll hold the phone and you press the numbers. Then I'll press Send, and I'll put the phone up to your ear. Okay?"

I nodded and licked my lips. I was so anxious I was forgetting to breathe.

Sharon flipped something on the phone and a light came

on with a slight beep. She waited a moment or two, then held the phone out in front of me. I pushed each number carefully and the phone shifted in her hand slightly with each push. Just as I got the last number I heard a series of beeps and the phone went dark then came back on again. I made a sound but Sharon shushed me.

"Try again," she said.

I did, pressing the numbers with even greater caution. This time I only got to the fourth number before the phone went out. "What's wrong with it?" I asked, feeling as if my hopes were dangling just out of reach.

She punched a few buttons of her own and finally shook her head. I think she was actually sorry. "The battery is going dead. I was afraid of that."

"No..."

"I'm real sorry, Miz Wyatt." Sharon slipped the phone into the sleeping bag beneath us and began to get comfortable.

I felt as if someone had ripped out my heart. It had seemed so easy, and then for the phone to be dead. "Sharon, there must be something else that we can do. What about Rory?" I asked. "Is he still here? Can't he get me home?"

She looked at me with her big soft eyes for a long time. Eventually she pursed her lips, then looked away from me. "I'm sorry, I don't know any Rory."

"Sure you do. Frankie." When she just stared, I added, "You know, your brother. Your older brother."

"I don't know what you're talking about."

"Please, I'm talking about your brother. F. Rory Stone. The news director of KSGE. He was here...before. Before I got sick. I heard him. I saw him."

She reached out and touched my forehead. "I'm sorry, Miz Wyatt, but there was nobody here. You must have been delirious."

"I wasn't—"

"I think you need to lay back down and get some sleep. That's the best thing that can happen right now." And with that she took me gently by the shoulders, one arm cupping my head, and laid me down. The inside of the cave spun a little at the movement. Sharon was right; the best thing I could do was get some sleep.

TWENTY-THREE

THE NEXT TIME I woke up there was light outside the cave and only silence inside it. I was on my back, my head turned to face the wall; gently, I moved my head and heard a grinding sound in my neck. It couldn't be helped. Slowly, I turned over, wincing at the pain that now flowed through both my head and shoulder. I closed my eyes again against the brightness from outside. It was going to take more than a couple of aspirins to knock this headache.

When I was finally in a sitting position, I opened my eyes: The cave was empty. At least that was my first impression. Then I glanced toward the entrance and found myself staring straight at James Elliott Jorgenson. He was watching me.

"Hey, there. How'd you sleep?" he asked, popping up from his crouched position. "All our guests rave about the accommodations, but then, come to think of it, we haven't had many guests since we chased that skunk out the first night."

I just stared at him, wondering what it would take to make him lower his voice.

"Cat got your tongue this morning?" he asked, moving back into the cave. "You don't have to speak to me if you don't want to, but a friendly nod wouldn't hurt any."

"It's my head," I said softly. "The tornado must have hit it and broke it."

He lowered his voice. "Think it was a personal vendetta?"

"Just bad luck. Wrong place, wrong time," I said, realizing the irony of that statement.

James grinned. "Don't I know that one. By the way, don't try it on a judge; they never buy it."

"Good to know."

James continued to watch me and I tried to smile, but it didn't get beyond a thought. I hurt and with that came an overwhelming desire to go home; I knew if I could, I'd feel better.

With as much firmness as I could gather up, I said, "James, I have to go home now. My husband and son will be worried about me."

James frowned and rubbed his chin, taking his time. "You know, that's a problem. See, you may have noticed, we don't have a phone." He gestured expansively around the cave. "We had a cellular, but the battery went dead. I suppose I could take you home in the pickup, but we're almost out of gas. I only have about five gallons left, and in that old thing, it won't get you very far. Can't waste it."

"I'll take my car—"

"That's another thought—you could take your car, except I don't think you're in much shape to drive. I could drive you myself, but your car's not in much shape to go anywhere, either. I'm afraid that tornado hit more than your head."

"My Mazda?"

"Unless it normally roosts in trees, it's got some bad troubles."

"Oh."

That ended my hopes of driving away. Not that I had believed it would be that easy, but now I was stuck. How long was I going to be here? When would I ever get to see Matt and Jeremy? My throat burned like there were tears back there. I didn't want to cry in front of James Jorgenson, but it didn't really matter anymore. My head and body hurt, I was more homesick than I'd ever been at camp, and there was a horrible pain in my chest, an ache that had nothing to do with my physical injuries.

James moved toward the entrance of the cave, his eyes avoiding mine. "Uh, hey, Sharon's right outside. She went to—uh, you know. And I'll bet you need to—uh, you know—too. Let me just see if I can find her." He slipped outside.

The back of my sleeve was dusty so I brushed it off before I used it to wipe my face. I did have to, uh, you know, but most important, I had to get out of there. If I had to walk, run, or crawl, I was going home. And then it hit me: James was probably lying about my car. It couldn't be in a tree, he only said that because he needed the Mazda to get to Mexico!

Hope bubbled up. I was ready to move on. I stood up abruptly and, just as rapidly, fell back against the side of the cave. My head began to throb again. I took a couple of breaths, but that only increased the intensity of the headache. It was worse than when I'd had my one and only migraine. I stood still, regaining control of my body. I could handle the pain. As for the rest of my aches, I told myself, they were just caused from sleeping on the ground. I straightened a bit more and took a tentative step. My knee cracked like a very old woman's and a shot of pain ran through it all the way to my hip. All I could do was suck in air and keep going.

It took several minutes, but I made it outside and my efforts were rewarded with a view that was nothing less than magnificent. The sky was a deep, clear blue without a single cloud. The temperature had to be in the seventies and there was the tiniest of breezes. The Hammond ranch was spread out in front of me. God, it was beautiful. My eye followed the gently sloping pasture land dotted with feathery green mesquites all the way down to the house nestled in among the yard and trees. It looked serene and pastoral.

Turning carefully toward the highway (between the fence posts and the foliage) I could just make out the black of the asphalt. There didn't seem to be any traffic, and certainly no one could see me.

By leaning against the side of the cave I could walk, and I took a few steps to try to spot my car. It wasn't where I'd left it, but then I wouldn't expect James to leave it in plain sight. Okay, so where would he hide it? I began to move along the outside of the cave, limping more than I liked, but still making progress.

The first thing I saw that wasn't as it should have been was a huge yucca, completely uprooted and lying on its side as if some giant hand had plucked it up and then tossed it down again. For almost fifty yards the earth seemed to have been stripped of all the algerita, the prickly pear, even the usual rocks and debris. A completely clean swath had been left behind by the tornado. I looked right and left of that path hoping to spot my car. Nothing. Damn. I limped some more, looking hard. Finally I saw it. The front wheel was hung over the V of a sturdy old oak tree. The windshield was gone and one door hung open at a crooked angle like a broken wing.

I wouldn't be driving home.

"How are you feeling?" It was Sharon, just a few paces behind me, one arm outstretched as if she intended to take hold of me. I didn't know if the gesture were one of concern that I would fall, or fear that I would run. I wasn't planning on doing either.

"I'm better," I said, trying to lift my slumping shoulders. I turned slowly and wobbled a little on my good leg.

"You're still pretty pale. I guess you need to go to the bathroom. Then maybe you should go back in the cave and lay down. Maybe eat something."

"Okay."

She helped me up the slope to a spot where there were bushes and a slender oak, handed me a roll of toilet paper, then left me in privacy for a few minutes. Afterward I began limping back toward the cave and Sharon moved in beside me. She stayed there the whole way. Several times she took my arm to support me. I hadn't seen James on our little outing and I vaguely wondered where he'd gone.

As we neared the cave I began to hear voices. One voice. It seemed to be jerky and sporadic. I knew it wasn't my hearing anymore—I was sure I was beyond that stage—but still the voice kept breaking up. Then I realized what it was: a radio.

"*...Although police won't give exact locations, rumor has it that officials are sweeping toward the north...*" Click.

"Shit!" James swore loudly and then added, "Sharon—" He swung out of the cave directly in front of us and I almost fell over attempting to get out of his way. "Oh, damn. Sorry."

"What's the matter?" Sharon asked, steadying me as we moved inside.

"We've got to get out of here; it's not safe anymore."

"Now?"

He shook his head impatiently. "Tonight. Soon as it gets dark, we're out of here. We'll head south, then straight to Mexico."

Sharon glanced at me as I gently lowered myself to the sleeping bag. "What about Mrs. Wyatt?" she asked.

"She's comin' with us."

"No!" I said. "You can just leave me here—in the cave. I'll be okay."

"I can't do that, and you know it. Just my luck, you'd die and then they'd pin a murder rap on me."

I looked at Sharon hoping for an ally, but she was frowning distractedly as she pulled granola bars, bananas, and little cans of Texsun orange juice out of a sack. "What looks good?" she asked me.

"Home," I said. "I want to go home. I don't want to go to Mexico. I want my family. I want to know that they're all right—did they say anything on the radio about the tornado?''

James slapped his forehead. "Oh, hell, I should've told you right away. The tornado hit the lake and tore up a golf shed out by the country club but it didn't do any major damage. No one was hurt, either. I'm sorry I didn't say something sooner.''

My sore muscles softened with relief; the pain seemed to ease. At least Jeremy and Matt were safe. I could stand almost anything now that I knew that. "I'm not going to die, James. Please, just leave me here. Maybe with a little water. I'll get home eventually, and by that time you'll be long gone.''

"Can't chance it," he said, sitting cross-legged on the floor. "Here's what we'll do. Everyone had better eat now. We'll pack and sleep the rest of the day—maybe I'll risk taking a load or two down to the pickup. Then, as soon as it gets dark, we head out. We'll drive all night. We can do it.'' His tone made it sound as if we were twelve and in some kind of club, as if this were a rite of initiation.

Sharon nodded. "Okay by me.''

"Well, it's not okay by me," I said. "I have a family— they're worried about me. Probably searching for me right now.''

"They are," James said. "Tell you what, soon as we get a different car, maybe in San Antonio, maybe as soon as Mason, you can call home. Just for a minute to tell them you're okay.''

"I want to go home. Why can't I just go home?''

"Because they'll ask you where the two of us are going and you'll tell them. Then we end up facing those damn roadblocks.'' He stood up, circled the cave, then quickly squatted down in front of me. "You are Sharon's insurance policy. You see, this whole mess has nothing to do with Sharon; she just got stuck in the middle of it. Well, it isn't fair, but no judge is going to let her go.''

"They might—"

"I've never had a judge believe anything I said. They take one look at me and decide I'm a bad un. Well, that's real fine for me, but Sharon deserves a normal life, and if I can get us to Mexico, she can have one. If I've got you in the pickup there won't be any roadblocks and no shooting." He stood up. "Sharon's been good to you, now you can return the favor. I'll let you go as soon as she's safe."

"That's not good enough...."

James reached into the duffel and pulled out a Beretta, probably the one he'd stolen from Henshaw's Hardware. He never did point it at me, just held it loosely in his hand, as if testing the weight of it. "I'm real sorry, Miz Wyatt, but that's as good as it gets."

TWENTY-FOUR

"JAMES, IF YOU don't stay inside someone's going to see you," Sharon complained. She had said similar words at least twice before, and James had ignored them each time.

"That was the last load."

"Then eat something. It's almost one and you haven't eaten anything."

James grinned. "Okay, Mama. Whatever you say, Mama."

"Well, you're making Mrs. Wyatt and me crazy with all your hopping around. Besides, if we're leaving at sundown and driving all night, you've got to get some sleep."

"I plan on it. I'll just get me something to eat and then I'll sleep."

"Finally," Sharon said.

James had spent the entire morning packing and repacking their things. Then he had taken most of them to the pickup, leaving behind only the sleeping bags and some food and water. Each of his trips took between ten to fifteen minutes, so apparently the pickup was hidden some distance from the cave.

While James had done the bulk of the packing I had dozed, but his nervous energy seemed to fill the cave every time he returned, waking me up. After several trips I'd stayed awake. My head seemed much clearer, the pain merely a recurring memory that didn't last. Perhaps because of that I had formulated a plan. It wasn't much of one, but it was the best I could come up with. I had hoped that he would turn on the radio again, but he'd taken it with him and must have left it in the truck. That meant noon came and went, and I had no more idea what was happening in the outside world than I had before.

I watched James fix himself a peanut butter and jelly sandwich and then I stood up. "I need to go out," I said to Sharon.

She merely nodded and stood, too. Together we started outside.

"Don't be gone long," James said. "We've got to do some sleeping."

Neither of us answered him. Once we were outside I sucked in air. It smelled much cleaner than it did inside the cave. I straightened my body and took a few seconds to assess my injuries. My head remained clearer. As long as I went slowly, I could stand and even move without getting sick or dizzy. The pain in my shoulder had become a dull ache, much like the ones in my back and neck. My leg was worse; I couldn't seem to prevent a limp and it hurt deep inside the leg, as if there were something wrong with bone or muscle, not just the flesh that Sharon had cleaned and bandaged. It was also swollen badly.

"Are you okay?" Sharon asked, watching my ungainly progress.

I leaned against the side of the cave and nodded as if it took the last of my strength. "Fine," I said in a weak voice. It was all part of my plan.

Sharon took me by the arm and helped me make my slow way toward our outdoor bathroom. "I'm really worried about you," she said.

A pang of guilt was added to the myriad of pains I was feeling. "I'll be fine." I paused for a second. "Maybe if I had a stick to help me walk...a really long one..."

She leaned me against a tree and went off to scour the hillside that was covered with debris from the storm. It gave me a moment to check out the landscape and add substance to my vague notion of escape. In front of me was the cave and beyond that the sloping ground that led down to the old house. On my right was nothing but pasture, stretching for miles. Behind me more ranch land that would eventually run into ours, but I wasn't sure how far that was, and what other obstacles might be in the way. To my left was the highway and, while my view of it was mostly obscured by a hill and trees, I knew I could get there on foot. Once I reached it I was sure someone would drive by and see me. It would just take some time.

"Here," Sharon said, holding out a thin, stripped tree branch that was almost six feet long. "It's pretty big, but I think I can break it in half—"

"No, no. It's perfect. Really. And thanks."

I took the stick from her and grasped it with both hands. I was going to leave the cave *à la* Indiana Jones, through a back way: the hole that had almost swallowed me the first time I'd been in the Rom Cursed Cave. I was going to use the stick, first to test the hole, and then to make it bigger if that were necessary. I was hoping it wasn't. The thought of squirming my sore body through a narrow place made the pains more acute.

I went to the bathroom, then slowly walked back to the cave. The limp was becoming more pronounced and I wasn't faking it anymore. I had to bite my lip to hold back the moan that wanted to accompany each painful step. I looked toward the highway, but there were no cars. I glanced up and spotted a vulture—no, two—circling above. Damn things.

The cave felt like an airless coffin. As soon as my eyes adjusted I saw that it was almost empty, much as it had been the first time I'd seen it with Diane, Trey, and Matt. Matt. Damn. I missed him, and knowing that he and Jeremy must be both worried about me strengthened my resolve to leave. I would get to the highway, somehow.

James was stretched out on his sleeping bag, his hands folded across his chest. His fingers were interlocked with his thumbs nervously circling each other. So far, James had been still only in sleep. Sharon, who'd been behind me, began to fold out the bag we shared so there would be room for both of us. I used my stick to go past them, into the far room.

"I've been here before," I said, trying to sound nonchalant. "It was just about a week ago." I turned the corner and spotted the hole. It seemed much smaller than I'd remembered.

"So that was you," James said. "We were staying down at the house when you drove in. Damn, you liked to scared us to death."

"It's our land...and our house. But, since we weren't using it, I guess it doesn't matter." By now I was out of their line of sight, and it was time to test my theory.

"Then I expect this is actually your cave, too?"

"That's right. We'd just closed on the land, which is why we came out here." I slipped the stick into the hole. It stuck after about four feet. "We found an old Coke bottle in here—the little ones that went out in the sixties. It was from Cleburne."

"I think I saw your bottle outside somewhere," James offered.

The stick wouldn't move no matter how I turned or twisted it. I leaned my weight onto it and it slipped only another inch or two before it stopped again. "The bottles are worth money these days." I quit talking because I could hear the effort in my voice and it was all futile anyway, there was no way I was going to be able to get out of the cave through this hole. Defeat washed over me.

"What are you up to?" James asked. He moved like a cat and he was up and around the corner before I'd pulled the stick up. "Are you drilling for oil?"

"Right." I hardly jumped when he surprised me. "I just wanted to see this hole," I said. "It's, uh, the one in the story. At least I think so." I pulled out the limb and once again used it as a crutch.

"What story?" Sharon asked from the other room.

"This is the Rom Cursed Cave. Haven't you heard about it?"

"No, ma'am." James grinned as I walked past him. "We found this place by accident one day when we were staying down at the house and figured it would be our own personal Hyatt. Not all the same conveniences, but we haven't had any reason to complain. So what's this about a curse?"

"There's supposedly a Gypsy curse on this cave," I said, moving over beside Sharon, who helped me down to the sleeping bag. She gave me two aspirins and held out a Thermos for me to drink from. When the pills were gone I lay flat and the pains began to recede.

I couldn't see James, but his voice came to me from ground level—no doubt he was already stretched out, too. "I love bedtime stories," he said. "Haven't heard a good one in years—ought to be just the thing to put me to sleep. How about telling me about this curse?"

"Will I disturb you?" I asked Sharon, who already looked drowsy.

"No. Go ahead."

I waited until both of them were settled and quiet before I began in a soft voice. "Well, you see, during the eighteen hundreds, Purple Sage was a rather God-fearing town. Maybe the people were a little beyond righteous...maybe self-righteous would better describe them—"

"I hear that," James said.

I softened my voice. "Anyway, it was during that time that a band of Romanian Gypsies came through...."

I WAITED ALMOST an hour until both of the Jorgensons were breathing rhythmically, then with a breath of my own and a silent prayer, I rolled over onto my stomach. I had made no sound, but I held still for a few moments to be sure they didn't move. When I felt safer I raised up onto my knees and almost ended my escape as excruciating pain seared through my leg. I clenched my jaws firmly and got quickly to my feet. The pain was so intense I couldn't even open my eyes. Tears stung, but they were a welcome distraction from the torture that was shooting up and down either side of my knee.

There wasn't time to give in to it. I had one chance and this was it. I moved toward the opening, limping, praying, fighting what I decided was just silly weakness. Once outside I grabbed at the side of the cave for support, and watched powerlessly as I dislodged a cascade of rock and dirt. It hit the ground sounding like muted thunder. If James heard it—

Now I really had to move quickly. I had forgotten my stick, so I pushed off, putting all my weight on my good leg, only allowing the injured one to touch down for balance. My head began to throb and my stomach churned ominously. Hop, little step, hop. Instead of going up behind the cave I went straight across, toward the highway. After a few feet I was in totally foreign territory. I spotted a broken branch and grabbed it up for a cane. Hop, little step, hop. In another hour or so I'd be with Matt and Jeremy. It was worth the pain. Hop, little step, hop.

The clear blue sky of the morning had given way to a darkness in the distance that told me another storm was coming. Already a breeze was beginning, kicking up little swirls of dirt, dust devils, they're called.

The ground began to rise and there was no way to go but up. I put even more of my weight on the branch and started up the incline. I came to a tangle of dead berry vines and had to skirt them carefully—there would be no good landing place in there and even the smallest bit of foliage or rock could trip me up.

My one leg had become almost useless. After five minutes or so I stopped to wipe the sweat off my face and see how far I'd gone. I looked toward the highway and realized I'd only made it about a fourth of the way. Then

I thought I heard a sound. The soft clip-clop of horses' hooves. I strained my eyes to search the area from the highway to the opening in the fence. There was nothing, just the green of the mesquite and the dusty algerita along the fence line.

Maybe it was a trick of the light wind, bringing with it some sounds from miles away. I was higher than the surrounding terrain; I could see and hear better than at cave level. Maybe that was it. Then I thought I heard a car, maybe voices, all riding the wind. I swung around and looked back at the cave. I thought I'd caught some movement out of the corner of my eye. The entrance was almost hidden from here, but I could see the level patch of ground in front of it and it was empty. No James, no Sharon.

I let out a pent-up breath and began to go forward again. Hop, little step, hop. A couple of vultures circled over me, but they were moving lazily, without intent—yet. Then I heard the unmistakable whinny of a horse. This time I looked more carefully, as if I could penetrate trees and bushes with my stare. I followed the fence line through each post, all the way to the gate, then on to the house, and finally up the barely visible road that eventually wound its way to the cave. That's when I saw them: a solitary horse and rider. They hadn't seen me; they were just following the road.

It was Matt's horse—I'd recognize him anywhere. A bay with soulful eyes. I began to wave my arms and I wanted to yell out, but I knew better. Then as I watched I realized that it wasn't Matt on the horse. The rider was too small, the hat too big. He had a canteen slung over the pommel and something else, long and thin, in a leather bag. A rifle. It was a rifle. I was studying the rider when I saw him whip his head up and look toward the cave. In that instant I realized it was Jeremy.

I whirled around to look at the cave, too. There'd been someone there, but I had been too slow to catch it. Someone just going back inside. I turned again to see if I could get Jeremy's attention, but he was too intent on his own actions. He was off the horse in a flash and with him came the long leather bag. Suddenly he was on the ground, on one knee. With fumbling movements he pulled the bag off the rifle. He brought it up to eye level and aimed at the cave.

A noise came from the cave—James was now standing in front of it. He was also holding a rifle, probably the one he'd stolen from Henshaw's Hardware. Attached to it I could see the very expensive scope that gave him deadly accuracy. It was pointed straight at Jeremy.

A vulture screeched. I screamed the word no but it was lost in another sound—the sound of a shot.

TWENTY-FIVE

THE WORLD SLOWED. The birds let out expanded screams before they wheeled away to the west. I pulled my head to the right, then the left. The figure to my right took one step back then fell, the rifle slipping from his hands. It was James.

Normal time resumed. I heard an anguished cry as Sharon flew out of the cave, saw James, and threw herself, sobbing, on his prostrate body.

Jeremy still had his rifle up, but it came down quickly as he swung toward his left. There was another figure I hadn't seen before, all but hidden behind an algerita bush. It was a slender boyish woman with blond hair. She was also holding a rifle, and still had it aimed at the opening of the cave. At Sharon.

"No!" It was Jeremy's word but he appeared only to mouth it as the sound blew away on the wind.

Lurline swung her rifle toward Jeremy. I saw his confusion at the gun that was now trained on him. He said something I couldn't hear. I watched as Lurline cocked the gun. This time I was the one who screamed. With every bit of breath I had, I screamed, "No!" I snatched up a rock, as big as I could hold, and flung it down the incline. It hit another rock and made a thud before it rolled to a stop. I yelled again, "Lurline, don't shoot!"

Her head popped up, and even from that distance I could see her surprise. "Don't shoot!" I yelled again. She didn't seem convinced.

I had to stop her. Moving as fast as I could with my splintery cane, I began to hop down the slope. Words tumbled out of my mouth, commands, pleas.

She looked like a puppet, jerking erratically. First she swung the gun toward me, then back at Jeremy and finally up toward the cave. Sharon had picked up the rifle James had used and now it was pointed at Lurline. I didn't know if Sharon knew how to shoot it, but neither did Lurline.

In that moment Lurline must have seen the futility of what she'd done and how she was trying to cover it up. For an instant she let the rifle drop. I relaxed my vigilance and my foot hit a rock; I lurched toward the ground. Even as I fell forward I saw Lurline swing her rifle up one more time. As my body slammed into the dirt I heard the second shot.

By the time my head was up again, the scene had changed. Jeremy's horse was charging off, pounding up the slope in a frenzy to get away from the gunfire. Jeremy was flat on the ground. Lurline had dropped the rifle and was running toward the fence and the house. What she couldn't see was that she was also running toward the sheriff's car that was racing along the road to the gate.

"Jeremy!" I screamed the word. Even if he couldn't hear my voice I wanted him to hear and respond to my need. "Jeremy!" Please, God, don't let him be dead, I prayed. He didn't move; his horse thundered past me. I was running, falling, hobbling, the pain merely an incentive to move faster.

I saw the sheriff's car brake in a cloud of dirt. Lurline almost ran straight into it. Then all the car doors opened at once and men jumped out. One of them stepped up to Lurline, but she jerked away. I yelled again, "Stop her!" Someone grabbed her—it was Linc Draper.

It all happened in a flash, and I was still trying to get to Jeremy's prostrate body. He hadn't moved.

A figure separated itself from the other men; it was Matt. He'd seen me and started toward me. I pointed to the spot where Jeremy lay. Puzzled but willing he began to hurry in that direction. A siren cut through the air. Matt must have seen Jeremy because he began to run. When he reached him he went down on one knee, stayed that way for what seemed like hours, then turned and shouted something at the other men.

I had finally gained the level ground; the road was just in front of me. It would be easier going, only my view was blocked by some heavy bushes. My lungs burned and my leg felt like a heavy weight, almost useless, dragging at me. I heard a car start up and I cut across the barren road until I could see it. It was the ambulance—they were loading a stretcher inside. I ran forward as fast as I could, my adrenaline carrying me. Skip Jackson jumped out of the driver's seat. "My God, Jolie. Here, let me help—"

"Jeremy," I said, "how is Jeremy?"

Before he could answer the ambulance's back door swung open and Matt stepped out. He reached me in two steps and grabbed me up with both arms, holding on to me for just an instant. I could feel his heart hammering as he clung to me for one brief second. "Oh, God, Jolie—" Then he swung me up into the back of the ambulance.

I lurched forward as he closed the back door and Skip began to turn the ambulance around. I almost fell on Marta Winters, the nurse who was bending over Jeremy. She had his shirt ripped half off, and there was blood everywhere. Marta was holding a thick wad of gauze on Jeremy's chest. His eyes were closed and his skin looked gray under his tan.

"How is he?"

"Can't tell yet what the bullet hit," she said, never looking away from what she was doing. "I've got to get the bleeding stopped."

I tried to bend forward on one knee, but the pain was excruciating and half a scream escaped before I could bite down on it. Jeremy's eyes fluttered open. He saw me.

"Mom." His voice was barely a whisper.

"It's okay, honey. Don't talk. Just relax. Marta's going to take good care of you until we get to the hospital."

He tried to lift his head to get closer, but Marta pressed him back down. "Stay still, Jeremy."

"Mom," he tried again, his eyes locked on mine.

"Save your strength—"

"I didn't shoot James," he persisted. "I didn't want you to be mad...." Then he closed his eyes and all his muscles seemed to go slack.

THERE IS a small sign outside the Wilmot County Hospital that reads, MIRACLES HAPPEN HERE. I hoped that was true.

Dr. Baxter did a quick examination of Jeremy, gave some terse instructions to several nurses, and then hurried to his office. He told me later that he'd made a phone call, and that call brought us a minor miracle: An old friend of his, a surgeon who'd been in med school with him in Dallas, was visiting in Fredericksburg. He was a surgeon said to have magic in his hands, and Jeremy needed magic because the bullet appeared to be lodged close to his heart.

They flew Dr. Amsmith in by helicopter. Matt and I waited, standing awkwardly outside the closed door in the wide and overly bright hallway. We were unwilling to go any further away from Jeremy, but not able to get any closer. People moved everywhere always hurrying, always nodding at me with their solemn eyes. A different doctor, young and new to Purple Sage, whisked past us and through the door, so that we could glimpse Jeremy being draped with light blue sheets. Then the door closed silently.

Within a few minutes the young man came back out, and headed straight for me. "Mrs. Wyatt?"

My heart plummeted. "Yes?"

"Um, I'm Dr. Edward Salinas—"

"What's happening to my son?" I asked. Matt slid an arm around my shoulders and steadied me against him.

Dr. Salinas cleared his throat and watched my face. "I know they're trying to get him stabilized...."

"What does that mean?"

"Mrs. Wyatt, I'm not the person to talk to. Only Dr. Baxter can speak with authority on your son's condition. I'm just here because Dr. Baxter said you could use some medical attention, too. Why don't you come with me and let me check you over."

"That's not possible. I can't leave."

"Jolie," Matt said, his voice gentle. "Honey, Jeremy's going to need you to take care of him in a few days; you have to be well for that." Then he looked straight into my eyes. "I need you, too." He kissed me lightly.

"It's okay, Matt. I'm fine."

"You're limping. There's blood on your face."

Dr. Salinas took me by the arm and moved me away from Matt; it felt like I was losing my lifeline. "No, I can't—"

"Your husband's right," he said, "and we won't go far. Just down the hall. Believe me, if anything happens that you need to know, they can find you in seconds." His arm around me was firm as he led me away. "Your son is going to be in surgery for a while, so this way at least we can put some of the time to good use."

He took me down the hall, left me to get undressed and into a hospital gown before he returned. He began by asking me how I had received my various injuries. Then he started examining me, speaking in a quiet, reassuring voice. He talked about the healing power of the body and how Jeremy was young and healthy, which was always important. He talked about how he believed in the power of prayer and in miracles.

When there was a knock on the door I stopped breathing, terrified that someone was bringing me horrible news. I watched Dr. Salinas walk to the door, and open it carefully to shield me. I heard him say, "Yes, she's here." And then

I heard Diane's voice, a little too loud, like it is sometimes when she's scared. "I'm her best friend. Her husband asked me to bring her some clean clothes and I have them here. And I have to see her. Now."

He turned to me. "Mrs. Wyatt—"

"Come in, Diane."

She rushed into the room, her arms outstretched, dropping the clothes on the floor as she came. "Oh, God, Jolie, I'm so sorry." She enveloped me in a hug.

"Jeremy is—?"

"He's in surgery. Oh, wait, you thought! Oh, God, no." She stopped and tears popped out of her dark eyes. "Oh, Jolie, I'm sorry. As far as I know he's fine. That other doctor is here. They're operating. I just came to be with you. I'm so glad you're alive and so sorry that Jeremy got shot."

"Then he's okay?"

Dr. Salinas stepped forward. "Mrs. Wyatt, bad news travels very fast, especially in a hospital. Your son is in the absolute best hands."

"That's right, Jolie," Diane said, sitting on the examining table beside me. "And how are you?" she asked.

"Fine."

She looked at Salinas, who said, "She has a concussion. And I suspect a fracture in the leg, but we won't know for sure until after we get some X rays."

I was taken in a wheelchair to X-ray, then sent to a room to shower and change. None of it seemed real at the time. Even in the shower when I got the water too hot, it only shifted my focus for a few moments. Finally, I went to sit with Matt in the small coffee room used by the staff. Diane and Trey stayed nearby, too.

Mac Donelly arrived to see how we were. There was a deputy with him to stand guard on James Jorgenson's room. James only had a minor wound, but he'd hit his head when he fell. I kept nodding like it mattered.

Then Mac brought a chair close to me, so that we were almost eye to eye. "Jolie, it's my fault Jeremy got shot and I don't know how you can ever forgive me."

"No, Mac—"

"Lurline was helping to search for James; a lot of people were. Linc even told me he suspected her, I just never thought…" He swallowed hard. "Jeremy was so worried, so intent on finding you. When Matt mentioned the cave, Jeremy went off on his own. I didn't think a thing about it and then when I realized Lurline had followed…and heard the shot—thank God we weren't far away."

"It's all right, Mac. It's no one's fault." I touched his shoulder, but it didn't really matter. None of it mattered except what was going on in that operating room.

"We'll talk more later," he said.

"Yes."

He left and others came. Nurses, some friends, Rhonda Hargis, IdaMae. They hugged and touched us, perhaps for strength, then left. Dr. Salinas told me about the break in my leg—I never really heard or cared what it was. Someone gave me a shot for the pain, but I don't recall any pain. I kept taking long, shuddering breaths, simply out of reflex. I'm not sure I was even in my body. I felt like I was in spirit somewhere, begging the angels to save my son.

THE SURGERY TOOK five hours. When they brought Jeremy out, we were near the ICU, Matt and me. I was in a wheelchair, and I stood up before I remembered that I had a brace on my leg. Matt caught me and sat me back down.

Doc Baxter looked exhausted. The other doctor stayed with Jeremy as he went past. Jeremy looked gray, but he was breathing, I could see that.

"He's doing much better," Dr. Baxter said, reaching down and touching my hands. "It's going to take a while—this was pretty serious—but I don't think it will be too long before Jeremy will be coming to me just like he always has. Needing stitches put in those cuts he's always getting, or..."

I didn't hear the rest. I was crying.

TWENTY-SIX

DR. BAXTER LOOKED UP from Jeremy's chart, his expression grave. "I have some real concerns about letting you go home, Jeremy," he said. "So I'm going to make some stipulations. First, you have to give me back my hospital and all the people in it. You have to leave all the Gray Ladies who've adopted you, and all the Sunshine Rays who have a crush on you. Even when they beg you to take them home with you, you have to say no. Understood?"

Jeremy grinned. "Yeah. Understood."

"Now, as for food. I know that the entire population of Purple Sage High will keep trying to bring you pizza and hamburgers with french fries, just like they've been doing while you were here"—Jeremy started to protest but Dr. Baxter kept right on going—"but I don't want you eating food that's high in fat. It's bad for you, especially now, when you need proteins, vitamins, and minerals to help your body heal. So no junk food. Got it?"

"Got it."

"And I also know that everyone in town will want to visit you and continue to glorify you for your heroic efforts—again, I do understand. What I don't understand is why nobody wants to glorify my efforts! I mean, I was part of the team that saved your life. But did I get a medal? Ha! Nothing. And you got all this!" He gestured to Jeremy's walls, which were covered with cards, a get-well banner, and even a medal that someone had made in the shop room at school. Every flat surface held flowers or Purple Sage dragons. Michelle Kleinsmith had brought him a stuffed Barney (her idea of a Purple Sage dragon), which sat on the foot of the bed. There were three balloon bouquets, now beginning to sag a little, as well as two cakes and several dozen cookies. Jeremy had not been neglected in his recuperation.

I looked up. "Tell you what," I said, "we'll be happy to leave most of this with you. And as for the food, I seem to remember that we forced you to take a dozen of Linda Beaman's snickerdoodles and at least that many of Mrs. Hammond's lemon bars."

"And half of that chocolate fudge cake," Jeremy added.

"Everything went to the staff at my office," Dr. Baxter said solemnly. "Of course, one or two of the cookies may have slipped out of the box before I got there...." He cleared his throat. "Now, back to business. Here is some information for you, Jolie." He handed me a sheet that looked like it had come off a computer. "Follow these instructions and keep this young man in line. I feel like I have a personal stake in his life and I don't want him going bad on me."

I took the sheet and glanced through it: instructions on food, rest, and exercise. It seemed simple enough. "Got it."

Jeremy reached out a hand for the paper and I gave it to him. He still looked pale to me, but I supposed that was to be expected after an extended stay in the hospital. At least his eyes were bright, and his smile, which was becoming more frequent, was like sunshine.

"I like this one," he said, pointing to the paper. "No heavy exercise. Guess I can't vacuum, either." It was his least favorite chore.

"Two weeks, then you'll be cleaning house with the best of them," Dr. Baxter said. He glanced at his watch, then back at Jeremy. "You can leave after lunch, but I want you to understand something: I do not *ever* want to see you back here with a bullet in you. Got it?"

"Okay."

"You only get one body, there's no need to be so rough

with it." He shook hands with Jeremy, then turned to me. "And you take care, too. I want to see you in a week to check on that leg."

"Aye-aye, Captain."

He left, and I began packing up the gifts Jeremy had received. Matt had brought boxes by earlier and had promised to return to fill them around lunchtime, but I figured the sooner that job was done, the sooner we could leave. It wasn't that our stay in the hospital had been unpleasant; everyone had spoiled us, especially when both Jeremy and I were official guests. Once I'd been checked out and Jeremy had moved out of the critical stage I had started spending some of the nights at Diane's house, although I still hadn't gone out to the ranch. I just didn't want to be that far away from Jeremy in case I was needed. I was very grateful that I hadn't been needed.

"Mom, why don't you sit down and let Matt do that. Or, I'll help—" He started to get out of bed, but a visitor arrived.

Rhonda was moving fast, as usual. "Hey, hi, Jeremy. Hi, Jolie. I hear you two are going home."

Jeremy pulled the sheet back up to cover his short pajamas and said, "Right after lunch."

I took the opportunity to sit down; I still hadn't completely found my balance with my broken leg. "What's up, Rhonda?"

"Oh, not much."

We did the polite chitchat as long as any of us could stand, then Rhonda jumped up from where she'd been leaning against the windowsill and said, "I got an exclusive interview with Lurline Batson! The hell of it is, I'm not going to print hardly a thing she said because it was all hogwash! Can you believe it? And what I can print, according to Mac, is all supposition. My stories have so many disclaimers you'd think they were car ads. The whole thing is killing me. Anyway, I hope that makes you feel better about being away from the radio station—at least you know you're not missing much.''

"I suppose so. But, hey, you can tell *us* the whole truth,'' I said, gesturing toward Jeremy. "We're dying to know.'' What I didn't say was that we'd already heard a dozen versions of the *whole* truth about Lurline Batson from a dozen different sources. None of them explained everything I knew, though, and I hoped Rhonda's information would fill in the gaps. Even if she couldn't always print it, Rhonda could ferret things out. She'd been known to snoop through official police records and talk to a mugger to get to the bottom of the story. I was hoping she had this time.

"Yeah, I'd like to know what Lurline thought she was doing,'' Jeremy said. "She seemed so nice, but I think she was wacko underneath.''

Rhonda nodded, her blond ponytail bobbing. "They may try the insanity defense; she's got some lawyer from Abilene who's supposed to be pretty good. It might even work; she did some pretty crazy things.'' Rhonda moved over to a green-and-white-striped hospital chair, sat down, then shook her head. "I guess it all starts with Tim. Lurline was the one who, well, uh, went after Tim.''

"Are you saying she seduced Tim?'' I asked. She nodded and I added, "It's okay, Rhonda; Jeremy deserves to hear what went on.''

"Oh. Well, yeah, okay. See, from what I've been able to get from the cops and everybody else, there was a staff party at the club one night and Tim got drunk. So Lurline offered to drive him home, only she took him to her home. Nice lady, huh? Her landlord, Ollie Rodriquez—he has the big house right in front of hers out at the lake—he says Lurline practically dragged Tim inside that first night. Lurline tells it a little differently. She claims they fell in love, but I think it was wishful thinking on her part. I mean, look at it logically, she was fifteen years older than Tim and he could get almost any girl he wanted.''

"Like Sharon Jorgenson," I said.

"Right. Only Lurline started following them around."

Jeremy sat upright. "No, that wasn't Lurline—" He stopped himself before he blurted out the name. "I don't think Lurline was doing that."

"Oh, but she was." I said, patting Jeremy's leg. "Sharon Jorgenson told me she saw a white car pull up in front of her gram's house one night when they were there. What else could it be but Lurline's Saturn? It parked right behind another car that was already out on the road." I hoped that was cryptic enough not to arouse Rhonda's suspicions yet clear enough for Jeremy to understand.

"I see," he said. He got it.

"So, go on," I said.

Rhonda took a breath. "Anyway, Lurline got so mad about Tim dating Sharon that she lured him out to the lake and then shot him. The night after Jorgenson escaped. And we can't prove it, but I think she started hunting Jorgenson right away. First on her own, then as part of the manhunt. She was stalking them."

"She wanted to kill Jorgenson?" Jeremy asked. "Why? Oh, wait, I get it. So people would think he murdered Tim. If Jorgenson was dead, no one would know the truth about Tim's death."

Rhonda nodded and took her time before she added, "And, I think, because Lurline also wanted to find and kill Sharon. If you ask me, that was pure D jealousy."

We were all silent. The visions that came to my mind, of Lurline and Tim at the lake, of Lurline the stalker, were unsettling ones. Texas had passed stalking laws, but they were weak, making the offense a misdemeanor with the same punishment as for drinking alcohol at a convenience store. And here was a case of stalking, only this was the reverse of the standard roles. A young man had been the victim and now he was dead.

I brought my attention back to the here and now. The

everyday sounds of the hospital filled the room. Those sounds were almost homey to me, nearly as familiar as the sounds at the ranch or those at KSGE. A loudspeaker paged one of the volunteers; a phone chimed insistently; I heard the whirr of the elevator as it came up from the second floor and the clatter of the lunch trays being loaded down the hall.

I wouldn't miss Wilmot County Hospital, but I would miss some of the people. I was grateful to them, and the everyday routines that had been comforting during the week and a half that I would have to call the worst of my life.

"I guess I'd better get going," Rhonda said, twisting around in her chair, "but I wanted to ask you first—do you know what Lewis is going to do about Rory? Is he going to fire him from K-SAGE, or what?"

"I don't think Lewis is going to do anything," I said.

"But he's James Jorgenson's brother! He moved there to be closer to him."

I nodded. "Yes, and to get reacquainted with Sharon, too, but Rory claims he never saw them after the prison escape until they were captured."

"I'll bet he did. How else did Jorgenson get a cellular phone? And how did he keep evading the law?"

"Rory's story is that James must have stolen the phone."

Rhonda stared at me, her mouth open. "And Lewis believes that? It's a crock! You aren't buying it, are you?"

"It's none of my business," I said firmly. That was the decision I'd finally come to after several days of soul searching.

Lewis had stopped by the hospital just two days before to tell me about Rory, and I had listened without comment. According to Lewis, yes, Rory did sometimes behave badly, but that was veneer. Underneath he was a sad and lost little boy. Rory had been sent away by the only real family he'd had after his parents died. He'd probably never felt the kind of love that most of us take for granted. When he'd come back to Purple Sage it was in hopes of finding his home, his family, everything he didn't have. Lewis said it was sad that things didn't turn out the way Rory had planned.

His grandmother had just died and his brother was in prison. His little sister hardly remembered him, and certainly didn't need, or want, some bossy stranger trying to run her life. So Rory had hidden his relationship with the Jorgensons, just to make sure it wouldn't hurt him professionally. When James had escaped from prison, apparently with Sharon's help, poor Rory had been in torment. He'd become physically sick and didn't know what to do. Mostly he'd worried. At least that was the way Lewis told it. I knew more.

I knew that Rory had been in contact with the Jorgensons after the escape. And I didn't really care how many times people told me I'd been in shock and had a head injury—I knew what I'd seen. Rory had been in that cave and he'd been helping the Jorgensons.

And maybe that's why I never said a word about Rory—because somehow I believed that helping James and Sharon had been the right thing to do.

Rhonda stood up. "Oh, there's something else I'm supposed to tell you. I have a message for you, from Lurline."

I didn't want a message from her.

"She wanted me to tell you," Rhonda went on, "that she's really sorry about shooting Jeremy. She said she feels real bad about it. She just got carried away and she's really glad that you're better, Jeremy."

No one responded until finally Jeremy shrugged. "Yeah, it's okay."

Rhonda nodded her head, patted me on the shoulder, and left.

"It's not okay," I said. "It's not okay at all. She could have killed you."

"It was me she shot—"

"But she didn't just hurt you. She hurt all of us. You and Matt and me. And all the people who love you."

"Mom, this is about me."

I stood up and looked him straight in the eyes, wanting him to understand. "Was Tim's death just about Tim? Or was it about hurting all of us? Even you."

Jeremy didn't say anything for a long time. Eventually he broke the eye contact and I began packing gifts again. It was almost five minutes later when I heard Jeremy's voice. "Mom?"

"What, honey?" I turned to look at him.

"It's about all of us," he said. "But we have to forgive her anyway."

I felt the words career against my heart. I could hardly respond, but I said. "You're right. Thanks for reminding me."

And someday, I hoped I would be able to forgive her.

EPILOGUE

I WAS SITTING in front of the judge's desk, reading his nameplate for at least the eighth time. THE HONORABLE DANIEL PETTEY. He was fortyish with thick dark hair and a wide face. He blinked often as if he wore contact lenses and they weren't comfortable. I'd never met him before we'd been introduced just a half hour earlier. Mac Donelly was in the room, as was the district attorney, Randy Inks, but I was the one who had to answer all the questions.

"So you're telling me that the Jorgensons did not kidnap you, is that correct?" Judge Pettey asked me again, blinking twice.

"That's correct. I ran into the cave on my own." I'd already explained the circumstances and I got the feeling Pettey was disappointed in my story.

"Did they ever threaten you with bodily harm?"

"Never. In fact, they took care of me. Sharon bandaged my cuts, gave me water and food, made a bed for me, and just generally nursed me."

"And what about James Jorgenson?"

"James was very kind. He never threatened me, either."

Pettey blinked. He was not looking happy. If he'd been less professional he might have rolled his eyes. Instead he said briskly, "Did they ever tie you? Gag you? Stop you from leaving the cave?"

Well, they'd never stood in front of me, I justified. "No. They didn't," I said aloud. "In fact, when I had to go outside to go to the bathroom, Sharon always helped me because I was in so much pain."

Judge Pettey asked the same questions again, I answered the same way, then he covered some other areas, and finally, in what appeared to be pure disgust, he blinked one last time and told me I could go. I stood up, and then sat back down again. "I think I have something else to say."

Pettey raised a heavy eyebrow. "Certainly, Miz Wyatt."

I looked at Mac, then at Randy Inks. These guys weren't going to like me much, but then sometimes things just work out that way. "Your Honor, the Jorgensons not only didn't kidnap me, they probably saved my life. I've already told you how Sharon said the escape happened and I believe her. I believe something else, too." I swallowed hard before I said, "James told me that people take one look at him and assume he's a 'bad un.' You know what? It seems to be true and it's not fair. He was outside the prison because he was comforting his sister. A younger sister who was trying to finish high school and keep a house, as well as get over the death of her grandmother. When the lights came on inside the prison, James got scared and ran. It was stupid, but I'm not sure any one of us would have done any better.

"I think that James Jorgenson deserves a chance to get back on the right side of the law. I'd like his brains on our side for once, and it would be nice to know that our legal system was still a justice system, too.

"As for Sharon, she didn't assist in the escape. She was just there. In the wrong place at the wrong time, and I don't think it should ruin her life."

No one spoke, although I thought Mac was going to. When the judge finally said, "Thank you," I picked up my purse and left.

Matt was outside waiting. "How'd it go?"

"Lousy," I said, as we walked toward the Bronco. I would have been stomping off, but one leg was still in a brace.

"Why is that?" Matt asked.

"I have this awful feeling they're going to hang James just to win a few political Brownie points. It isn't fair. We have killers running loose, and rapists getting out after a few months, and this kid who's never physically hurt anyone in his life is probably going to be locked away forever!''

The sound of hurrying footsteps penetrated my anger and I turned around to see Mac coming toward us. He was grinning. ''Hey, Matt,'' he said, shaking hands with him.

''How's it going?''

Mac was still grinning, only now he was looking at me. ''Well, I can only say that right at the moment, I'm doing fine and things are definitely looking up for the Jorgensons.''

I was stunned. ''They are?''

''Jolie, I don't know how far that little speech will carry, but I do know that you gave the Honorable Daniel Pettey something to think over. And he is. It's about the best we can do for the moment.'' Then he took my hand and shook it. ''Nice work.''

UNTIL THE END OF TIME
Polly Whitney

An Ike and Abby Mystery

First Time in Paperback

IN DYING COLOR

Roller-blading duo Ike and Abby return—still divorced and still working together. Ike is the gorgeous producer of "Morning Watch," Abby is the director.

Abby is mugged walking to work by a man who promises a story. Abby suspects his attacker knows something about a crime wave sweeping Manhattan: the Yellow-Man murders. The victims are homeless, their faces are painted yellow, a cryptic message left behind.

But when a "Morning Watch" guest becomes a victim right outside the studio, Ike and Abby are drawn into the murders, trying not to kill *each other* in the meantime.

"...clever, effervescent, and jam-packed with acid-spiked tidbits about broadcast news."   —*Mystery News*

Available in April at your favorite retail stores.

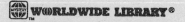

WORLDWIDE LIBRARY®   TIME

Take 3 books and a surprise gift FREE

SPECIAL LIMITED-TIME OFFER

Mail to: The Mystery Library™
3010 Walden Ave.
P.O. Box 1867
Buffalo, N.Y. 14240-1867

YES! Please send me 3 free books from the Mystery Library™ and my free surprise gift. Then send me 3 mystery books, first time in paperback, every month. Bill me only $4.19 per book plus 25¢ delivery and applicable sales tax, if any*. There is no minimum number of books I must purchase. I can always return a shipment at your expense and cancel my subscription. Even if I never buy another book from the Mystery Library™, the 3 free books and surprise gift are mine to keep forever.   415 BPY A3US

Name	(PLEASE PRINT)	
Address		Apt. No.
City	State	Zip

* Terms and prices subject to change without notice. N.Y. residents add applicable sales tax. This offer is limited to one order per household and not valid to present subscribers.

© 1990 Worldwide Library.

MYS-796